FORKED LIGHTNING

BY
MARY DURHAM

THE THRILLER BOOK CLUB
121, CHARING CROSS ROAD, W.C.2

This edition 1952

TO
JOAN

MADE AND PRINTED IN GREAT BRITAIN BY
EBENEZER BAYLIS AND SON, LTD., THE
TRINITY PRESS, WORCESTER, AND LONDON

THE thunderstorm was the last straw. It had threatened to break all day, darkening the sky to slaty purple and filling the air with dank humidity which could almost be smelt. When the first flash of lightning flared above the tree-tops Jess put down her book and gave up the struggle to occupy her mind with the amorous adventures of an elderly pawn-broker. The conspiracy against her was too strong. She began methodically to count her troubles.

Foremost in her mind was the date—September the nineteenth. It confronted her with aggressive clarity from the turnover calendar on the mantelshelf. It was the second anniversary of the day on which she had married Derek, and the first anniversary of the day on which they had parted. The swift agony of the break and the slow torment of the frustrated year which followed united now to form a wall of pain which entrenched her thoughts within narrow limits. Whatever extraneous ideas strayed into her mind were instantly coloured by the dominant gloom of her mood.

In spite of all the hours she had spent brooding over Derek's conduct it still remained an unsolved problem, challenging her tired brain with nagging persistency to return to it again and again. Had any other man in human history, she wondered, bludgeoned a woman into marrying him against her will, spent a year with her in harmony surely not often achieved in marriage, waited until her feeling for him had become the most vital factor in her life, and then coolly announced without preamble or explanation that he had reached the conclusion after careful thought that only by living alone could he develop his personality to the full extent of its potentialities and make the best use of the gifts with which nature had endowed him. His pompous phrases were as fresh in her mind as on the day when she had first heard them; in fact she seemed to recall them more clearly in retrospect because at the time she had been too stunned to appreciate their full significance. She smiled grimly as she remembered how he had "chivalrously" acknowledged that she was in no way to blame, implying at the same time that neither was he. It—by "it" she supposed he meant their marriage—was just one of those false steps which anyone was liable to take now and again. Fortunately they were both old enough to realize the wisdom of retrieving their error and making a clean break before they became so firmly entangled in the ties of marriage that the break would be painful.

Jess could remember very little of her stumbling words of protest. In any case they had been wasted for Derek was ready with an answer to everything. He assumed that she was pretending for his sake, so as not to hurt his pride, that she had been happy during the year they had spent together, and assured her that now the decision to separate had been taken there was no longer any need of pretence between them. The important thing to remember was that they were both, in their different ways, creative artists, and no creative artist can produce his best work while he is living under a sense of strain.

"You see how much more sensible you were than me," he said cajolingly. "You didn't really want to marry me, now did you?"

"Not at the time, Derek," she admitted. "But I *am* married to you now, and that makes all the difference. . . ."

"It *would* make all the difference," he amended, "if we had a child or if you were financially dependent on me. But as things are I feel we can part quite amicably and with perfectly clear consciences. After all a year is long enough to test a thing and decide on its merits one way or the other, and yet it isn't a very big slice of one's life to devote to an experiment."

"I wish you wouldn't keep calling marriage a 'thing'," Jess had protested.

Derek looked hurt. "I'm sorry if I don't make myself clear." And he ran through his arguments a second time in the indulgent tone of a teacher recapitulating a lesson for the benefit of a backward child.

Of course his cousins came into the picture somewhere. Rupert was full of half-digested psychological theories, and was constantly enlarging on the importance of a sympathetic background in the life of a creative artist. "Frustration" was one of his pet words. Any kind of tie or responsibility was classed as a frustration, and in Rupert's view a man who did not ruthlessly free himself from all frustration-producing encumbrances was irrevocably doomed to professional failure. What happened to the careers of the cast-off encumbrances if they happened to have any was not taken into account in Rupert's philosophy. Althea was bitten by the same bug as her brother and was even more dangerous since she devoted a large part of her time to reading the works of various schools of psychologists all of whom seemed to have unpronounceable names, and was invariably able to quote passages to lend weight to Rupert's arguments. Also she was probably in love with Derek—she was only a distant cousin—and so she had a personal motive for wanting to break up his marriage. All the same it was hardly credible that Rupert and Althea had directly incited Derek to dismiss his wife as though she were a cook or a secretary—only, Jess reflected in parenthesis, with another of her grim smiles, one would put up with a good deal of "frustration" in these days before getting rid of an "encumbrance" in such short supply as either of these commodities. The methods used by the two cousins must have been indirect and subtle, and to suppose that Derek had been influenced by them one was driven to assume the co-operation of some other factor which she had so far failed to discover. Had she done or left undone something, which had fortified Derek's strange decision? And so her thoughts returned to the well-worn track and gyrated fruitlessly around it for a miserable quarter of an hour until she jumped up in exasperation and began to wander about the room.

The storm had taken its cue from her thoughts and was moving round in a circle with the village as its centre. Except that the slaty tinge in the sky was a shade deeper, there was little change in the view since the last time she had looked out of the window. The rain had not yet begun to fall though the clouds looked ready to burst at a pin-prick; the wide open windows caused no draught to stir the stagnant air in the room. Jess was allergic to electrical disturbances in the atmosphere, and the difficulty of breathing combined with the feeling of pressure across her fore-head produced a condition of physical restlessness which seemed to aggravate her distress of mind beyond the limits of endurance. When the rain came the air would cool but she did not feel able to trust to nature for relief from a tension which had become intolerable. She fetched a glass of water from the kitchen, extracted some aspirin from the bottle in her handbag, and swallowed the dose in the desperate hope that it would ease the pain in her head. She returned to her chair, lit a cigarette and sat smoking with her eyes half closed, waiting. . . . She did not know quite what she was waiting for, perhaps for the rain, perhaps for the aspirin to take effect. But she seemed now to be always waiting for something; it was a state of mind she had grown used to and could not shake off.

For weeks she had been waiting for a letter from Derek. With the dramatic sense of timing—a part, she supposed, of his playwright's craft—which had led to his choosing their wedding anniversary to announce his intention of ending their partnership, she had allowed herself to hope that he might. . . . Again, she was not sure exactly what she had hoped. There had been varying degrees of hope to which she had yielded in turn according to her mood. Suppose that his year of living in solitude had proved dis-appointing, one could imagine him thinking in terms of reunion when the experiment had been given a fair trial. If a year was a fair test of marriage, surely it was a fair test of separation. If that was the way his mind had been work-ing, one would expect him to write when the anniversary drew near suggesting a meeting to talk things over. September the nineteenth, falling on a Friday, would have been an ideal day for such a purpose, because Derek could so easily get away from Rupert's office for a long week-end.

If he had not cared to stay with her—and there were difficulties about that since she was known locally as Miss
Munro—he could have put up in the village. This had
been her most optimistic forecast, and was responsible for
her recent habit of living with her ears half-cocked to hear
the postman's knock. When no post was due there was
still the chance of a telegram since Cairn Cottage had no
telephone. In other more realistic moods she had thought
she might receive a letter on the day itself, a kind of feeler
to find out how Jess was liking her spinster existence—not
that Derek had paid much heed to her reactions when he
made his startling proposal, but before that he had been as
considerate probably as the average husband, and he might
have reverted to his normal self in the interim since they
had parted. Now she knew with humiliating certainty that
all her dreams had been inspired by the most foolish and
unwarrantable type of wishful thinking. She had built her
future on a tinsel foundation, and nothing lay before her
but eternal inescapable loneliness. . . . "You don't understand the difference, my dear Jess," Derek had told her,
"between loneliness and solitude." Maliciously she had
hoped that some day he might not feel quite so sublimely
clear about the distinction himself, but it seemed that she
had hoped in vain.

Crushing out her cigarette end, Jess began to think about
the book she had finished writing in the small hours of the
morning. It had reached the stage a few days earlier when
she could scarcely put down her pen to eat or sleep without
fearing that the words which were crying out to be written
down would float away somewhere like feathers in a wind
and never be caught. It was like that always, and even her
anxiety about the posts had made no real difference. One
part of her mind seemed to dictate the words to her skurry-
ing fingers while another was aware that the time for the
second delivery was approaching, or had passed and
brought nothing. . . . It did not seem to matter so long as
one went on and on and on; it was the time spent in eating
and sleeping which were the danger zones. One felt used
up in the morning and lethargic after meals. Indeed the

approach of September the nineteenth had goaded her to a supreme effort so that nothing should hamper her enjoyment of Derek's letter. . . . Derek's letter which had never come.

Jess began to lose patience with herself. She was giving rein to a wishy-washy sentimentality which would make her sick if she came across it in a book. It was degrading to encourage these orgies of self-pity, and humiliating to hang on to a man who did not want you, even in your thoughts. But her headache combined with the spent sensation which followed the completion of a book, as though one had lost mental weight, and would not feel oneself again until one had made it up, made it hard to concentrate on anything, and a breakdown of concentration left the way open for a host of undesirable invaders to enter the mind.

She turned her thoughts back resolutely to her book. Inevitably it was at present either the best or the worst she had ever written, and it would be some time before she would recover enough mental energy to discover which. While she composed the last few chapters she had felt assured that it was a masterpiece. Now the usual doubts had made their appearance. Perhaps there was too much talk and too little action; perhaps no one would understand the main theme; perhaps . . .

She was cocking her ears now as the time for the delivery of the second post drew near. It was very unlikely that a letter from Derek would be delivered in the afternoon; letters from London always came at breakfast time, and only local or long-distance letters by the second post. Almost dead on time came the sharp double-knock, just as a prolonged rattle of thunder died down into silence.

Derek might have been away from London the day before. . . . Jess went out into the dark little hall and peered at the white envelope lying on the doormat. The address had fallen face downwards. She swooped forward to pick it up, telling herself it was probably a bill or a circular.

It was the doctor's bill for attending her when she had had 'flu in the spring. "One pound thirteen and six," she said to herself. "I suppose that's seven and six a visit, and the extra three and six is for that filthy tonic I poured down the sink."

She went into the kitchen and put the kettle on for tea, then sat down on a hard chair and cried her heart out.

2

It was when the rain began that she remembered Angela's letter. The rain came suddenly; one second the air was as still as a becalmed sea, the next it was violently stirred by a rush of water falling in straight columns from sky to earth. Almost instantaneously the air inside the room cooled, and little puddles appeared in the uneven surface of the gravel path outside. Listening to the rhythmic sound of falling water, Jess reflected that a few moments' exposure to its force would drench one to the skin, and then she thought of Angela, whom she had forgotten all day in the pressure of her own troubled affairs. She would have to go to the pillar-box nearly half a mile away to post her answer to Angela's appeal. And she would have to go at once if she were to catch the five p.m. collection. But it was, of course, impossible to go at once. One could hardly stand up, let alone walk, in such a deluge. The best she could do now was to get her letter ready and slip out as soon as the rain diminished so that she would catch the six o'clock collection the following morning. That ought to ensure that Angela, who was staying in some remote town in the north of England, would receive her reply by the first post on Monday morning. She could not risk waiting for the Saturday evening collection because Angela had mentioned that she wanted to travel on Monday morning to her next destination.

Angela had written to borrow money. In her disappointment that the solitary letter which had arrived at breakfast time was not from Derek, Jess had not read it very carefully at the time. She determined at once to respond to Angela's request, but her vague intention to write after breakfast and give the letter to Mrs. Bradshaw to post in the village had fizzled out because she had mislaid her cheque-book. She fetched Angela's letter, switched on the standard lamp, and read it through with forced attention. Her friend was playing in a Repertory Company which was touring the smaller towns in the north country. It sounded rather a rocky affair from her description; a mixture of unsuccessful professionals, ex-amateurs, and dramatic students crazy to gain experience anyhow and anywhere. But Angela described it as all "tremendous fun" until after a month of playing to poor houses in a small town in Westmorland the manager had announced that he had not sufficient funds to pay the last week's salaries in full. They were due to appear at a more promising cultural centre in Durham the next week where they hoped to recoup their losses, and meantime everyone was feverishly wiring and writing to relatives for cash. Angela had no near relatives and so half airily and half apologetically she had written to Jess. She only asked for the loan of ten pounds.

Jess scribbled a note on a writing-pad, found her cheque-book, after ransacking all the drawers in her sitting-room, behind the clock on the mantelshelf, wrote a cheque for twenty pounds, and placed the stamped envelope, which she had marked "Urgent", on the little table in the hall where it would be impossible to lose it. The thunder was now only a distant intermittent rumble, but the rain showed no sign of slackening. The gravel path was under water, an indication that Cairn Lane would be a small river. Jess put her gumboots ready under the hall table and returned to the sitting-room where she once more sat down and waited. This time she was waiting for the rain to stop. . . .

It was almost dark when at last she set out on her errand. The rain was still fairly heavy but it had lost its tropical intensity, and it was falling with a steady persistency which gave no promise of clearing before morning. Jess could face neither the prospect of getting up to catch the early morning post, nor the even unpleasanter one of being kept awake by a nagging conscience. So she struggled into gumboots and mackintosh, tied a dark scarf firmly round her head, set her teeth and paddled out into the lane. A faint

sense of virtuosity provided some compensation for the
discomfort of ploughing through mud and splashing into
unseen pools under the dripping trees, and even allowing
for the bad going she expected to be home again in less
than half an hour. She braced herself to squelch recklessly
through and into whatever lay in her path, thinking of the
hot bath she would have when she returned, and Angela's
joy when she opened the letter and found it contained
double the sum she had asked for. But she did not want
to think of letters. . . .

When she reached the corner where Cairn Lane entered
the wider lane which contained the pillar-box, and was
no longer sheltered by overhanging trees, she found the
rain had quickened its tempo and it was driving into her
face instead of coming straight down. As she turned the
corner a jagged flash of lightning played about in the sky
for what seemed like several seconds, and automatically
counting until it was followed by a sharp thunder clap
she reckoned that a fresh storm was brewing about seven
miles away. If the direction of the rain was any indication
of its movement it was coming towards her. She hesitated,
wondering whether to turn back or to battle on to the post
and hope for the best. It seemed feeble to give in when
she was already more than half-way to her objective, and
she recalled hearing that storms often moved against the
wind. She lowered her head and butted her way forward. . . .

She posted the letter with a sense of triumph. The rain
had soaked through her scarf and was running down her
neck. Her mackintosh clung to her knees and made it
difficult to push her legs forward. The last remnants of
twilight had been superseded by full darkness relieved
only by occasional yellow streaks of lightning which be-
mused her eyes and made her way seem blacker than
before. It was a labour in such conditions to keep moving
and one needed a sixth sense to maintain one's direction.
Several times she had stumbled on to the grass verge and
almost slid into the ditch. The thunder had kept its
distance but was threatening enough to exacerbate her

strained nerves. But now she would have the moral stimulus of knowing she had accomplished her purpose and was moving towards home and shelter. She turned quickly and, throwing the weight of her body backwards, allowed the wind to propel her, and concentrated her mind on keeping her slithering feet on the track.

Afraid of missing the turning to Cairn Lane she kept on the left side of the road and found herself half running and half sliding along, sometimes striking mud and sometimes grass with her rubber boots. Moving with diminished effort and without any sound which could compete with the sound of the storm, Jess had the sensation, associated with moments of exhaustion, that her mind was detached from her body and was unaffected by anything which happened on the physical plane. This must be how the lotus eaters felt, she thought. . . .

> "With half-shut eyes ever to seem,
>   Falling asleep in a half-dream. . . ."

The shock was the more stunning because she had failed to notice that the storm was coming closer. . . . She was at the junction of the two lanes when a vicious display of forked lightning, more spectacular than fireworks, lit up her surroundings with crude brilliancy. The simultaneous clap of thunder was like gargantuan cymbals clashing in mid-air, but her ears were rendered insensitive by the melodrama played out in swift seconds within a few feet of her eyes. . . .

She saw the scene with the acute perceptive vision of a deaf person. There were no petty noises to divide her interpretive power between seeing and hearing. There were only two actors on the miniature stage, that was no more than a patch of mud and grass, with a single tree for scenery and a bank of earth as a back-drop. The larger figure sprang from behind the tree with a perfectly judged leap. An outstretched hand grasped the small man by the collar. A knife was poised high in the air . . . pointed downwards with calculated accuracy . . . the blade caught the artificial brilliancy of the light . . . it fell like a meteor, and as it fell the clang of the giant cymbals died to a low echo. A human shriek filled the hiatus, rising to a mad crescendo and petering out in its turn to silence. Darkness came back like an iron curtain and in the black stillness Jess heard nothing but the soft swish of the rain, and the groaning of the wind which was like the sound of women kneeling. She tried to move her feet which seemed embedded in the soil, jerked herself forward a yard or two, then staggered and fell backwards . . . down a deep shaft, on and on until the walls closed in upon her, and space and time ceased to exist.

3

JESS burned her bedside lamp throughout the night, assured
only by the chiming of the clock downstairs that time was
not at a standstill, as it had been while her body lay in
the ditch and her mind slept in the dark pit of oblivion.
Twice before in her life she had fainted from shock, and
the doctor had warned her to avoid excitement as though
excitement were a dish which you can eat or abstain from
at will. But there had been no doubt on either occasion
as to the tangible nature of the circumstance which had
upset her, none of this gnawing indecision as to where
the boundary lay between fact and fantasy. The forked
lightning had been real; she knew precisely where she had
been when it dispelled the darkness with the suddenness
and effectiveness of a mammoth flash lamp. But after
that all was haze and uncertainty, until she came round
with the groping bewilderment of a patient recovering
from an anæsthetic. She had been aware first of little
except the aching chill which pervaded her body and
impinged more forcibly on her consciousness with every
second of renewed sensation. It must have been several
minutes before she was able to translate the impulse to
move into action, and her exploring hands encountered
slime and sodden grass. Trying to raise herself to a sitting
position she found that her resting-place was not a flat
surface but a ditch, but she was still too stunned to feel
surprise. Only the painful effort of scrambling out of its
depths on to the grass verge restored her faculties, and
then her first thought was of her letter to Angela, and she
began to fumble in the pocket of her mackintosh to see if
it were safe. As though to make up for its recent black-
out her mind began to race. . . . The letter? Nothing
crinkled in her pocket. Angela needed the twenty pounds
. . . oh, the pillar-box and that moment of triumph after

17

the frightening battle up the lane; of course, she had posted the letter, feeling with her fingers for the mouth of the box because of the stinging rain in her face and the inky blackness in between the lightning flashes. . . . Oh God, that terrible flash of forked lightning—that angry pattern of crude exposing light! Exposing . . . the figures, too, had been crude . . . caricatures of life: the big man and the small man, symbolizing strength and weakness, power and impotence . . . the destroyer and the victim.

She was standing erect now on the level grass, her head clear though her legs shivered like jelly under her weight. The storm had abated and the rain was no more than a faint patter coming through the trees. . . . He could not have lived with that blade in his shoulders. He must be lying dead a few yards away; there was no ditch the other side of the lane, so he would be lying on the flat ground. She had only to take a few steps and she would find him; five steps or perhaps ten—he could not have moved with that knife in his back. She was steadier now; she began to count her steps. . . .

There was nothing except wet grass, clean-smelling in the rain-washed air. She had been down on her knees, painfully probing the whole area round the tree; she had searched much further than a body could fall. Everything was flat and featureless; there was no dark hump on the ground, no contact of fingers with the substance of a human form—only wet tufts of grass and the debris of twigs and leaves under the tree. Puzzled and yet relieved, she went on her way home, stumbling because her legs were still shaky, but impelled to hurry for fear she should collapse again before she reached shelter. She was conscious of little as she covered the last lap of her journey, but the urgent need to shed her wet clothes, take a pull at a strong drink and relax . . .

Later, refreshed by food and a hot bath, she faced the problem squarely. She did not know whether she had fainted from exhaustion after her struggle to the post, coupled with the fear caused by the bursting of the storm directly over her head, and dreamed the melodramatic episode of the stabbing, or suffered perhaps from some obscure form of hallucination induced by shock, or whether . . . The alternative was petrifying to contemplate. If it were true, and how real it had seemed to her at the time—she shivered to remember—she ought to do something about it. But what? . . . Mrs. Bradshaw was always telling her that it was unsafe for a woman to live alone without a telephone, but the fact remained that she had no telephone. She was certainly not capable of walking a mile to the village to-night. Even if she were it would be difficult to know what to say to the stolid young man who represented the law in Grassmere. He would probably scratch his head and advise her to see her doctor.

The temptation to believe that the whole frightful episode was a figment of her overstrained brain was powerful. So long as she remained downstairs, sipping hot milk and brandy, and warming herself by the electric fire, she was more than half convinced that this was so. It was after she had dragged herself upstairs to bed that she realized that one cannot believe what one wants to believe, and that the night which lay before her was to be one long wakeful nightmare. Urgently she tried to argue herself back to her earlier conclusion, till the sweat soaked her nightclothes and a ball of fire seemed to press on her forehead. Again and again she pictured the ghastly scene unwillingly and every time it appeared on the screen of her imagination it seemed more vivid and more real.

She saw the assailant spring from cover, the upraised knife, the vicious blow, heard the helpless agonized scream of the victim, felt herself falling down a deep shaft which seemed to have no bottom. She saw the dazzle of light on steel and the grip of a relentless hand on a dark coat collar. She saw something more dreadful than any impersonal horror; the face of a man in the act of killing. . . . It was not a brutal face; there was a grace about its sharp outline and something in the set of the dark hair and the clean sweep of the jaw reminded her of Derek. But every muscle in it had been contorted with purpose,

like the face of an athlete making a supreme effort—only
the purpose stamped on the features had been not human
but devilish. Could one see a face so clearly which existed
only in one's own mind? It was hard to believe, doubly
hard because she had always found it necessary for descrip-
tions in her writing to build on what she had actually seen.
It was difficult, she knew, to picture a human face *in vacuo*.
Difficult, but was it impossible? . . . pray God, it was not
impossible.

Between five and six she began to drop off to sleep for
a few seconds at a time, waking with a start and the
impression that she had been falling through space. If
her head had not ached she would have tried to prevent
herself from dozing by reading; it was better to be fully
awake than to experience the alternating horrors of falling and being jarred back to consciousness. Even the
pawnbroker's amorous problems would be preferable to
her own—to the still unsolved riddle of the scene at the
corner of the lane. She got up and drank some water,
bandaged her head with a handkerchief soaked in eau-de-
Cologne, and placed an extra pillow under her head,
hoping that if she fell asleep she would not have that
paralysing feeling of falling with nothing beneath her but
emptiness. She turned on her side and shut her eyes.

She was really asleep when Mrs. Bradshaw brought her
cup of tea at eight o'clock; she had not heard the charwoman let herself in at the back door. Saturday was
Mrs. Bradshaw's day for coming an hour early, leaving
her thirteen-year-old daughter to cope with the family
breakfast, in order, as she put it, to give the cottage a
thorough "do". For one of her size and weight she negoti-
ated the stairs with amazing speed, and slopped half the
tea she was carrying into the saucer as she burst the bedroom door open.

"Miss Munro—a norful thing 'as bin and happened.
You won't never believe it. Some murd'ring devil 'as
bin and stabbed Mr. Seely to death right in this lane, an'
he died in the 'orspital soon after they took 'im there.
Murder—that's what it wos, I'm telling you—right here

in Grassmere, not more'n a stone's-throw from your very door. I says to Bert, I says, Miss Munro won't never believe it."

Jess had no difficulty in believing it.

4

"Gracious, miss," Mrs. Bradshaw exclaimed as she set what was left of the tea on the bedside table, "you do look poorly. P'raps I didn't ought to have broke the news to you so sudden like, but I feel all of a dither myself, and I was that worried thinkin' about you when I heard the dreadful news, that I took and run nearly all the way from the village, to see if you was safe and sound. I 'ope as Miss Munro locked her front door last night, I says to Bert, 'er being only a quarter of a mile from the spot where the murder was done."

"Five yards," Jess amended to herself. Aloud she said, "Oh yes, I always lock the door at night, Mrs. Bradshaw. I do feel rather ill as it happens. The storm seems to have upset me."

"There's some as can't stand thunderstorms," sympathized Mrs. Bradshaw. "I ought to know, for my poor mother was one of them sort; always had a fit of hist'ricks, she did, when there was a bad storm. And last night the lightning was something wicked. Struck a chimney at Beech Lodge, it did, as if it wasn't misfortune enough poor Mr. Seely being murdered without his house being damaged and all. Seems like troubles never come singly, don't it?"

Jess felt she could face the situation better when she had drunk the half-cup of tea which had survived the passage upstairs. Mrs. Bradshaw drew the window curtains back and "returned to her muttons".

"Lucky thing 'e wasn't married," she continued, leaning against the bed-rail. "Leastways, they say he had been married twice, but his first wife died and the second took and divorced him. 'Tanyrate there's no woman to fret over 'im now."

"You're sure it *was* Mr. Seely who was . . . who was murdered?" Jess said weakly.

"Certain sure, miss. 'Dentified 'im afore he was dead, they did."

"How do you mean they identified him?"

"Why, miss, 'e was picked up lying half dead in the lane by the doctor drivin' home through that awful storm, 'aving been to see Mrs. West's baby as 'ad the croup. Not old Dr. Tom Leigh—'e's gorn for his ollerday—but 'is nephew who does locum for him when he's away. Lucky thing it warn't the old doctor, for he could never 'ave carried the body to the car—not but wot he wasn't still alive when he was found—and rushed 'im off to 'orspital like the young doctor did. It wasn't a mite of good though, for 'e passed away at midnight, so the postman told Bert, and he 'eard it off the p'liceman. They give 'im a blood 'fusion first, same as they did Bert when he had his operation, but 'e was too far gorn, I reckon."

"Have they caught the . . . the man who murdered him?"

"They don't know from Adam who 'e was. Seems like 'e got clean away in the storm. Mr. Seely not having been in Grassmere long—I reckon he only bought Beech Lodge just afore you come 'ere—Bert don't think it could be anybody local. I reckon they'll have a rare job to catch the brute; it'll be one of them big cases, I dessay, with big noospaper headings and suchlike. But he'll hang in the end all right, Bert says. Look here, miss, you look right feverish to me. I don't reckon you ought to get up to-day. You lay here while I slip down and get you a bit of breakfast. Daisy being home from school, I can stop to dinner if you like. It will give me a chance to give the sitting-room a real turn out and I reckon it wants a proper 'do', murder or no murder."

Jess had not the energy to refuse Mrs. Bradshaw's offer. It was so much simpler to let the woman have her way, and she felt so queer when she went to the bathroom to wash that she was thankful not to have to dress and go downstairs. Her legs ached and her back was stiff, which was hardly to be wondered at since, if her calculations were right, she must have lain in the rain-logged ditch for the best part of quarter of an hour.

After Mrs. Bradshaw's "bit of breakfast", garnished with titbits about the crime which she was now too drowsy to take in, Jess slept soundly for several hours—too soundly; it was the feverish kind of sleep which leaves the head thick and the body languid. She felt even less like rousing herself when Mrs. Bradshaw brought her some soup and toast at lunch-time, apologizing for the poverty of the fare by opining that her charge "didn't ought to take nothing solid, not while she was looking so flushed".

As though from some lofty perch, Jess looked down upon Mrs. Bradshaw's bulk rolling here and there, assuming extraordinary shapes and attitudes as its owner cleaned the room and made the bed. Jess did not attach names to these operations; it did not seem to be her room which was being swept nor her bed which was being tidied. After a time she had the impression of watching a huge seal flapping in and out among the rocks on a carpet of sand; then the seal dived into the water and the sand began to turn black. . . .

It was late afternoon when she awakened. The room was half dark because someone had pulled the dove-grey curtains across the window. Someone was moving about downstairs; not Mrs. Bradshaw—it was someone with a light tread. They were coming up the stairs now. Jess answered the knock on the door and turned her head with faint interest to see who entered.

It was Mrs. Bradshaw's Daisy, a mousey child with timid eyes and a long brown pigtail. She carried a tray almost as large as herself, and balanced it anxiously as she put it on the table.

"Please, miss, Mum said to tell you as she come away without waking you, you was sleeping so heavy she thought it would do you good. And she said to say as she sent me to get your tea, her legs not being so good as they was, and taking her a half-hour to walk from the village."

"Thank you, Daisy."

"And she said," the child went on as though fearful of forgetting her part, "that if you'd like to have the doctor, Dad will fetch him for you and to tell you Dad'll come to

take me home afore he goes to the club, Mum not liking
me to go home alone in the dark, becos' they ain't caught
the murderer yet, an' he may be lying in wait somewhere
ready to pounce again." Daisy looked fearfully round the
room as though wondering whether the murderer was lying
in wait behind a chair. "Ain't that awful, miss, to think
of that pore gentleman 'acked to pieces with a carving
knife?"

"But he wasn't hacked to pieces, Daisy," Jess corrected
the child. "At least, I don't see how he could have been if
he didn't die until he was in the hospital. But I should try
not to think too much about it if I were you. I expect the
m . . . the man who attacked Mr. Seely is a long way away
by now."

"Can't help but think about it, miss. They ain't talking
of nothing else up in the village. Standing at their gates,
they are, a-calling out acrost the road. An' I had to come
right past the spot where the doctor found him. They've
put stakes in the ground and roped it off so as you can't
walk that side of the lane. There's a p'liceman there too—
not our p'liceman; I ain't seen this one afore. I run past
as fast as I could and he called out to me there wasn't
nothing to be scared of."

The child went on babbling with low-toned suppressed
excitement while Jess drank her tea. Jess was trying not
to face the fact that she had to take some action in the
near future; action that was already overdue, but Mrs.
Bradshaw could testify that she had been too unwell to
talk or think in the morning. The obvious course was to
let Bradshaw fetch the doctor, tell him the whole story and
let him take whatever steps were necessary to inform the
police. But had not Mrs. Bradshaw said that old Dr. Leigh
was away on holiday? Jess was vague about the morning's
conversation, but this scrap of information had lodged in
her mind. It was because something had been said about
the young doctor carrying the inanimate victim to his car.
She had had a bill from Dr. Tom Leigh though, the afternoon before. But that had probably been sent by his sister
who kept house for him. Reaching the conclusion that

Mrs. Bradshaw had definitely said the old doctor was away she made it the excuse for putting off action until she was able to go out. It would be intolerable to tell her story to a stranger, and she would almost certainly be pestered that same evening for details by the police. After all, the delay was of little importance from the point of view of the investigation of the crime. The murderer was unknown to her; although she could picture him plainly in her own mind, she could not convey her impression to others; it must be clear to anyone who examined Seely that he had been stabbed in the back; and she had not seen what took place after the blow had been delivered. To-morrow she would feel better; to-morrow she would do whatever had to be done—if it still had to be done. Perhaps the police would have arrested the stranger who had stabbed Seely by then. She remembered that Derek, quoting Rupert or Althea, no doubt, had told her once that she had the *mañana* complex. But no one could expect her to get up and take action when it was painful even to turn over in bed.

Later, when Bradshaw had taken Daisy home, she began thinking about Ambrose Seely. It was odd that it had never occurred to her that he might have been the subject of the attack. She had taken it for granted that the victim as well as the aggressor was a stranger. It was more than odd, it was really absurd, because Seely was a small man and the spot where he had been attacked was close to the footpath leading to Beech House. Probably her unconscious desire to deny reality to the episode had clogged her power to reason. Althea would call it the domination of the sub-conscious mind or something of that sort.

Ambrose Seely. . . . Well, if someone in Grassmere had to be the victim of a brutal murder, it might as well be Seely as anybody else. Jess felt no regret at the knowledge that her neighbour had been precipitated into another world with melodramatic suddenness. She had known Seely personally only slightly. Her real knowledge of the man had been derived from his dramatic criticisms in the *Intelligentsia*, above the well-known pseudonym *Ambrosia*.

Everyone who wrote for *Intelligentsia* used pen names, and everyone took particular care to make their real identity plain to their readers. Jess had analysed Seely's character from his reviews, and found him less interested in plays and playwrights than in Ambrose Seely. His criticisms were carping and insincere; the style was brilliant but the brilliancy was shallow; behind the flamboyant façade of language there was no solid cultural background.

Curiously enough the two occasions on which Jess had spoken to—or more aptly, been spoken to by—Seely, had both been in London during the year she had lived with Derek. She had met him once at a cocktail party at Rupert's flat and a little later at a meeting of a Literary Society at which Seely had condemned modern novels as lacking in humour. Seely had been living in London then; she had an idea that Derek or someone else had mentioned that he had retired to the country after a nervous break-down, but she had been quite unprepared to find him her neighbour when she in turn retired to the country after being superannuated by her husband. As a neighbour, however, Seely might as well not have existed. He had shown no sign of recognition when he came face to face with her in the village post office, and she had had no wish to remind him of their former meetings. When he met her in the lane he took off his hat and gave the greeting appropriate to the time of day, but this, she was sure, was simply because he wished to follow the country custom of saluting passers-by.

Well, *Intelligentsia* would give Ambrose Seely a fulsome obituary notice, she supposed. She began to predict the phrases . . . penetrating mind . . . discerning judgment . . . scintillating wit. . . . "The death of Ambrose Seely," she murmured, "has robbed the artistic world of one of its most . . . most ardent . . . (or would trenchant be better?) . . . The death of Ambrose Seely . . ." With a baffled sigh Jess gave up groping for words and fell asleep.

5

"ALL the world loves a murder," said Chief Detective-Inspector Christopher March. "But happily not as a rule enough to commit one. I wonder how Ambrose Seely came to blot his copy-book."

Detective-Sergeant Peter Cowie produced a perfunctory grin and returned to his novel. He was bored and annoyed for a number of reasons and he wished the Chief Inspector would not talk so much. That was the worst of March; he would talk shop or semi-shop whenever he had the chance. Who on earth wanted to think about murder on a train journey, let alone discuss it? There would be plenty of that later—unfortunately.

Peter was furious with the fate that sent him to Grassmere with March that sun-drenched Sunday afternoon. Sunday was a bad day to start an investigation, he thought. He was to have been off duty that evening and he had secured a date with a young woman who was notoriously difficult to book a date with. His forced defection, he reflected ruefully, would not enhance his prospects of success next time he chanced his luck. He considered too that Grassmere was near enough to London to warrant the use of a police car for the expedition, instead of crawling down in a train that stopped at every other station. What were police cars for anyway? A further grievance was that the Chief Inspector was to be housed in comfort by the Deputy Chief Constable, while he was to put up at a pub in Grassmere, where he supposed gloomily, he would sleep in damp sheets and feed on tough beef and stale cheese. And no doubt he would have to slog through country lanes, questioning dumb yokels, while March rolled about in his host's car, or sat about at official conferences, talking big and manipulating the data his subordinate painfully collected to pin the crime on to the guilty person. Peter loved comfort and he disliked the country—except so much of it as one saw from a racecourse or golf links, and he turned the pages of his book with peevish roughness which expressed his displeasure with life.

Reaching the end of a chapter, he slammed the book to and began to fill his pipe. March had ceased trying to converse with his unresponsive companion and was smoking and gazing out of the window with unshifting eyes—a habit of his when he was concentrating on a particular train of thought. He was not a bad-looking chap, Peter reflected; his well-defined profile would show up to advantage under a barrister's wig and one could imagine him gesturing with his long fingers as he made his points. His hands were his most striking asset; Derwent had told him that painting in water-colours was March's hobby. Perhaps he was selecting a subject for his canvas now, but more probably, judging from his withdrawn expression, he was still thinking about Ambrose Seely. Not an unbearable loss to the community —Seely, Peter thought. Peter was a discerning theatre-goer, and *Ambrosia's* comments in *Intelligentsia* had infuriated him. Self-satisfaction leered at one from every paragraph. Seely was an unreliable judge of the pioneer efforts of some of the younger playwrights to break new ground. That play of Derek Garle's, for instance; it was immature and bristled with technical faults, but it had good stuff in it. *Ambrosia* had damned it not with faint praise, but with burning contempt; he had not alluded to a single one of its merits. He had the reputation for being outspoken; the easiest of all reputations to acquire, Peter thought cynically, when the victim had no chance of hitting back. Seely had invariably chosen the wrong play to boost, too; not that he often boosted anything except, Peter suspected, to provide a foil to his habitual cavilling.

Setting a light to the tobacco, Peter gently chid himself for catching the tone of the Chief Inspector's thoughts. Before the week was out he would be sick to death of Seely and all his works, and be ready to clap the fellow who had given the dramatic critic his *quietus* enthusiastically on the back—if the poor devil was ever tracked down. If only

Seely had had the grace to get himself bumped off a few weeks earlier, Peter would have had no hand in the investigation of his murder, for he had only recently been detailed to assist March, in succession to John Derwent— promoted to the rank of Detective-Inspector and assigned to other duties.   Derwent would have revelled in this excursion to rural surroundings.

The train, without—it seemed to Peter—having to slow up appreciably, entered a gravel-paved country station and halted.   March swung his wrist up and looked at the time. He remarked to Cowie that Grassmere was the next station and that they did not look like being more than ten minutes late.   Cowie was to alight at Grassmere and make his way to the Buffalo Inn.   The Chief Inspector was going on to the next station—Heathmere, which was nearer to his host's house.

Peter nodded.   "Pity Derwent is out of this, sir," he remarked.   "It will make a fair-sized stink, I guess; well-known dramatic critic bumped off during the most devastating storm for thirty years—and so on.   Derwent loves publicity."

"Not more than most of us, I fancy.   Anyhow, Derwent is not completely out of it.   I was able to arrange for him to make the initial inquiries into Seely's background at the London end, and I expect we shall see him at Grassmere during the week."

Peter checked a snort.   "I suppose he will hoof me out of my bed just as I've absorbed the damp of ages into my system.   I dare say I shall find a barn or an outhouse to sleep in, but I wish I'd brought my ground-sheet."

March looked amused.   "Don't look on the black side— or the damp side," he enjoined.   "There may be plenty for Derwent to do at a distance; Seely was a comparative newcomer to Grassmere."

"And Derwent will have to write up his murky past—if it is murky, and I'll hazard a guess that it is."

"More or less—that is, we need all we can get about Seely's background, whatever its colour."

Peter reached for his bag as the train pulled into Grassmere station. He surveyed the empty platform with distaste; it was gravelled like its predecessor, and backed by a patterned flower-border, reminiscent of a cemetery. A solitary porter chewing a piece of straw was hovering in search of prey, apparently without much hope of its appearance. Peter stepped out on to the platform and waved a hand to March as the train jolted forward on its leisurely way. He inquired of the grass-chewing porter how far it was to the Buffalo, and on being informed that it wasn't "no more'n ten minutes", and advised to turn left when he left the station, he mentally doubled the distance and set off towards the village.

The room the landlord offered Peter was a small attic, permanently condemned to semi-darkness because the window was shaded by projecting thatch. Picturesque but unhygienic, thought Peter. The bed did not look very promising; it was studded with lumps and covered with a decaying blue bedspread. Peter did not investigate any further. Probably it harboured bugs, and he dared not hope that the sheets were aired. He decided that he had received as much discouragement as he could stomach for the moment, and that his next move must be to secure some tea before he set out to explore his surroundings.

6

BRUCE NORTON's welcome to his guest was almost ecstatic. Christopher March and he were old friends. They had been colleagues in the C.I.D. at Manchester, before March gravitated to Scotland Yard, and Bruce accepted the post of Superintendent at Heathmere, and was later appointed Deputy Chief Constable. It was a shattering experience to be saddled with a murder—particularly the murder of a distinguished citizen—in one's sphere of jurisdiction while the Chief Constable was away on sick leave, and Norton had scarcely allowed himself a moment's relaxation since the crime had been reported at police headquarters. Now he felt that he could shift part of his burden—and the greater part—on to March's willing shoulders. He knew no one more ready to accept responsibility than Christopher March and the tacit way in which he assumed that any blame for failure would accrue to himself, while at the same time creating the impression that success was only a matter of time and patience, and therefore a virtual certainty, engendered in Norton a confidence which smoothed the harassed creases out of his face within ten minutes of the Chief Inspector's arrival.

"So you've run into a spot of bother," March said as he balanced his teacup and bit into a piece of bread-and-butter. They were sitting close to the open french window, facing a neat garden of the small town-residence type, and the sun was streaming gaily into the bright little room behind them.

"You've said it, Chris. And I don't mind confessing that it had me bothered, good and proper, until you turned up."

"That's very nice of you, Bruce. Do you feel like giving me an outline of the business right away, or do you believe in the theory of banishing unpleasant topics at meals?"

"My dear chap, I'm just bursting to talk the whole thing

over. The trouble is, I'm afraid, that the outline is rather blurred, not to say broken."

"That's why I'm here, I take it. Let's have it."

"I must tell you first that we know practically nothing about Seely here. He was a newcomer, he had no friends in the locality, he made no contacts. So it is difficult to know where to begin."

"Begin at the end—with his death."

"He died at midnight on Friday, in the Cottage Hospital here."

"Without recovering consciousness? He didn't speak at all?"

"You've put your finger on the sore spot right away, Chris. He did recover consciousness to some extent, but unfortunately—*most* unfortunately—it was soon after he was taken to the hospital and before our man was on the scene. They telephoned from the hospital to police head-quarters directly Seely was admitted, and the Sergeant-in-Charge sent a constable off at once on a bicycle. The storm had died down by then but the streets were greasy. He made the best pace he could, and there seems to have been no unreasonable delay. I don't think one can fairly blame anybody, but the fact is that Seely's brief spell of lucidity—or semi-lucidity—was over when he turned up, and though he remained by the injured man's bedside until he died, he got nothing at all. If Seely had been able to make a statement it might have changed the whole complexion of the case."

"If he knew who attacked him, it would certainly have simplified matters," March said dryly. And seeing that Norton's fair skin was beginning to weave itself into its old pattern of anxiety he added: "But as the police were not to blame, it's not your worry, Bruce."

"All the same one wishes . . . It was a case of 'so near and yet so far', you see. Seely did speak a few inco-ordinated words, but no one is able to swear to what he said. The doctors were preoccupied with trying to save the man's life; it was not their primary concern to get information out of him."

"You know, Bruce, if one of your men made a report to you in this rambling, tantalizing way, you'd haul him over the coals! Exactly, and in chronological order, what *did* happen from the moment Seely was admitted to hospital?"

Norton responded to the Chief Inspector's banter with a wry smile. "Seely was unconscious on admission, and was examined immediately by Matthews, the best surgeon in the district, who happened to be visiting a serious case he had operated on earlier in the day. Assisted by Leigh, he removed the knife from Seely's back in the operating theatre. Leigh had not attempted to do this earlier as he had no means in the car of dealing with the subsequent bleeding. Matthews formed the opinion that Seely's recovery, owing to the location of the wound, was extremely doubtful. Seely opened his eyes and began to mutter soon after the knife was extracted and, before giving him an injection to deaden the pain, Matthews asked him if he knew who had attacked him. Seely did not reply, but Matthews fancied he understood the question, so he framed his next one differently, and asked him if he knew of anyone likely to try to harm him. Seely then tried, it seems, to answer the previous question and said something to the effect that he did not, or could not, see anything. Even that is uncertain; the nurse who was present said she thought he said something about lightning—forked lightning. Leigh was standing behind Seely's head, and heard only the '-ing' sound which was repeated as though it had some special significance. And that was all. The injection quietened Seely and he lapsed into a stupor. The constable was on the spot a few minutes later and was present while the blood transfusion was given. But Seely lost ground steadily all the same. He never spoke again."

March betrayed no disappointment. His sole comment was that it was by no means certain that the police representative could have coaxed a coherent statement out of a dying man.

"Maybe not," agreed Norton. "But he would have done his damndest. . . ."

"No doubt, and hastened Seely's death, I dare say."

"He would have been under medical supervision. With skill and patience he ought to have achieved something better than Matthews anyhow. What is the use of 'ing . . . ing . . .' I ask you? Enough to make one crave for more—a mere appetizer——"

"I'm not sure that we may not be able to make use of the fragment later. But go on with your story."

"Leigh will tell you how he found Seely lying in the lane, near the footpath to his house, on his way home from an urgent case. The time was within a few minutes of nine o'clock. It is quite clear how Seely came to be there. Since he came to live at Beech House just over a year ago, he has kept in touch with his work in London by going up to Fleet Street twice a week, on Tuesdays and Fridays. He returns always by the last down train which stops at Grassmere, arriving at eight-thirty-five. Normally, it would take him about twenty minutes to walk home; on a night like that perhaps five or ten minutes longer. The train was punctual and Seely was seen to leave the station. Grassmere station does not boast any taxis; there is a car for hire in the village, but it has to be ordered, and as a matter of fact it had been ordered that evening to drive some people home who were going in the opposite direction from Seely. So Seely set off on foot and may be presumed to have reached the junction between Cairn Lane and the road the local people call Pillar-box Lane about twenty minutes later. He was then within three or four minutes' walk of his house."

"Which he never reached because he was stabbed and fatally wounded between, say, eight-fifty and nine-five."

"Those are about the time limits. Seely was admitted to the hospital at nine-thirty; Leigh drove carefully on account of the weather and the risk of jolting the injured man. I don't think he could have made it in under twenty-five minutes. The time of the attack is about the only thing we are definite about. Leigh saw nothing of Seely's assailant; no one was likely to be out unnecessarily in such a storm; no stranger was seen that day in the locality. The knife was an ordinary steel carving-knife, such as one might find in any house. The surface of the handle was too rough to register finger-prints. By the time our police car reached the scene of the attack, the murderer had had a good hour to make his getaway. Search of the ground where Leigh found Seely yielded nothing. The lane was practically under water; no use looking for footmarks. If the assailant got away by the fields, which is indicated by the fact that Leigh didn't meet or overtake him—he would find meadow land one side of the lane and a deep ditch on the other. No doubt he would avoid the ditch and the grass would show no footmarks."

"Anything else you can find to put on the debit side, Bruce?"

Norton shook his head with a grin.

"Not just at the moment, Chris. There's no knowing what I may think up later."

"Let's consider the credit side then. The dirtier the night, the less likely, as you aptly pointed out, that anyone would be abroad unnecessarily. Unnecessarily, that is, for some purpose of his own. It need not have been a good purpose, Bruce. The murderer, having decided to lie in wait for Seely and stab him—I am assuming premeditation because people do not normally carry carving-knives about with them—found it necessary to his purpose to brave the storm. When we come to the little matter of alibis, the weather will be a favourable factor for us. Sensible people remained under shelter; no one can plead that he just went out for a walk alone. And when our man reached cover he must have been wet—very wet indeed."

"Oh well, if you can find comfort in that . . ."

March's grey eyes twinkled. "I find quite a lot of comfort in it, Bruce. And in other things. Chief Constables, for instance, have a pardonable if regrettable habit of backing their local fellows to solve a crime, and only falling back on the Yard when their own lads seem to be exceeding the reasonable time limit, or, less euphemistically, when they get stuck. In this particular instance——"

"I'm afraid I deserve no praise, Chris. The motive was not modesty but sheer cowardice."

"None the less I reap the benefit. I'm faddy about corpses; I like 'em fresh."

"Talking of corpses, the inquest is to-morrow morning. We shall get an adjournment, so it won't take up much of our time. I don't know what you would like to do this evening? My car is, of course, at your disposal."

"Thanks, Bruce. I don't think I need go far afield. I've told my assistant to get in touch as soon as possible with your man at Grassmere, go over the ground with him, and ring me up if there is anything there which calls for my immediate attention. I've acquired a new sergeant by the way—a young man of the name of Cowie, he's the son of Chief Inspector Cowie of Manchester fame. You remember him, perhaps?"

"Gerald Cowie? Of course I remember Gerald. If his son is anything like him, you are well placed."

March smiled at the suggestion. "I think Peter must take after his mother—without offence to the good woman, whom I haven't had the pleasure of meeting. Between ourselves, I am doubtful whether Peter will make the grade. So far as I am concerned he is on probation, though he doesn't know that. It is reported that he cast himself as an actor, was turned down at his first audition with un-flattering comments, and decided in a fit of pique to gratify his father's wish. However that may be he is in on this case for better or for worse, and it's my job to avoid the second alternative, if I can. Peter has some assets. He is pleasantly unofficial in appearance and he makes friends easily, if he wants to. But that is a digression. If I hear nothing from him this evening, I am to meet him to-morrow morning at Grassmere. Meantime I should like to get in touch with Dr. Leigh, and whoever was in charge of the party which 'proceeded', as they say, 'to the scene of the crime' on Friday night."

"You can do both those things, Chris, without stirring from your arm-chair. I took the precaution of asking Leigh to keep me apprised of his movements to-day and at the moment he is playing golf on the Heathmere course. He promised to call here on his way home if I gave him a ring.

Inspector Norman is at police headquarters, tying himself into knots over the reports and statements available to date about the crime, and trying to make them look less like a jigsaw puzzle before submitting them to you. He also will appear, complete with dossier, at a word from me. Which of the two will you begin with?"

"Give your man a little longer to play with his puzzle. I should like to meet the doctor first."

Returning from the telephone, Norton announced that Dr. Leigh would be along inside half an hour. "While we await him, Chris, there is one small request I should like to make. I know you love talking; keep me *au fait* with your methods of handling this case as you go along. I've done nothing but routine work since I left Manchester, and I feel I've lost touch with the art of crime detection."

"My dear fellow, I should have done that in any case. As you say, I love talking and Cowie is as responsive to a confidant as the dagger which stabbed Seely."

"Carving-knife."

"Figure of speech. You may regret before the end of my visit that you invited me to talk."

"No fear of that. Begin now and tell me where I've gone wrong already, there's a good fellow. I mean it; I'm not angling for praise."

March smiled as he shook his head. "I don't think you've committed any fatal error. You may perhaps have presented me with one or two unwarrantable conclusions."

"For example?"

"Your assertion that Seely made no local contacts. Is that really true, Bruce? Did a busy dramatic critic live entirely alone in his country retreat and do all his own cooking and housework? Seely, unless I have built up a false picture of him from his literary self-revelation, had considerable regard for his stomach. . . ."

"Of course he didn't live alone. When he bought Beech House, he was lucky enough to persuade the very respectable married couple who had worked for its late owner to stay on and look after him."

"There you are then; that gives us two contacts for a

start. Then you mentioned that Seely came to Grassmere on account of his health. He had been there for over a year. Had he no need during that time of the services of a local doctor?"

"I understand that old Dr. Leigh—Dr. Tom as they call him locally—attended Seely since he came to Beech House. Dr. Tom has reached the age when he ought to retire; he takes long holidays to prolong his active career and he has no partner. For some time now his nephew, Jerome Leigh, has acted as locum for him during his absences. I think Seely must have consulted Jerome Leigh while his uncle was away, because Jerome stated that he recognized the injured man as soon as he got him inside his car and turned the ceiling light on."

"Good; that gives us four contacts, including the absent Dr. Leigh."

"But . . ."

March held up his hand. "I know, I know, Bruce. You didn't mention any of those people because they were so obvious as to be mentally invisible to you, like Chesterton's famous postman. And I'm not questioning their respectability till I know more about them. But we have to get at Seely's murderer *via* someone. And who is more likely to know something helpful about Seely's affairs than his doctor and his domestic staff? And were you perhaps a little rash in saying categorically that no stranger was seen in the locality on the day of the crime?—unless you are prepared to vouch personally for all the inhabitants of Grassmere. . . ."

"Of course I can't do that, my dear fellow. I simply meant that my men have made inquiries without result— and of course the news was all over the village by Saturday morning."

"No doubt, and no one has come forward with an oblig-ing description of a sinister-looking stranger. That does not preclude the possibility that our man may have been seen. Perhaps he was a mental 'invisible'; perhaps some-one has a reason for not betraying him or perhaps even is holding back for no better reason than dislike of publicity.

I wouldn't say that no man, woman or child in Grassmere, saw anyone on Friday to whom they couldn't put a name, unless I could see inside all their minds—all of which sounds terribly 'Holmesian' I'm afraid."

"I asked for it—but here, I think, comes your first 'contact'—Dr. Jerome Leigh. I hope he will prove a useful one."

7

PETER sauntered through the village towards Pillar-box Lane. He had to admit grudgingly that it was quite pleasant strolling along the country lanes in the late afternoon sunshine, provided one did not have to go too far or too fast. He had no intention of communicating with the Chief Inspector unless asked to do so by the local police; he thought it would be much more amusing to poke about for himself. A certain morbid interest attached, even to one of his cultural standard, to the spot where the celebrated critic had been stabbed, and communicated itself to the home where the victim had spent the last year of his life. Murder, reflected Peter, casts a glamour, even though it be a sordid glamour, over scenes which would normally not attract a second glance. There was no need to feel shamed by the slight anticipatory quickening of his pulses as he turned out of the village street into Pillar-box Lane. Was it not acknowledged that reading detective fiction was one of the recreations of the intellectual and had not Dorothy Sayers pointed out that Aristotle, who had "a stout appetite for the gruesome", had accepted the detective story as a worthy subject for serious treatment? For once, since his instructions were to visit Beech House and the scene of Friday's tragedy, Peter found that duty coincided with pleasure and, little as he had wished to forego other more commonplace pleasures in order to visit Grassmere, he decided that now he was there he might as well extract what enjoyment he could from the situation. He did not propose to exert himself unduly, but if he could laze his way into the late Ambrose Seely's environment and discover therein some clue to the mystery of his death, he would have the additional pleasure of surprising March with his brilliancy. The Chief Inspector, Peter was aware, considered his new sergeant a feeble substitute for the in-

defatigable, painstaking Derwent. He might learn that
some people could achieve without effort what others had
to toil after. Like Adrian Winterton in *Good-bye to Murder*,
which Peter had read without in any way identifying himself with that unattractive character, he believed himself
capable of success in almost any career which he chose to
adopt. The stage was barred to him by the unfortunate
lack of discernment which characterized the selectors of
castes. It was not unlikely that the stage's loss might prove
the Yard's gain. So long as the opportunity for a brilliant
coup was forthcoming, without the need for any excessive
exertion. . . .

That others had shared Peter's Aristotelian appetite for
the gruesome was evidenced by the boot-crushed surface
of the lane. A regiment of soldiers would hardly have
flattened the mud more thoroughly. Apparently two days
had sufficed to satiate the emotional cravings of the villagers,
for the road was now deserted, or perhaps they were all at
home discussing the tragedy over their tea and would return
later for more mouthfuls of titillating food. Peter reached
the corner of Cairn Lane where rope and stakes still marked
the spot where Seely had been struck down by the assailant's
knife. Evidently the necessary police survey had been made,
and the site photographed from every aspect, for there was
now no one on guard to warn off sightseers. Deliberately
Peter swung a leg over the rope, lifted his other foot carefully, and stood beneath the tree which had sheltered
Seely's murderer. He lit a cigarette and measured the
enclosed ground with a speculative eye.

There was nothing apart from the barrier raised by the
police to denote the grim significance the little patch of
rough turf had lately acquired. An observer had to draw
on his imagination to re-create the dark episode of Friday
night. With the knowledge he had obtained from his host
at the inn, Peter began to build up the picture, stroke by
stroke. The storm was flashing and raging overhead as
Seely struggled home from the station, his mackintosh
collar turned up and his hat jammed down to protect his
face from the rain. He was not a strongly-built man and

he had not been in good health. He would have been tired
when he reached the turning and perhaps anxious about
his safety as the storm grew more intense. He must have
turned the corner with a sigh of relief. He was nearly home
now and beginning to think, perhaps, of dry slippers and a
stiff peg of whisky. He kept close to the hedge as he entered
the narrow lane, for who would want to take a step out of
his way on such a night? He was abreast of the tree now
under which Peter was standing and Peter mentally transferred his own body to the other side of the tree. For there
it must have been that fate stalked Ambrose Seely, ready
to strike at the very moment when his spirits were rising,
and his tired steps quickening. Peter abandoned Seely for
a moment and saw himself as the killer; a strong man,
perhaps a big man, for the blow which pierced Seely's
mackintosh and jacket had needed force behind it. Turning his head, he measured with his eye the space between
the trunk and the hedge. Room enough there for a larger
bulk than Peter's. A most convenient waiting-place. A
spring as the small man passed the tree, a single blow, with
power and weight behind it, and the little matter of sending
Seely to his last account was settled. And after . . . ?
Escape over the stile that Seely was making for, perhaps
. . . yes, almost certainly, for there was a deep ditch the
other side of the lane.

Throwing away his cigarette end, Peter approached the
stile. At Beech House, he understood, the local sergeant
was expecting him. He took a couple of steps forward and
checked himself abruptly, drawing aside just in time to
avoid collision with the young man who vaulted the stile
from the other side. Peter had felt so much alone a moment
before that he stared in surprise at the intruder. The first
local resident he had come across was, he reflected, no
yokel but a man of his own standing. Only his leather
jerkin and whipcord breeches suggested that he was a
farmer rather than a professional man. He was a strapping
well-set-up fellow, but his face was not that of a country
dweller. The thickness of the black hair, clinging like a
cap to the well-shaped head, led one to expect a swarthy

complexion. But the man's skin was almost ivory white, and though his hands showed signs of manual work—Peter always had an eye for hands—they were slender and graceful. The leap, too, with only the slightest contact of fingers with the bar of the stile, had been graceful; in fact there was something of the athlete in the build of the young stranger who had sprung so unexpectedly into Peter's path.

The stranger stared back at Peter in equal surprise before he found his voice.

"Afraid I nearly jumped on to you," he apologized, speaking in a pleasant low-pitched tone. "Were you going over the stile?"

"I was and I am," Peter responded with a smile.

"Perhaps I had better warn you, they—the police, I mean—are turning reporters away from Beech House."

Peter was not sure that he appreciated being classed as a reporter, but he contrived to look disappointed.

"Is that so?" he said, looking regretfully at the footpath.

The unknown nodded. "If that leaves you with time to kill—there's no train back to town for a couple of hours—why not come along with me? I've been taking a look at the damage done by the storm, but I'm on my way home now. My farm is only half a mile away and I can give you a drink."

Peter decided that the local sergeant could wait and, accepting the stranger's offer, tried to suit his step to that of his longer-legged companion as they set off down Cairn Lane.

"I wouldn't have taken you for a farmer, except for your clothes," he remarked, to set the conversation going.

"I wasn't—until two years ago. I was a journalist before the war, joined the Navy as a temporary bluejacket, was invalided out with arrested t.b. and advised to take up outdoor work. I had a course of training—provided by the Government and took Cairn Farm—also provided by the Government. So here I am."

"Hard luck," Peter murmured.

"I don't know; they tell me I may live to be ninety in

the right surroundings. I've put on a couple of stone in weight since I came to Grassmere."

"But does one want to live to be ninety—in exile?"

"You haven't time to feel exiled."

"But isn't farming terribly boring?"

The young man laughed quietly. He seemed to be enjoying Peter's ignorance. "It's exhausting and exasperating, but boring is the last word I should apply to it," he asserted.

Peter, off his guard, was on the point of saying that he had once contemplated going in for journalism, and thought he could have made good in that line, when he remembered that at the moment he was a journalist. He retrieved the situation by asking what paper his companion had been on.

"I free-lanced for a year or two—didn't make much of a living, though. *Intelligentsia* gave me my first regular job; that was when they had just started, before their rise to power. I didn't last long there, though. I was booted out when they became established and was free-lancing again when the war broke out."

Peter had pricked up his ears. "Did you know Seely in your *Intelligentsia* days?"

"Vaguely, I think. He didn't make much impression on me; he hadn't made a name for himself then. He and the paper waxed mighty together. Apparently I made even less impression on him; he didn't remember me when he came here."

It struck Peter as odd that only an oblique reference had been made so far to the fact that Seely had been murdered two days ago. Perhaps as a nosy newspaper man it was appropriate for him to introduce the subject his companion shunned. He was just about to do so when his eye was caught by a low white cottage, picturesquely dappled with reddening virginia creeper.

"Very rural and charming," he exclaimed. "Who lives there?"

"Another ex-Londoner, but whether she feels exiled or not I can't tell you; I've never spoken to her. Her name is Miss Munro, and I believe she writes novels."

"Jessica Munro?"

"Maybe; the name means nothing to me, I'm afraid."

"You know, you're shattering my conception of country life. I imagined neighbours were neighbours in a village and that everyone knew all there was to know about everyone else and a good deal more. I suppose you'll tell me that you didn't know Seely?"

"I shouldn't be far out if I said that. I passed the time of day with him—no more."

The end of Cairn Lane degenerated into a slough caused by the tramping of cattle to pasture. Peter zigzagged in an attempt to preserve his shoes from contamination, but gave it up as hopeless, and squelched after his guide through a gate leading to a small farmyard. Beyond the yard a cheerful red and brown farmhouse shone in the slanting sunlight.

"By the way," said the owner, leading the way over the threshold, "I should have told you that my name is Ling— Ivan Ling. I'm afraid my wife is away for the week-end, but I'll do my best to entertain you while you're marking time. What will you drink—whisky or beer?"

Masking his surprise at hearing that Ling was married, Peter expressed a preference for beer.

8

BRUCE NORTON closed the french window as the sun dipped
behind the roof-tops at the bottom of the garden. As soon
as one was deprived of sunshine the chill of late September
crept into one's bones; he was a little stiff already from
sitting still while he listened to the other two talking, Chris
unobtrusively questioning and prompting, and Jerome
Leigh narrating and explaining. As they faced one another
they reminded Bruce of counsel and friendly witness. March
looked like a distinguished barrister completely at ease as
he drew the information he wanted from the doctor and
pigeon-holed it in his mind for future reference. Bruce
admired the skill with which he recalled Leigh to the point
whenever he strayed from it, without appearing to interrupt
him. He had created an atmosphere of informality, while
at the same time, Bruce noticed, certain formalities were
being carefully observed.

Jerome Leigh was facing the light, his long legs stretched
in front of him, and his head pressed comfortably into a
soft cushion. His skin still glowed from his round of golf,
and Bruce noticed that it was tanned almost to the shade
of his brown hair. He had one feature which reminded
Bruce of old Dr. Tom; his blue-green eyes, shaded by heavy
lashes. He had told March how he had acted as locum for
his uncle for several years in succession; he was a member
himself of a partnership of four doctors in a west country
town, and this enabled him to absent himself for a month
each year to look after Dr. Tom's practice. He knew most
of the regular patients fairly well now. On Friday night
he had gone to visit a sick baby a couple of miles or so
beyond the spot where he had found Seely.

"Were you sent for?" March had asked him.

"Not that night; they would have had to send someone
on foot and I doubt if they would have done that in such a

storm unless the child were dying. I was sent for on the
Tuesday night just after dark. The baby was in a bad way
then—I hardly hoped to pull it through.   But in the
astounding way babies have of clinging to a thread, it hung
on through the night and the next morning it was a little
better. I saw it the two following mornings, and I'd had
it on my mind all Friday. But I was pretty busy and I
had no other case in that direction. It wasn't till after tea,
when I was entering my visits in the case-book, that I
found I still had to see the child, and I decided to go over
directly after my evening surgery. It was the hell of a
night to turn out, but there was no help for it. I found the
baby had turned the corner, and I only stayed for a few
minutes, rather wishing I hadn't been quite so conscientious. It took all I knew to keep the car on the road driving
home. My shortest way was by Pillar-box Lane, and the
rain was pouring on to the windscreen in a solid sheet. I
was about half-way to Cairn corner when the whole world
seemed to go up in flame and there was a deafening crash;
it was just as though an ammunition dump had blown up.
I braked instinctively and switched off the engine; I
wondered for a minute if I'd been struck; I felt a bit dazed
and numbed. It was that flash, evidently, which struck
Beech House, about a quarter of a mile away on my right,
so it's not surprising that I thought it had got the car.
After a couple of minutes the shock wore off and I pushed
on cautiously in bottom gear. The rain began to slacken
soon after the climax, but it was still heavy enough to make
driving a strain on the eyes. When I reached the corner of
Cairn Lane my headlights picked up—and only just picked
up—a dark hump on the grass verge. If it had been a little
further round the corner I should have missed it. I thought
in terms of 'it' rather than 'him' at first sight, but of course
I stopped and got out to investigate. When I drew close I
saw it was a man; I wondered if he had been struck by
lightning, or was perhaps just stunned by shock. I swung
round one of the headlights of the car, and at once I saw
the knife. My mind began to work from the police angle;
I was a police surgeon at one time. The only thing I had

handy to mark the spot with was my pen-knife. I sacrificed it, sticking it into the ground just behind Seely's head. As it happened, I drove it in so deep it disappeared, but the police dug it out and marked the spot in their plan. I carried Seely to the car and put him under the ceiling light to see if he were still alive. It was then that I recognized him, and finding there was still a spark of life in him, decided to rush him to hospital—if you can use the term 'rush' in such conditions. I made the best speed I could having regard to the weather and his comfort."

March had intervened at this point to ask whether Leigh had seen anyone on the road between the cottage and the corner of Cairn Lane.

"Not a creature," the doctor replied. "And I saw no one after I picked Seely up either, until I reached the main road to Grassmere where I met an occasional car—still no pedestrians. I don't think I saw anyone on foot until I was in the town. It wasn't an encouraging night for promenaders."

Jerome Leigh had described the fight for Seely's life at the hospital, every detail of which was already familiar to Norton. None the less, the doctor's matter-of-fact recapitulation, punctuated by March's requests for more detail, captured Bruce's attention, and he derived added interest from his effort to follow the working of the Chief Inspector's mind.

March was taking the doctor back over some of the ground now.

"How did you fix the time when you picked Seely up as within a few minutes of nine o'clock?" he asked.

"Roughly, at first, from the time we reached hospital. My guess was confirmed later by Inspector Norman who told me the chimney at Beech House was struck at five minutes to nine, according to the people present there."

"When you pulled up, thinking you had been struck yourself . . . think back, will you, and tell me just what happened."

"Nothing happened. I just sat and recovered."

"Were you in a condition to hear any unexpected noise?"

"I think so. You mean if Seely had screamed . . . ?"

"I was thinking of something like that. You didn't move on, I take it, while the thunder was still deafening you?"

"I'm rather hazy as to what I did."

"Was it a sharp crash, or a prolonged growl?"

"Sharp as . . . I can't find a simile."

"Never mind. Sharp and *short*, was it?"

"Relatively short—that is my impression. If there had been a shout for help or a loud shriek after it died down, I should say my ears would have registered it, though I doubt if my brain would have interpreted it till later."

"But you would have done so when you found Seely?"

"Undoubtedly. Either Seely had no time to cry out, or I was too far off to hear him. I stopped by a gateway in a bend in Pillar-box Lane. The Inspector has it taped on his plan."

"Good. We will return to the hospital then. I understand three people were present when Seely spoke. Which of the three was in the best position for hearing him?"

"Matthews, undoubtedly. He asked the questions and bent over Seely to catch his reply. I was the worst placed; I couldn't see his lips."

"But you did hear something?"

"As I said, he seemed to be repeating a word ending in '-ing'. His breathing was bad, and his voice not much more than a whisper."

"Did it strike you that he was definitely trying to convey information or did he seem to be just rambling? I want your original impression—before you compared notes with Matthews and the nurse."

"I thought he was anxious to give a message; I hoped Matthews had made sense of it. But it was more difficult than perhaps you realize. I heard a number of indistinct sounds as well as the one I picked out, but the breathing broke the words into monosyllables with distinct pauses in between. Any sound might have been one word, or part of another word. There was no guessing the meaning from the rhythm of the sentence."

March declared that nothing was farther from his mind than to blame anyone because Seely's last words had not been clearly recorded. Leigh grinned, and said the doctor generally got a kick at the inquest, a statement which Bruce interrupted reproachfully.

"You must have been unlucky in the west country, Leigh. Coroners and police are all charitable creatures in this part of the world, and I believe March is the Yard's champion diplomat. What about a spot of sherry while he prepares the ground for his next—I won't say attack . . ."

"Expedition," supplied the Chief Inspector. "I'm really exploring Leigh's mind, to see if there is more inside it than he realizes."

Jerome Leigh raised his glass and shot an impish glance at the Chief Inspector. "Here's luck to the inquisition!"

"Thank you, but my vanity prefers the word 'success'."

"One way or another I hope you get your man—and get him quickly."

"One way or another, I mean to do just that. By the way, when did you first meet Ambrose Seely?"

"I didn't meet him here last year at all. My uncle took his holiday earlier; the late owner of Beech House died while he was away. As it happened, I met Seely the night I arrived at Grassmere a couple of weeks ago. I always come down the day before my uncle leaves, so that he can turn things over to me personally. Seely looked in to fetch some tablets my uncle had ordered specially for him; it was out of surgery hours and my uncle brought him into the sitting-room and introduced us. It was understood then that I was to look Seely up now and then during the next month. Actually I had not yet done so when he called me in last Thursday."

"The day before his death?"

"Yes. I got the message in the morning and called late in the afternoon. He only wanted a routine inspection; perhaps he thought I had forgotten he wanted me to call."

"You didn't gather that he called you in because he was worried about something?"

"I understood from my uncle that he had been worried about his health ever since he came to Grassmere."

"Nothing specific? Did he make any personal confidences?"

Leigh shook his head. "I wasn't inside the house more than about five minutes. I had to get back for a surgery."

"Don't take this amiss, but were you sufficiently hurried and abrupt in your manner to check any confidence he might have intended to make? Suppose, for instance, that he meant to tell you that his health was being undermined by some specific worry, such as fear of violence at the hands of someone he had offended; did you give him a chance to unburden his mind?"

"To be honest, perhaps not. I wasn't expecting anything of that sort from a man I was visiting professionally for the first time."

Norton quietly refilled his guests' glasses, remarking as he stooped over March's chair that one of his avenues seemed to be blocked.

"I wasn't hoping to get very far," the Chief Inspector said cheerfully. "This is very good sherry, Bruce—where do you get it—black market? . . . What I was thinking was that it looks as though someone with a grievance against Seely deliberately laid in wait for him at a spot he knew he would pass at a certain time on Friday night. You both agree? . . . Good. Now, when I say 'grievance' I mean something of a substantial enough nature to rouse very strong passions."

"The desire to kill," put in Norton.

"Just so. Can we conceive that Seely was blissfully ignorant of the injury he had done this hypothetical person? I think the odds are that he knew, and that the knowledge brought fear; he may possibly have been threatened. If I am right, he was probably trying to name the object of his fear when the surgeon questioned him in hospital. Now, is there——?"

"Good God!" exclaimed Bruce. "Why didn't I think of it before? The sound he repeated was 'ing'. . . ."

"Well?" prompted March sharply.

"The married couple I told you about who look after Beech House—their name is King. The man is George King!"

9

PETER had some difficulty in shaking the mud of Cairn Farm off his shoes, for his host was persuaded that he had time to burn until the next train up to London was due. He congratulated himself on the resource which had inspired him to develop a passionate interest in architecture; fortune had favoured his boldness, for it appeared that part of Grassmere Church was fourteenth century—no doubt, Ivan said, his guest would discern the original among the hotch-potch of restorative work—for himself, he had no time to study any art except the art of farming. He directed Peter to the church; he would offer to act as guide but he had chickens to feed and sundry other small jobs to do—Peter smiled with relief. He set off alone through the mud, shuddering a little with distaste, and hoping the Buffalo would provide an efficient shoe-cleaner, for he had no mind to pollute his hands as well as his feet with the stench of the farmyard.

His destination was not the parish church but the chaste little white cottage, hiding shyly behind its veil of autumn leaves. "Chaste" was a good word to describe it, he thought. He had a flair for language; he might have made good as a novelist, if he had not given in to his father's whim and followed in his footsteps. He would like to meet Jessica Munro; she had a flair for the right word too, but she ought to develop a sense of drama. There was insufficient plot and action in her books, a fashionable fault, but a fault none the less in Peter's view. A book in which nothing happened from cover to cover was a dull book however well it was written. One didn't want to be told how people would behave in various contingencies; one wanted to see their reactions for oneself. He was confident he could construct a book with a sound plot, and adorn it with prose no less graceful than Jessica Munro's—but one must first

live. . . . Jessica had a convent mind; she ought to come
out of her virginal cottage and . . . Peter broke his train
of thought as he approached the white gate. He began to
prepare his entrance speech.

He probed among the tawny leaves with an exploring
finger, found a bell and pressed it, but heard no sound
from within. He seized the brass knocker and beat a cheerful tattoo. That would rouse her if she were enjoying a
Sunday siesta. . . . It had roused her, for a door banged
overhead, and stairs began to creak, the sound intensifying
as the responder to the summons descended slowly. Feet
clopped on a wooden floor and the door was pulled open
with a jerk. An immense woman, wearing a blue checked
gingham apron over a bursting Sunday dress, confronted
Peter with displeasure.

"That's the third noospaper man I've creaked down
them stairs to send packing," she announced.

Peter was slightly disconcerted for a moment but recovered his confidence before the door was closed in his
face. He edged forward with a foot over the threshold.
"I'm not a newspaper man," he disclaimed. "May I see
Miss Munro?"

" 'Ooever you may be, you can't see 'er to-day; Miss
Munro is very poorly, else I shouldn't be here meself,
Sunday being a day I reckon to bide at home. But I
couldn't let her lie abed with no one to see her, so I leaves
my Daisy to see to the dinner, and I says to my husband
as they must get on best way they could, for Miss Munro,
I says, needs lookin' after more'n what they do, not but
what my feet ache cruel bad and I could do with a good
lie abed myself."

Peter, rehearsing his apologies while the good woman
wheezed and rumbled on, showed such a charming interest
in Miss Munro's indisposition that Mrs. Bradshaw was
mollified. "No, I don't reckon as it's nothing worse than
a thorough chill, and no wonder this weather, raining cats
and dogs one day, and pipin' hot the next."

"You had a bad storm on Friday?" Peter ventured. He
had wheedled the whole of his slim person through the

half-open door, and he leaned a shoulder against the panelled wall as he spoke.

"Shocking bad, that was; I don't reckon the folk here will forget it in a hurry, what with the harvest bein' spoilt and pore Mr. Seely murdered, and all. Lucky we was all safe indoors though the wireless crackled that bad we couldn't hear the noos, same as we always does, but I'm sorry for anyone as was out that night—might 'ave bin struck or drownded, or stabbed in the back by that 'orrible man."

"I don't suppose anybody *was* out after dark, except Mr. Seely and the man who attacked him——"

"Not for choice, they wasn't, but there's some as didn't have no choice. The doctor was out, and lucky 'e was as it turned out, and pore Hannah Green was half drownded a-runnin' home after Beech House was struck. . . ."

Peter showed a polite interest in the unfortunate Hannah. Hannah, Mrs. Bradshaw explained, was general help at Cairn Farm and lived in. "Which many won't do these days, but her 'aving no home it suits her well enough." Hannah, Peter also learned, was aunt to the late Mr. Seely's housekeeper. She had gone to tea with her niece on Friday afternoon, which she often did when Mr. Seely was in London, and been caught by the rain. She had waited as long as she dared, but she had to leave before the rain stopped; people went to bed early in a farmhouse. "Fell down twice, she did, the path was that slipp'ry. 'Twas lucky she didn't break her neck, nor she wasn't the only one to get a ducking. . . ."

"Really?" prompted Peter gently.

"That she wasn't. Mrs. Ling was in a rare taking when she got home, Hannah says to me Saturday afternoon when I see her in the shop, along of Mr. Ling being out in the storm, and him supposed to be careful of 'is chest of a night-time and all."

Oho, thought Peter. So Master Ivan *had* been out in the storm, had he? This was definitely intriguing—in fact it was peculiarly suspicious. For Peter, anticipating that one of his routine tasks the following day would be a house-to-house canvass in search of villagers who had been abroad on Friday night, had adroitly extracted from Ling the information that he had remained at home after dusk. And the information was false! His mind rapidly constructed a newspaper paragraph under the heading of "Grassmere Murder" . . . "Detective-Sergeant Peter Cowie, who accompanied Chief Inspector March to Grassmere to investigate the murder of Ambrose Seely . . . obtained information which led to the arrest . . ." There might be a photograph inset—the one he had had taken recently, which made him look rather like Rupert Brooke; Derwent had said it reminded him of a head on a postage stamp—John was not always particularly tactful. . . . But the iron was hot and, if he did not strike, his informant might flit; she was casting a speculative eye at the staircase already.

"I hope neither Hannah nor Mr. Ling were any the worse for getting wet," he said, infusing a note of anxiety into his voice.

"Hannah is that tough I don't reckon nothing 'ud harm her, without she fell in the duck pond and was drownded outright. As for Mr. Ling, he didn't take no harm neither. His wife made him take a hot bath and get right into bed the minnit he got home, Hannah says."

"Very wise," remarked Peter with a grandmotherly air. "Nothing like a hot bath and a good swig—and a nice hot drink when you get your feet wet."

"Feet! I reckon Mr. Ling got more'n his feet wet! Dripped all over the kitchen, he did, Hannah says, when he got in. Bert says he reckons we 'ad a cloud-burst bang on top of the village and lucky we wasn't flooded right out."

Peter thought he had gleaned all there was to glean from playing the part of sympathetic commentator. It was time Detective-Sergeant Cowie set off in search of fresh worlds to conquer. His informant seemed to have reached the same conclusion for she swept the door wide open with unexpected swiftness directly he made the first move, remembering to ask him what name she should tell Miss Munro only when he was on the doorstep.

"Oh, don't worry her now," he said, turning so that his

farewell smile might not waste its sweetness on the gravel path. "I'll call again when Miss Munro is better."

If Peter's interest in architecture had been real and not feigned, he would have been enchanted by Beech House. It was the remains of an old Tudor manor, known for two centuries as Grassmere Manor—before its Georgian purchaser rechristened and restored it. The footpath from the top of Cairn Lane joined the old drive to the manor close to the inner entrance gate; the outer entrance had been covered by a fine archway which had crumbled into disuse, and the drive itself no longer belonged to the house. It was indeed now no more than a broad cart-track across a meadow, and beyond the meadow it joined a small open road which wound circuitously towards Cairn Farm, forming a rough triangle with Cairn Lane and Pillar-box Lane. Some half-mile or so beyond the farm it ran into a secondary road connecting with the main road to Heathmere. Anyone approaching Beech House by car from the station or the village had therefore to go a very long way round, and tradesmen usually stopped their vans at the corner of Cairn Lane and delivered their goods on foot.

Stationed at the gate Peter found a constable standing with his feet well apart, and wearing the patient expression of one inured to long periods of waiting. Peter gave his name and the constable swung the heavy gate open.

"Sergeant Dew is inside the house, sir; he's been expecting you some little while."

"Good," said Peter. "Has there been much activity here this afternoon?"

"We've had some local reporters nosing round for news, and one chap who came on a motor bike from London and took me a half-hour to get rid of. Prowled round the fence, he did, trying to find a way in while my back was turned. Inspector Norman's orders is not to let any of them in here; all inquiries are to be made at Police headquarters. But they want to get inside the house, so they can write up something spicy for the public."

"Same old story," said Peter. "Half a column for the foreign news and front-page headlines for the chap who croaked Seely." He saw two four-letter words in stark black against a white background. Ivan Ling. . . .

"When he's caught," the constable amended, and by his tone it was plain he had no great faith in such a climax to the police activities.

Peter checked his impulse to assuage the policeman's doubts even by a bare hint of his own discovery. No one—not even March—no, certainly not March—should know the clue he intended to follow up, until he had substantiated his suspicion, and was prepared to produce circumstantial proof of his hypothesis. The plodding Derwent had never solved a case unaided; he had played a laborious but very minor part in the Chief Inspector's investigations. It just went to show the absurdity of associating genius with a capacity for taking pains. Either you had a flair for a thing, or you hadn't, and if you had, you didn't need to take pains. Your brain worked like a flash of lightning, picking up in a split second what the other fellow took weeks. . . . Peter was so absorbed in his thoughts that he almost walked into the wall of the house.

The sergeant was just packing up to go back to Heathmere. He was thin and grey-haired, and looked, Peter thought, more like a clerk than a policeman. He was not surprised when Dew told him later that he had been engaged on clerical work in the Army for several years. Dew had been looking through Seely's writing-desk in search of any letters which might give the police a clue to the identity of anyone who had a grudge against him. Seely's lawyer was coming over in the morning; Dew had been making sure of the first innings.

"Not that Mr. Blackie won't pass on anything he finds of interest to us," he added. "But the Inspector was anxious to save time."

"Got anything?" asked Peter.

"Nothing to suggest that Seely had been threatened by anyone—at least not recently; there's an accumulation of old correspondence that I haven't had time to examine thoroughly. Most of his private correspondents seem to be women."

"Ah!" said Peter. "Are the letters intimate in tone?"

"Some of them—extremely so," replied Dew, smiling reminiscently, and exchanging an understanding glance with Peter. "Anything you want to do here before I clear off?" he asked. "I shall make my report personally to Superintendent Norton to-night."

"I should like to see whoever is in the house. Who is here, by the way?"

"George King and his wife; they comprised Seely's domestic staff. And a woman named Green. She doesn't live here, but she is Mrs. King's aunt and a frequent visitor. We let her come in to-day because Mrs. King is knocked up after the shock of Seely's death."

"Good," said Peter, keying his satisfaction down to a professional level. "I'll see them all individually in here. But there's no need for you to hang about, Dew. You might tell Chief Inspector March that there's no call for him to come over here before the morning."

Dew seemed glad to be released. "I'll send King in here," he said. "Or will you take the women first?"

"King will do for a start, thanks."

Peter took out his note-book and set the stage for his operations. He pushed a comfortable chair into the window embrasure, followed it with a small table, arranged a high chair at right-angles to his own for his successive examinees, put a delicate point on his pencil and waited. A faint anticipatory smile lighted his face. The last traces of his discontent had vanished.

THE first witness was a long time in answering Peter's summons. Sergeant Dew had ridden off on his bicycle and Peter had ornamented his margin with silhouettes of most of his girl friends, before the door opened to admit a middle-aged man, who shuffled reluctantly forward, responding only with a grunt to the detective's greeting. He seemed still more reluctant to take the chair Peter had so carefully placed for him. He was obviously going to be a difficult witness, Peter thought; well, this was where a knack of handling awkward customers came in useful. No use to rush the fellow; better put him at his ease first.

He offered King a cigarette, remarking that he only wanted an informal talk to enable him to get his bearings, and took stock of the man while he was lighting up. His most remarkable feature at the moment was his brow, which was cleft by a deep frown; Peter fancied that the heavy-lidded eyes beneath it looked sleepless. There was something stark and gaunt about the face which was lit up for an instant by the flash of a cigarette lighter; the taut skin had a greyish tinge, so that there was no sharp contrast between it and the close-cropped hair. Yet the face was not repellent, Peter thought. The features were well-defined; one felt that a sculptor would take pleasure in modelling them; he wanted himself to keep his eyes on them longer than was permissible without being impolite. He turned away and picked up his pencil.

It was King who spoke first. "More questions?" he said. "I've answered so many questions since Friday night, I don't know what I've said and what I've not said."

Peter dropped his pencil and essayed a disarming smile. "I expect you've told the Grassmere Inspector all you know."

"I know nothing at all, except that Mr. Seely didn't

turn up at his usual time on Friday night. We didn't know what had happened to him until the police arrived about half-past ten. We don't know much now."

"Were you alarmed when he was overdue?"

"We didn't give it much thought. We were thinking about the storm; it upset my wife and when the house was struck she got hysterical. I thought perhaps there was a bad storm in London too, and Mr. Seely had decided to stay the night."

"You haven't a telephone?"

"We had, but he had it taken away. He said he wanted peace and quiet; he was only just getting over a nervous breakdown when he came here."

"You were here first then?"

"That's right; we were here with the last owner. It suited us to stay on because——"

"Yes?"

"There isn't much else I can do except this sort of work."

"But you look strong."

"I've got good muscles, yes. But I had an accident at football—I was a professional the best part of twenty years. Just thinking of retiring; I wish I had retired, by God, I do."

The man's voice was flat-toned, and did not reflect the bitterness of his face. He had a bare soupçon of a north-country accent, Peter thought, which he had partially learned to control. Peter asked whether he had been badly hurt.

"Badly enough," King replied. "I did something to my spine. They operated several times; I was an interesting case, they told me. In the end they put in a steel plate. I'm all right as long as I don't lift heavy things or get over-tired. I wasn't educated for a black-coat job, so what was there for me? I was out of work when I met Sibyl—my wife. We fixed to get married and her aunt found us this job. That was ten years ago. . . ."

"What will you do now?" asked Peter, losing touch with his planned sequence of questions in his interest in King's story. He was thinking the man would be an interesting character to develop in a novel. He had thawed since he began talking, but still seemed to be holding himself in, or keeping something back. The hint of tragedy in his eyes was a challenge to one's powers of interpretation.

"We haven't had time to think, much less talk things over. Go on as we are, I dare say. It depends. . . ."

"On who buys the house?"

"That, partly. But my wife hasn't been well lately. A change might do her good."

"Especially after what has happened here."

"Yes, it shook her up. . . . I dare say she'll be glad to get away from the place."

"It must have been a pretty grim shock to you both."

King made no comment and Peter added, "Particularly if you had grown fond of Mr. Seely," but again evoked no response.

"Was he a pleasant sort of person to work for?" he asked. "Or was he very nervy?"

"A bit fussy, but not too bad. He had plenty to do with his writing and he was out all day twice a week, and now and then for a night or two. We didn't see so much of him."

Peter asked whether Mrs. King was well enough to see him for a few minutes. King said she had been resting all day but had come down at tea-time. He didn't want anything said to upset her again and she knew no more about Seely's death than he did.

Peter was curious to see what sort of woman the enigmatic King had married. "I'll be careful not to upset her," he promised.

"Women are squeamish about blood," King said. "It turns her sick to think of him being stabbed—with a big, clumsy carving-knife."

"I won't speak of that," Peter assured him.

King went in search of his wife with the same shuffling reluctance he had displayed on his entry. But he left Peter with the conviction that he had handled him adroitly. That brooding reticent type could be as mute as camels if they were so minded.

Peter did not speak of carving-knives to Sibyl King. He did not speak of any aspect of the crime. . . . He drew in a sharp breath as she came in. For she was an "eyeful"— by God, she was the negation of anything he had thought to behold in a dreary village. Of course, in trying to make the best of herself, she had achieved the opposite effect. Her hair was pure Titian, but it was too long to be worn hanging down; her lips were too dark a red and her cheeks too colourless. The contrast was bizarre. The green glass beads round her bare neck were a monstrous error. But what a margin there was for error! She had done everything she ought not to have done and yet her beauty took your breath away.

The dusk was invading the room and as Peter rose to pull up an arm-chair for Mrs. King, he turned the light on. She sat down, scarcely looking at Peter, and folded her hands in her lap. There was silence, and Peter knew he had to break it, but he did not want to speak—just yet. He did not want Sibyl to speak; he feared her voice would not accord with her looks. And there was nothing he wanted to say now that would be consonant with his status as a detective officer. But custom decrees that the human species must converse; there was an expectancy in Sibyl King's stillness. . . . Peter cleared his throat and plunged into the first subject that entered his mind.

"Your husband told me you had been married ten years. You must have been very young."

"I was eighteen."

The voice was not so disillusioning as Peter had feared. It was a little husky, and had the same hint as King's of an acquired habit of control. But one could listen to it without shuddering. Peter tried to measure the difference in age between the husband and wife, and, as though she followed his thoughts, Sibyl said, "George was much older —twenty years older."

Peter would have liked to ask whether she were happy with a man old enough to be her father. Instead he asked whether the pair of them had been happy at Beech House.

She shrugged her shoulders. "We had to get a living.

There was a lot of unemployment when we married. George didn't have a chance with his back; there were plenty of strong fellows out of work."

In a few minutes they were talking naturally, Peter leading, and Sibyl, finding the young detective made no reference to unpleasant topics, content to follow. In fact she seemed more than content; her passivity gradually gave way to animation—shy and restrained animation, but it brought colour to her face and light into her eyes. Peter diagnosed that she was releasing some of the dammed emotions of the past two days. Whether she took any personal interest in him, or was merely using him as a means of escape from repression, was not clear. There was nothing of the coquette about her on the surface; it would be interesting to explore the possibilities . . . but the time was not propitious.

He did not allude to the recent tragedy until the close of the interview and then only by implication. "You know, Mrs. King," he said, "it isn't good for you to shut yourself up here and brood over things. You're feeling better for this talk, I think?"

"I think I am—a little."

"You look better. You need to get out and meet people. I shall be in Heathmere to-morrow afternoon. What about a cup of tea and a cinema?"

"Oh, but I couldn't do that! George——"

"I'll talk to your husband. If I fix him will it be O.K. by you?"

"It would be nice to get out of this house. . . . But George——"

"Leave him to me."

Peter made serious preparation for his interview with Hannah Green. The neglected note-book was reopened and the original chair placed directly under the electric light. This was the crux of his visit—from the official point of view. Hannah was to provide the skeleton which he would cover later with solid flesh.

As Peter had been informed, Hannah was tough. The description was, if anything, an understatement. Regarding her with awe, Peter wondered whether any part of her squat body was vulnerable. Her brown face, patched with moles of a deeper brown, was shaped like a bulldog's, and her round eyes stared at Peter as though she was prepared to snap her jaws on provocation.

Peter asked her whether she had recovered from her fall on Friday night.

" 'Oo said I fell?" she demanded in a voice half-way between a croak and a growl.

"Oh, I heard it somewhere," said Peter vaguely. "You had a pretty bad storm here, didn't you?"

"Bad! It was offal! Not that I minded it, but it upset some."

"You were here when the chimney was struck, weren't you?"

"Just packing up to go 'ome, I was. We was drinking a cup of tea, when I noticed sudden-like it only wanted five minutes to nine. I got up to say I must be off, when we was knocked all of a 'eap by an offal crash. Sounded like the roof was fallin' in. ' 'Ouse as bin struck,' I sez, and George run out to see for 'isself. I dursen't wait being later than what I reckoned, though my niece didn't want me to go along of the storm. 'Might wait all night for that to stop,' I sez, and Mrs. Ling wanting to get to bed, I dessay. The road was that slushy I fell over twice and was covered in mud up to me face. Good thing I didn't wait no longer though, for Mrs. Ling was scared of the storm and fretting herself sick becos' the master was out, thinking he'd catch his death if he weren't struck by lightning. I tell 'im what I thinks of 'im leaving the missus alone in a storm like that, and 'im supposed to be delicut."

"I suppose he made some excuse?"

"Sed 'e had to go out to the cowhouse to see to some cow as was sick. 'That didn't ought to take you the best part of an hour,' I sez."

"Is the cowshed near the house?"

"It ain't above five minutes' walk. He said he waited becos' the rain was so heavy and 'e thought I'd be back by nine o'clock. I tell 'im it wasn't so easy to get back, and he didn't ought to 'ave scared the missus. I give him his hot cocoa as soon as he'd took off his wet things, and the missus made him get to bed after his bath. He weren't none the worse next day, I will say."

"I expect that was due to the hot drink and the hot bath. I don't expect he was as wet as you were either if he hadn't been far?"

"You should 'ave seen the pool he made in my kitchen! Lucky it was Saturday next day when I always has a scrub through."

Peter was searching for an opportunity to switch the conversation to Seely to find out whether Hannah knew the extent of Ling's acquaintance with the late owner of Beech House. Hannah saved him the trouble by taking the initiative and remarking that it was "an offal thing, this murder".

Peter could have shaken her knotted hand.

"Coming here so often, I expect you saw a good deal of Mr. Seely?" he suggested.

But Hannah had seen very little of Seely. She generally came round when he was in London, or on a Sunday afternoon, when he was writing or resting. "Them book-writing people ain't like ornery folk," she declared. "He kep' in one room hours on end, same as that dark young lady at Cairn Cottage. Not like neighbours, they ain't."

"Did he never call at the farm?"

"Not above two or three times since 'e come here, and then only to worrit the master about suthing. . . . No, I dunno what it was, but I heered Mr. Ling getting right angry with 'im—a thing 'e don't often do. Mustn't say nowt against Mr. Seely with 'im not yet in his grave, but I reckon 'e was one as liked his own way."

Peter asked whether Seely had been at the farm lately.

"'E come in Wednesday evening. Missus was gorn to Heathmere and I let 'im in meself. He didn't stop above a half-hour. Mr. Ling had to go to meet the bus so I reckon he showed 'im out as quick as he could."

"Was that the time you heard the quarrel?"

"I heered words, that's all. I didn't say nowt about a

quarrel. I shouldn't have paid no heed, only Mr. Ling ain't one to raise 'is voice, and I thought to meself, I reckon as Mr. Seely is in one of 'is aggravating moods, like as folk gets what stops indoors too much a-worriting their brains. I dessay 'tis their livers wants shakin' up."

Peter smiled, but behind his smile his mind was busy marshalling the ideas Hannah's story had suggested. He let her go home to see to her master's supper and sought out King. This was a matter which needed superlative tact. He intimated that he thought Mrs. King looked over-wrought and might have a breakdown if something was not done to take her out of herself. "What do you think?" he asked.

"She's had a shock," King agreed. "I'd like her to go right away for a bit, but we can't leave here at present, either of us. There's the funeral . . . and we don't know how long the inquest will drag on."

Peter said a day's outing might take Mrs. King's mind off the recent tragedy.

"Someone has to be here to see to the police," King objected.

Then Peter made his proposition, hinting that if he took Mrs. King to a cinema the following day, perhaps the police would have finished at Beech House by the end of the week, so that King could take his wife out himself. He won his point without further opposition.

"We mustn't put too much on this, Bruce. I mean you can't run a fellow in because his name ends in 'ing'." March spoke half jokingly but his face was thoughtful.

Norton slowed the car down to negotiate a corner.

" 'Spose not," he agreed. "But it's a tantalizing situation—or will be, if you can't find enough supporting evidence to make a case."

"It will be a damned sight worse than tantalizing! All the same, Bruce, I don't like your choice of language."

"Eh? Why not?"

"Strictly speaking, it's evidence pure and simple and not supporting evidence we're after. Seely's dying words are not evidence. You heard what Matthews said to me after the inquest? He sticks to his first impression, that Seely said he couldn't see anything—or he might have said 'Not a thing', with the accent on 'thing'. The nurse admitted that she may have thought of forked lightning because she had been watching the storm from a window, and that Seely may well have been trying to say a name—but, well —that doesn't help much, does it?"

"Perhaps not," said Bruce regretfully.

"Don't sound so dismal, my dear chap. If King killed Seely we shall get him all right. But I'm forgetting Leigh's evidence for the present. Apart from that, there is every reason for looking closely into King's movements at the time of the crime. If his name had been Robinson I should have been bound to begin by investigating him keenly. Seely was stabbed within a few hundred yards of Beech House, with a common or garden carving-knife that King could easily have procured. From Norman's statement I see that King was outside the house during the period when the stabbing took place. There is the woman Green's evidence for that, and only his wife's statement as to how long he was absent. As to motive, I scent a possible motive; I can't say much more at present."

"Don't hold up on me, Chris. Let's have it."

"As you like, but I'm only speculating, remember. John Derwent, my ex-sergeant, rang me up while you were getting the car out. Derwent's a first-class ferret; if there's anything to nose out he finds it, even if he has to forego sleep for a week and cover the whole of England. I put him on to Seely's past—the private aspect of it. It isn't very savoury. . . ."

"In what way?"

"Women."

"I'd like to know who's being tantalizing now!"

"Sorry. I was sorting Derwent's fragments out. I have not had a written report from him yet. Seely's two marriages both ended in disaster. His first wife committed suicide in mysterious circumstances; she was only twenty-one at the time; they had been married just two years. That was fourteen years ago, however. His second venture was made three years later. His second wife divorced him in under two years, alleging, among other things, both physical and mental cruelty. The case was heard outside London; there was not a great deal of publicity. Seely hadn't made his name then, and international crises monopolized the headlines. The woman subsequently remarried and is now living in Canada. Well, that's a start."

"Any more women in his life?"

"Plenty, I infer, but he didn't marry them. Before his illness, he lived in a flat in Chelsea. Derwent believes he associated with various women—fairly discreetly; it isn't easy to obtain definite evidence. The indications are that none of the associations lasted more than a year or so. When he came down here, he kept on his flat for the convenience of having somewhere to sleep when he attended a first night. It was also convenient in other ways. He lent it to a woman—according to Derwent she's a familiar type; as glamorous as you make 'em, but not unduly weighted with grey matter. There we leave London for the moment."

"And translate ourselves to Grassmere?"

"Exactly, but this is where we begin to speculate. Seely takes Beech House, and with it the services of the Kings. George King is forty-eight; his wife twenty years younger. I only have Norman's word for it that Sibyl King is an 'eyeful'—I hope to remedy that very shortly."

"Tut, tut, Chris!—and you a crusted bachelor."

"On the contrary, if I were a married man you might say 'tut tut'. But you needn't bristle, Bruce; my interest in the woman is purely scientific. I'm wondering whether Seely's was."

"You suppose . . . ?"

"I suppose nothing. I merely wonder. Seely lived over a year at Beech House with only intermittent meetings with his glamorous blonde in Chelsea. I wondered quite a lot; I wondered particularly whether King was ever away from Beech House. There was nothing to suggest it in Norman's report."

"That was why you asked me to stop at police headquarters, you secretive devil."

"Norman gave me some sidelights on King he hadn't incorporated in his report. The man has a spinal injury as the result of a football accident. He has to go to Leeds every now and again to see the surgeon who operated on his spine. He has only been away once for that purpose since Seely bought Beech House, but the date set me wondering still more. . . ."

"If I weren't driving the car, Chris, I'd wring your neck! You're as bad as a comedian waiting for applause."

"No, no, you misjudge me, Bruce. I've not had time to think things out quietly. I'm doing it as I go along. King travelled to Leeds last Wednesday, spent the night there, saw the surgeon on Thursday morning, and came home on the last train that evening."

"Leaving his wife alone in the house with Seely. And the next night Seely is stabbed near his house. I don't wonder you wonder! It would be the first chance King had of getting him after his wife told him——"

"Exactly—if there was something to tell."

"By Jove, Chris, don't you see! It fits like a jigsaw.

Leigh heard nothing of Seely's assailant making his get-away. Of course he didn't. King had only to run across the meadow; he could meet Seely at the corner and be home again in five or ten minutes. He couldn't start till Hannah Green cleared out, so he was bound to run it a bit fine."

"Ever tried to do a jigsaw with a missing piece? The missing piece is the knife. With Seely dead, who is to say what cutlery there was at Beech House. Unless Seely enter-tained people to dinner?"

"I've told you he didn't."

"And he employed no charwoman?"

"No, the Kings did all the work between them." Norton sounded crestfallen.

"Never mind, Bruce. These sudden changes from elation to depression are bad for people of our age, you know. Keep the ship on an even keel. There are ways and means of finding out. . . . I want to stop at the Buffalo to pick up young Cowie."

Norton brought the car to a standstill outside the inn. Peter was sitting on a rustic bench in the sunshine, smoking his pipe. Apprised of the morning's programme he re-strained a cynical smile. Of course the Chief Inspector was blinded by the obvious; that was the drawback of being over forty—the mind tended to run in grooves. Still, if his false scent kept March occupied for a few days, it was all to the good. Peter needed time to plan his own more subtle line of approach. When he was ready to make his dis-closure—and it would need exact timing to procure a dramatic effect—the Chief Inspector would discover that more than one local name ended in "ing". He almost chuckled as he lounged in the back of the car.

When they reached Cairn corner, March called a halt.

"I want to place the time of the actual stabbing as exactly as possible," he explained. "We know there isn't much margin. Seely left the station at eight-thirty-five. Leigh got him to hospital at nine-thirty. Seely could hardly have been attacked before Leigh pulled up for a couple of minutes or so in a gateway down the road. He hadn't time to get so far ahead of the doctor; I rather think that if Leigh hadn't pulled up and waited he might have overtaken Seely before he reached the corner."

"And saved his life," Norton interjected. "But go on, Chris; what are you getting at?"

"Just this. It is difficult to stab a man accurately—even discounting the darkness—when he is moving forwards. Instinctively one would use one's free hand to grab him, don't you think? What would you do, Bruce, if you felt someone suddenly seize you from behind in the midst of a storm which had already strained your nerves to snapping point?"

"I should yell blue murder!"

"I think Seely would have had time to scream. Leigh heard nothing, but to hear a yell on a night like that, both nature and the doctor's car would have had to be temporarily at peace. Now the two or three minutes which passed after the thunder died down before Leigh drove on is a long space within the narrow limits we're concerned with. I want to know whether Leigh would have heard a scream then. If not, let it pass. If he would, then the inference is that Seely was stabbed after Leigh started the car up again; say at approximately a minute or two after nine. The assailant had got away before the doctor picked Seely up at—well, not later than nine-five, according to the time he reached hospital."

"Which would just give King time to dash across the field and do the job."

"Provided his back allows him to run—I won't say sprint —the going was too bad for that. I must find that out."

"I knew a chap who was a rattling good tennis-player— and he had a steel contraption in his spine."

"We can easily test King on that point. Meantime I want to try a little experiment. Cowie, you stay here. Get inside the ropes to make it more realistic. Allow Mr. Norton time to drive me to Leigh's gateway. In a couple of minutes from now yell blue murder. Got it?"

"I'll bust my lungs," declared Peter.

"But don't keep it up too long. You've got a carving-

3*

knife in your back within a matter of seconds, don't forget that."

Peter's agonized wail pierced the quiet of the country-side. It rose to a rapid crescendo, and died abruptly to a significant silence.

March looked at his companion and smiled at the exultation in his eyes. He forebore to say anything to damp his spirits. "Now we'll get Master Peter to do a little running," he said. "If King is as little affected by his plate as your tennis-playing friend, he ought as an ex-footballer be able to give Peter a start and beat him. We'll allow for the weather, of course."

Peter, with an indulgent smile for the whimsicalities of Chief Inspectors, loped across the field in two and a quarter minutes.

12

Bruce Norton was present at March's interview with King in the role of passive observer. Peter, warned to remain on hand in case the need arose to take a statement from the witness, wandered out into the kitchen where Sibyl, looking more pleasing than ever in her plain working overall, greeted him with a friendly smile and offered him a cup of coffee. She repeated her husband's comment of the previous day. "I suppose they're asking more questions," she said, jerking her head towards the wall beyond which the inquisition was in progress. "Won't they ever finish and let us get a bit of peace? How can George and I tell them what we don't know?"

"You'll get away from it all this evening," Peter said soothingly. "It must be irritating to be pestered when you're busy, but inquiries have to start somewhere and Mr. Seely's home is the natural place to kick off from. I say, you make good coffee, Sibyl—better than the muck I had at the Buffalo for breakfast, if it was coffee. It was impossible to tell from the taste."

Peter babbled on but Sibyl, though she poured a cup of coffee for herself and sat at the table opposite the detective, made only a feeble pretence at listening.

"Something worrying you?" Peter asked, pushing his cup away and leaning across the table. "Yes, I can see there is. Why not pour out your troubles to me? I expect they'll be talking next door for the next half-hour, so you can take your time."

"You're very kind, but . . . I don't know if George would like it. He told me—— Well, he said the less we said the better. The police might get the wrong ideas."

"Like that, is it? George is jittery, and you've caught it from him, eh? Can't you tell me?"

"He made me promise. . . . It was something that hap-

pened last week when he was away. He says it has nothing
to do with Mr. Seely's death, but the police might think it
had. I'm scared that if the Scotland Yard man keeps on
at me, I might give way. I get muddled when I have to
answer questions."

Peter weighed the matter carefully in his mind. So King
had been away the previous week. The inference was plain
to someone with his flair for deduction. Seely, with his
unsavoury record with women, had been alone with Sibyl.
There was no need for Sibyl to tell him anything. Whether
March would also put two and two together was another
matter. If he did it was of no great consequence. It was
only a question of a few days before he would himself be
ready with his damning case against Ling, which would
draw the limelight away from Beech House once and for
all. But he did not like to see Sibyl looking harassed. He
made his inevitable response to beauty in distress; stretched
a hand across the table and pressed her limp fingers
consolingly.

"What ought I to do?" she asked, letting her hand
close round Peter's mechanically without returning his
pressure.

Flattered at being consulted, Peter became portentous.
He could not tell her it didn't matter in the long run what
she did.

"Whatever worries you least," he said.

"I don't know. . . . I don't like to upset George."

"Keep your promise then."

"If I can."

"I'm sure you're too smart to be jockeyed into saying
anything you mean to keep to yourself. The Chief Inspector
is very quiet in his manner; not at all the bullying
type."

The Chief Inspector, whose character had been thus
vouched for by Peter, was at that moment questioning King
quietly but with relentless persistence. Bruce Norton was
following his methods with intense appreciation. A question
with little significance was followed without change of tone
by one of vital import to the investigation into the Grass-

mere crime. March, Norton realized, was on the alert to detect whether King knew which were for him the dangerous questions.

King had been asked whether the injury to his back gave him any trouble. It was uncomfortable at times, he said, but nothing much to complain of.

"Bearable, is it?" asked March. "I suppose the most serious thing from your point of view was the effect it had on your capacity for work."

"There wasn't much choice," King agreed.

"I suppose you have to move carefully so as not to jar the spine?"

"It was lifting anything I was warned against."

"You can still run then?"

King's face darkened and Bruce saw that he was unwilling to commit himself one way or the other.

"Not the way I could before. I get tired easily."

"But I dare say you could manage a short sprint; three or four hundred yards, say?"

King avoided his interrogator's keen eyes.

"I wouldn't risk it," he mumbled.

March stared out of the window. "No, I dare say you would be unwise to risk it—except in an emergency. Then no doubt you would forget your disability."

He looked back quickly at King. Bruce wondered whether he had turned in time to see the antagonism in the man's eyes. This game of cat and mouse, played with a veneer of suavity, was beginning to make Norton feel jumpy. What effect it must be having on the mouse, he could only guess. Instincts of humaneness prompted him to wish March would spring, and bring the unequal duel to an end.

"You knew something of Seely's reputation with women?" the Chief Inspector asked.

"I heard he had been divorced; nothing more."

"Your wife is a very attractive woman."

King's eyes lit up again, but this time he faced his tormentor squarely. "I can look after my wife."

"No doubt, when you are here. Were you happy about

leaving her alone here with your employer last Wednesday night?"

"I didn't think anything of it. My routine examination was due; I couldn't get to Leeds and back in a day."

"You thought nothing of it at the time. But afterwards? When you returned did your wife make any complaint to you about Seely's conduct?"

For the first time King hesitated. Bruce felt that he could read the thoughts that were germinating behind his wary eyes. He wanted to deny March's insinuation categorically, but was uncertain whether his wife would be strong enough to follow his lead when her turn came to face the inquisition. Afraid to defend himself by denial he launched a blustering attack.

"What call have you to ask about what goes on between me and my wife? I can look after her if you let us alone."

"Perhaps you *have* looked after her, King, unwisely but effectively. I asked you a fair question; by fair, I mean it concerns events within forty-eight hours of Seely's murder —events which I am bound to inquire into. If you don't wish to be frank with me, I must ask your wife."

"It's no use pestering her; she hasn't anything to tell you. Nothing happened while I was away—nothing that was worth taking notice of."

"Nothing that was worth avenging by drastic means; for instance—by murder?"

King changed his tone and became almost conciliatory, but the colour had drained out of his face, and against the ashen background the furrow in his forehead looked as though it was etched in charcoal.

"If you won't trouble my wife, I'll tell you all there is to tell, sir."

"I won't trouble your wife if I can avoid it. Go on."

"There was a little trouble while I was away; nothing much—it was just that Mr. Seely started playing up to my wife when she served his coffee in the evening. She's a nervous woman and it scared her more than it would most women. She told me when I got back. I thought she was exaggerating the way women do and making too much of

Mr. Seely getting a bit too familiar with her. He'd never tried anything of the sort before, and it gave her a shock. I promised her I would never leave her alone here with him again. Next time I went to Leeds, I'd fix it for a date when he'd be in London. That was all there was to it, sir, I assure you."

"When did your wife tell you this?"

"Not till we went to bed on Thursday night. I didn't get home till the last train."

"Did you speak to Mr. Seely about it?"

"I never said a word about it, to him or anyone else."

"He went up to London early the next morning, didn't he? So if you had meant to speak to him you would have had to wait till the evening. And in fact he never came home that evening."

"I wasn't going to say anything if he had. A man can't warn his employer off his wife. All I could have done would be to give notice for the pair of us to go. If it had been worth it that's what I would have done. But it wasn't. . . . Mr. Seely only acted the way a lot of middle-aged men act when they find themselves alone with a pretty girl. That's all there was to it——"

"So you said before."

"And you won't upset my wife, sir?"

"I'm not going to see your wife at all just now. I have some other business to attend to. If you're ready, Norton, shall we be moving?"

Bruce concealed his amazement at this tame denouement to the scene, just when he had believed it was approaching its climax. He said as much to March when they had dropped Peter in the village, primed with the instructions he had anticipated, to canvass the villagers in search of anyone who had been abroad on the night of the storm.

"Why, Chris, you'd got him, if you'd only pressed home the attack. The man was as jumpy as a cat on hot bricks, and scared to hell you were going to squeeze the truth out of his wife."

"I shall be seeing him again—and his wife next time."

"But you've given him time to cool down. You'll have to begin all over again."

"Oh no, I shan't. And I want him to cool down. I'd like him ice-cold next time I tackle him; his reactions will be much more revealing than if he's worked up to fever pitch already. Wait a bit, I don't want to go back to Heathmere yet."

"Where, then?"

"Could we split forces for an hour? I feel less formidable and official without a bodyguard."

"I'll drive on to Beckthorne; I know a chap there I can cadge a drink off. Pick you up outside the church at twelve-thirty—that suit you?"

"Fine. I won't keep you waiting."

Bruce drove on, ruminating about his friend's strange behaviour. To draw back on the very brink of success seemed to him to be tempting the gods to withdraw their patronage. King would have time to tell his wife how much he had revealed to the police and to coach her to tell the same story. He found his friend at home and continued to muse over a glass of beer. When chaffed for his absent-mindedness he claimed that a Deputy Chief Constable with a murder on his hands must be pardoned for seeming preoccupied. . . .

Christopher was sitting on the low churchyard wall waiting for him. It still wanted five minutes to the half-hour, but March looked as though he had formed part of the landscape for some time. Norton hoped he hadn't been too long.

"Oh no, I'm enjoying the air. I got what I wanted in half an hour."

"What was that?"

"They held some Victory sports on the recreation ground here a couple of years ago. George King won the over-forty race. The distance was two hundred and fifty yards. Back to Beech House, I think, Bruce, don't you?"

13

PETER experienced what was for him the almost unprece-
dented misery of being unable to sleep. He was uncomfortable both in body and mind. In trying to flatten out the
hillocks in his mattress he had damaged the springs of his
bed, and was forced to lie half buried in a depression.
Threshing about restlessly with his feet he had ripped a
long tear in an already disintegrating sheet, and was now
irritated by the contact of a harsh blanket. Nostalgically
he thought of the well-sprung divan and soft linen he had
left for this Spartan rigour, and cursed into the darkness.
There was no electric light in the attic and the hand-lamp
with which he had been provided smoked and filled the
tiny room with black smuts and a choking smell. He could
not even pass the wakeful hours by reading. Thought was
extremely distasteful to him.

For his brilliantly conceived plan had unaccountably
eluded his ability to execute it. It was no fault of his that
he had been unable to have a talk with Mrs. Ling. He
had shadowed Cairn Farm most of the afternoon so as
to ensure that he did not encounter Ivan Ling when he
called at the house. Ivan was to be avoided at all costs,
because the moment he saw Peter again he would know he
was no reporter. He would certainly reveal nothing to a
policeman which he had withheld in friendly converse with
a civilian, and he might thwart Peter's attempt to interview
his wife. Peter had no desire for a showdown with the
young farmer who was some inches taller and considerably
heavier than himself. Dodging Ling he had eventually
called at the farm to find only Hannah in possession.

"Missus ain't back," she replied to Peter's query.

"When do you expect her back?" he asked.

"I don't know nothing about it. I never knew as she was

going till she'd gorn. Never even told me she wouldn't be in for dinner, she didn't."

"Oh! How was that?"

"How do I know how 'twas when I weren't here? When we heard the news of the murder first thing Saturday morning, I thought I'd pop out after breakfast and git one or two things I needed in the village and maybe 'ear a bit more about how it happened. Not that I'm 'quisitive in the ornery way, but murder ain't ornery. So I pops up to the village and when I gits back there ain't a sign nor a sight of the missus. When Mr. Ling comes in for his dinner, he says she's gorn to stay with 'er mother for a few days, she needed a change of air, he says. Made up 'er mind sudden like, it being a bright morning after the storm and 'er mother living by the sea. An' that's all I know, so it ain't no use worriting me no more, I got to git on with me work, being single-handed."

Sauntering to the station to catch the slow train to Heathmere—he had deemed it injudicious to accompany Sibyl King on the bus—Peter reflected that Mrs. Ling's disappearance was entirely consistent with his theory of the crime. To pack his wife off somewhere where she could not easily be got at and questioned about his movements was what one might expect a man with a murder on his conscience to do. But at the same time it put Peter in a dilemma to which he failed to see the means of resolving. "By the sea" was vague. Mrs. Ling might be hundreds of miles away at Blackpool or Scarborough, or she might be easily accessible on the South Coast. In the latter case he could slip away to see her, while ostensibly engaged in interviewing the residents of Grassmere. But how to obtain her address without tackling Ivan Ling was a thing one did not learn from any manual on the art of detection. A detective was not conceived of as playing a lone hand.

Peter had not solved this problem when he received a second and more severe shock. He had arranged to meet Sibyl in the café of the Playhouse cinema. She was to wait there for him as her bus arrived before his train. He found her huddled up in the darkest corner, crying bitterly. . . .

For some time he could get no coherent information from her, but after drinking some tea—she refused food—she stifled her sobs and told her story. The police had come back to Beech House just as she and her husband were sitting down to their midday meal. The Heathmere Superintendent had taken George aside. The London man had frightened her by taking a carving-knife out of his bag and asking her whether she recognized it. She was too terrified to speak. She felt queer like she had done on the night of the storm, wanting to laugh and cry at the same time. In the end she had foolishly wept and been unable to stop.

"But why—if you didn't recognize the knife?" Peter asked, puzzled.

"It gave me a turn. . . . It was quite a common knife—but to think it had been used to stab Mr. Seely!"

"Did you tell the police the knife didn't come from Beech House?"

"I did, later—but they didn't believe me. I showed them the carving-knife Mr. Seely used in the dining-room and the old one we used in the kitchen. But they found—oh, Mr. Cowie, I can't bear to think of it!"

"What did they find?" Peter asked gently.

"They ransacked all the drawers and plate boxes and sorted all the cutlery out in rows. And they found three carving-forks and only two knives."

"How was that?"

"That's what they asked. I couldn't explain. We never used but the two sets, but there was a lot of odd stuff in one of the drawers. It was put there when Mr. Seely's things were unpacked, because there was no room for it in the boxes. George unpacked the things and put them away. He always cleaned the plate; I never touched it. I didn't know what spare things we had. I told them I didn't know, but they wouldn't believe me. I said they must ask George, and he told them there never had been a knife to match that fork. But——"

"Yes?"

Sibyl's voice sank to the level of inaudibility. Peter leaned across the table, and prompted her again.

"But the knife they found in Mr. Seely's back *did* match the fork. George asked them—what of it? Weren't there scores of knives and forks like that all over England? They never took any notice of what George said, nor of what I said. They wrapped the fork in a parcel and took it away with them. . . . And they took—George—away—too——".

"Good heavens! Do you mean they arrested him for murder?"

"They told me he would be detained while they made some more inquiries. But they'll never let him come home again—never. . . ."

Peter's attempts at consolation had fallen flat. Sibyl was in no state to go to the pictures; he could only advise her to go home and get her aunt to keep her company for the evening. He could not make her believe that unless her husband were actually charged he would be sent home the following day. That was the law, he explained patiently. The police could not shut people up at will; they must either charge them with a crime or release them within twenty-four hours. This was all Greek to Sibyl. George was gone and she never expected him to return.

Peter went to the pictures by himself and was bored by the film which he had seen half a dozen times before under a different title. Why couldn't they think up something fresh?—if he had gone in for film production he would have utterly banned all recurrent themes. The film world needed new blood, but it was a handicap having to make a steady income from the start; it limited one's choice of occupation. He went on to the best hotel in Heathmere for dinner; the food filled him without pleasing him; the beer was little better than what passed under that name at the Buffalo. And so he returned to the inn in a frame of mind which was ready to make the worst of everything.

"Damn this mattress!" he muttered as he counted the strokes of the church clock striking three. Striking clocks ought to be prohibited in residential areas. He dug himself out of his groove with a groan and reached for the matches. Whether he was smoked out or not he must light the lamp and have a cigarette. His discomfort palliated though not banished by the cigarette, he began to readjust his plans.

The Chief Inspector had worked altogether too fast for him. Certainly he had a better case against King than Peter had supposed from what he had heard in the morning, but in the young man's opinion it was a long way from being water-tight. The less educated people were, Peter reasoned, the more prone they were to consider themselves in danger if they were in any way connected with a crime. It was natural that the Kings should show fear, and that Sibyl should give way to panic when confronted with the weapon which killed Seely. It was tactless, no, that was too mild a word—it was heartless of March to use such a crude means of securing the evidence he wanted. He was out, no doubt, to cover himself with glory by hook or by crook, and was too impatient for results to use the subtler methods which Peter would have favoured. His crowning blunder was to interpret the odd carving-fork as a definite clue. The conclusion he had reached was a palpable *non sequitur*, Peter sagely reflected. True, one naturally associated carving-forks with knives, but one was not forced to buy them in pairs. One partner might be broken or lost; he was certain they had several serviceable knives for every one fork at home. But evidently March had never studied logic. He ought, however, to perceive that if King had taken the knife to stab Seely, he would have taken the elementary precaution of getting rid of the fork at the same time. There ought to be refresher courses for senior detective officers.

The fact that Ivan Ling had volunteered a lie about his movements on the night of the crime was, thought Peter, a much more significant circumstance. Unless Ling was guilty there was no reason why he should suppose that he, more than any other inhabitant of the village, would attract the interest of the police. Peter had a notion that Seely was a bit of a social as well as an intellectual snob. No doubt he took some advantage of King's absence, but he would hardly be likely to go far enough to embroil himself seriously with his manservant. One would give a lot to know whether Ling's wife was the type to take Seely's fancy; if there had to be a woman in the case—and though not a *sine qua non*, a sexual motive was as likely a one as any other for a murder of a man of Seely's stamp—Mrs. Ling might well fill the bill more satisfactorily than the glamorous Sibyl. Peter found his thoughts getting more and more intricate and his eyes actually beginning at last to feel heavy in the ruthless glare of the oil lamp. He blew it out, and after a last struggle with the mattress coiled himself up with his knees against one wall of his trench. He had one inspired thought before he finally closed his eyes. He could obtain a description of Mrs. Ling by discreet inquiries in the village. At the same time he would find out who her friends were; surely it was not extravagant to hope that one of these would know where she was at present staying. Cheered by this happy inspiration he fell asleep.

At about the time when Peter Cowie extinguished his smoky lamp, Jessica Munro turned on her bedside light. She had been sleeping, but had wakened with a start, and an impression that she had had a nasty dream. It did not come back to her clearly at first, but as she lay in the darkness it began to take shape in her mind. The dream had re-created the scene of Friday night, but with a difference. It was Seely's face which the lightning had revealed, the small pale features livid with terror. She had heard again his ghastly cry of fear and pain. She could not sleep again nor lie awake in the darkness in which nightmare pictures had power to take shape. She would burn the light until Mrs. Bradshaw came with her tea—Mrs. Bradshaw who had kindly promised to leave Daisy to see to the family breakfast and to come before her usual time. There was something comforting in Mrs. Bradshaw's solidity, and her frequent injunctions "not to fret yourself about nothing".

There were five hours to go . . . one could not just lie and do nothing. Thoughts were only a degree less desirable than dreams. She picked up a magazine and chose a commonplace story, thanking heaven that while some writers chose the dark experiences of human life for their themes, there were others who could weave a story out of the harmless trivialities which form a large part of existence. If only one could become absorbed in petty things, in ordering meals, planning clothes, matching curtains and adding up weekly accounts, and immunize oneself from the horrors and cruelties of life! She read until her eyes began to ache.

She emerged from a torpor half-way between sleep and wakefulness to hear Mrs. Bradshaw's steps shaking the old staircase. One wondered sometimes that the slanting treads did not reject the task of carrying her massive bulk. But always she reached the top safely, and now she burst open the door and stood puffing on the threshold.

"Miss Munro, whatever do you think 'as bin an' gorn an' happened now? The p'lice have took George King away—'rested him for the murder, so they say in the village. And Mrs. King was took bad last night, so Hannah Green had to stop with her."

"George King!" exclaimed Jess, staring incredulously at Mrs. Bradshaw's red face. "But King is—I mean, are you sure?"

"Certain sure, I am. Hannah come in last night to borrow a drop of Bert's brandy, what he's kep' for a 'mergency ever since he had his operation. But you take and drink your tea, miss; you're looking right queer again. 'Tain't no use for you to fret yourself. If he done it, he gotter swing for it, Bert says."

"I'm all right, Mrs. Bradshaw. It was just the surprise—I couldn't believe it. I'm much better this morning. I . . . I shall go out for a little while to-day, I think."

"You didn't ought to go far, and you been lying three days abed, miss. You'll feel right weak when you get on your feet."

"The pain has gone; it will do me good to move about a bit."

"I doubt you won't want to move far when you gets downstairs. Let me bring you a nice bit of fried bacon for breakfast to put some strength into you first. And I'll light the Ideal so you can take a nice warm bath."

Left alone, Jess slowly sipped her tea. Her hand was

shaking. George King! . . . Whoever had stabbed Seely, it was not his manservant, with his square build and uncompromising grey hair. The assailant had been taller, less solid though strongly built, and his hair had been as near black as made no matter. He had been a younger man than King, and from the snapshot view she had had of his features a more cultured man. George King had been falsely accused and arrested because she had lain in bed three days, wrapped in a fog of sleep, pain and indecision. No doubt the man had been tormented to breaking-point before the final blow had fallen. Mrs. King might be seriously ill. The inaction must end and end quickly.

By ten o'clock she was dressed, and disregarding Mrs. Bradshaw's advice not to go outside the garden, she began to walk shakily towards the village. She could entrust her mission to no other person. No one but herself and the recipient must know the subject of the telephone call to police headquarters at Heathmere.

14

Bruce Norton was holding a conference in his office with Christopher March and Inspector Norman when the telephone rang. He lifted the receiver himself, listened attentively, made a note on a writing pad, and turned to the Chief Inspector.

"That was a young woman from Grassmere saying she has information for us about Seely's murder. She wants to see the officer in charge of the case. Here's the name: Miss Munro, Cairn Cottage."

March whistled. "Information, eh? And why the three days' delay?"

"She says she has been laid up with a chill. Know anything about Miss Munro, Norman?"

"Cairn Cottage is at the bottom of Cairn Lane, sir. I asked the local constable who lived there and he told me it was a young woman who makes her living by writing books. I understood from him—and he had it from her charwoman's husband—that Miss Munro was ill in bed, but I made a note for Sergeant Cowie to include the cottage in his routine round of inquiries."

March turned to Norton. "I doubt if Peter has got down to studying his instructions yet. He seems to be playing a lone hand. He'll have to learn better if he wants to hold his job, but for the present I'll let him be. Well, I suppose I must see this young woman straight away."

"Do you mind if Norman drives you over? I have a good deal of correspondence to get through with the Chief Constable away."

"That will suit me admirably. Don't expect me back to lunch; I'll get a bite at Peter's pub."

"Right you are, Chris. You can either keep Norman, or send him back and ring up when you want to be fetched."

Half an hour later the car, with Norman at the wheel, drew up outside Cairn Cottage. March turned to his companion, an earnest-looking young man with carefully brushed fair hair. "Mind waiting in the car, Norman? If this young woman is temperamental—as most of her craft are—she may be less nervous of one policeman than two."

"Very good, sir. I'll run down to the end of the lane and turn the car."

March's knock was answered by Jess in person. She had hustled Mrs. Bradshaw off home, on the grounds that she had come early, and finished her work. She had not wished it known in the village that the police had visited the cottage. She looked shaky but composed as she confronted the Chief Inspector.

"You are Miss Munro?" he queried, regarding with interest the intelligent-looking young woman with the careless and yet pleasing attire. March approved the absence of make-up which in his opinion was more often abused than used to effect. On Jess's invitation he followed her across the dark little hall to the sunny sitting-room. They sat in the window and March was again delighted to see that Miss Munro did not fidget.

"I am sorry you have not been well," he began. "I hope you feel up to a short catechism?"

Jess smiled. The opening was so unlike what she had expected that some of her repressed nervousness left her.

"I had a stupid sort of chill. I feel much more myself to-day. Shall I tell you why I asked you to come over, or will you ask me questions?"

"Both, I think," March smiled back. "Perhaps you will begin?"

"Well . . . I—the fact is, I saw Mr. Seely murdered."

March showed no signs of shock. "Indeed?" he said quietly. "How was that?"

"I'm a very careless and forgetful person and I landed myself in having to go out in that terrible storm to post a letter. The nearest pillar-box is in the lane which runs at right-angles to this one."

"Yes, I have seen it. Have you any idea what time you set out on this pillar-box expedition?"

"Yes—it was soon after half-past eight. I reckoned that even though the going was bad I would be home by nine o'clock. The going was worse than I expected and it took all I knew to get to the pillar-box. Coming back, I had the wind behind me, and I was scurried off my feet to the corner of Cairn Lane. Just as I was turning the corner there was a spectacular flash of forked lightning and a simultaneous thunder clap—absolutely simultaneous—one couldn't have counted half a second. The corner of the lane was like a lighted stage. That was the moment when I saw Seely attacked and stabbed."

"Can you describe the assailant?"

"He was a stranger to me. I must tell you straight away that he certainly was not King. But though I saw him clearly, it is hard to give the kind of description you want."

"Of course it is, but try in general terms. You had some impression of his age, height and clothing, I expect?"

"Oh yes. He moved like a young man; not a boy—he had too much character in his face. Say, perhaps, between thirty and forty. He was tall and had very dark hair, almost black. All I took in of his clothing was that he had no hat and wore a mackintosh or storm coat with the collar turned up."

"A dark rain-coat?"

Jess closed her eyes. "No, I think the ordinary colour, a sort of neutral shade."

"Fawn?"

"More or less."

"Did you recognize Seely?"

"No, I had no glimpse of his face. I didn't even think of his being Mr. Seely, oddly enough, though I saw he was a smallish man."

"Just what was your impression of the actual attack, Miss Munro?"

Jess described faithfully the drama of the fateful moment before she lost consciousness. "And then I stupidly fainted and fell into the ditch," she added.

"So you saw nothing more?"

"Nothing. I heard later that the doctor had picked Mr. Seely up and taken him to hospital. That must have happened while I was in the ditch; when I crawled out and investigated, the . . . the body had gone."

"Do you know how long you lay in the ditch?"

"I worked out when I got home that I must have been there something like quarter of an hour. You must be wondering why I kept all this to myself. I am a fearful procrastinator. I hoped at first the whole episode was a kind of hallucination. When I heard the truth I felt too ill to do anything. Until this morning—when I heard King had been arrested; then I felt ashamed of myself and went to the village to telephone."

March made no expression of condemnation. "King has been detained, not arrested. He has not been charged, and now, of course, will not be charged. So your information, though tardy, is extremely valuable. Can you add any detail to the description you have given of Seely's murderer?"

Jess made a deprecating gesture. "I'm afraid it is hardly a description. I think he was—well, for want of a better word, I'll say cultured. A man in Seely's walk of life— that was my impression."

"Figuratively—a black-coater, though he wore a light raincoat?"

"Yes."

"Miss Munro, are you positive you never saw this man before?"

"I'm positive I didn't recognize him. There was something vaguely familiar about him. It is just possible he was someone I had seen without knowing who he was, in a bus or a shop, or something. But my real feeling is that he was a stranger to me and the village. People run to some extent in types and one often sees something familiar in a person one meets for the first time. I've never met you, for instance, but I get that impression with you."

March laughed. "I'm often told I look a typical barrister. But would you know this man if you saw him again?"

"Yes, I would know him anywhere. It must sound absurd to be so confident when I can't describe him better now. You see, I hadn't time to study his face, but the impression —fleeting as it was—was almost supernaturally vivid. I was keyed up by the storm, and my senses were sharpened by horror. If I saw him again that impression would be repeated—I'm sure of that. But at the moment I'm afraid I have said very little to help you."

"On the contrary, you have not only let King out, but a host of other possible suspects as well. In fact you have made it almost certain that Seely's murderer will be brought to justice."

Jess gasped. "*I* have? But I don't follow you."

March spoke indulgently. "Use that excellent brain of yours, which just now, I fancy, is a little below par. Do you ever think in terms of statistics?"

"Never. I hate figures. And, anyhow, statistics are not very reliable, are they?"

"There are practical difficulties in making use of them. I don't suppose the statistics I am thinking of have been worked out. But just think for a moment how many people your elementary description rules out. We were tolerably sure that Seely's attacker was a man; the force of the blow seemed to indicate that. But there are exceptionally strong women and Seely might have fallen foul of some Amazon. So you have effectively cleared the whole of your sex— more than half the population. Carry the process a step further. The word 'tall' rules out, I suppose at a guess, well over half the male population. The word 'dark' more than half the remainder. To say nothing of 'cultured'. . . . And so on. Even the fawn raincoat is an eliminator, though fawn raincoats are rather common, and anyone out in such a storm would wear whatever waterproof coat he possessed. Did you notice Seely's coat, by the way?"

"It was dark—very dark grey, I should say, at a guess."

"A very good shot. Seely was wearing a dark grey showerproof overcoat. That tests your observation of the whole episode. You have also fixed the time of the murder to a minute."

"I am much cleverer than I realized! How did I do that?"

"We have had several graphic accounts of the storm. There was only one flash of forked lightning such as you described right overhead and accompanied by a clap of thunder. It was the one which struck the chimney of Seely's house and occurred at five minutes to nine precisely. Incidentally, we have evidence that King was in the kitchen at Beech House when the house was struck, with his wife and her aunt. So your evidence eliminates him on two counts. Now we have only to look for the tall, dark stranger."

"And if you find him?"

"We shall have to hold an identification parade, and include other tall, dark men as well. Don't be alarmed. If you can't identify him positively, we shall find other evidence."

"That wasn't why I shivered. It was the thought that I shall be able to identify him. When there's a hunt on, I just can't help being on the side of the hunted. I'm the ostrich type of coward; I know dirty work has to be done, but I prefer other people to do it."

"Stabbing a man in the back is dirty work, Miss Munro."

"I know. I don't defend it. I just wish I hadn't seen it happen."

"The law doesn't often make a mistake, but King was in a nasty spot. It was partly his own fault, but he would probably have had to stand his trial. Even if he had been acquitted the affair would have cast a shadow over his life —and his wife's."

"Yes. I want it both ways, I suppose. Well, I'll do my best, if I'm needed to identify the stranger. Perhaps I shan't be called upon after all."

"We shall get him, I think, but there's no need for you to cross that particular fence yet. Do you feel up to coming to the corner of the lane with me?—I have a car outside. I should like you to show me exactly where Seely was when he was attacked, if you think you know?"

"I know almost to an inch, I should think. I know the

bit of ditch I selected to collapse into; of course it was the deepest spot I could have chosen."

"Excellent—not your nearly drowning yourself, but your being able to fix Seely's position. Sure you're not feeling too tired? We could call back later."

"I'd prefer to get it over."

Norman drove the car up the lane. March stood by Jess's side as she peered into the slimy ditch in which the water was now no more than a sluggish stream. "Just here," she said confidently. "There was a lot more water than there is now. It was exactly opposite here in a straight line that—look, I'll show you. . . . Mr. Seely was here; the stranger jumped from behind that tree; he grabbed Seely's collar so he couldn't take another step forward; he would have fallen with his head about here; the lightning faded and it was pitch black; I staggered about and then I fell too, so that's all I can tell you."

"Seely was five foot five. Measure up the ground, Norman, and mark the position of Seely's body, as Miss Munro estimates it, in the plan. I'll drive Miss Munro home while you get on with the job."

Norman produced his apparatus and Jess climbed back into the car. She was glad of the lift home; her head was beginning to feel light and her legs to tremble beneath her as they had done on Friday night when she searched for a dead body and found only tufts of grass and fallen twigs.

15

"I'm going to take advantage of Mr. Norton's offer and keep you, Norman," said March, as he pulled up at the corner.

The young Inspector was palpably delighted. Acting as A.D.C. to Scotland Yard's representative was high adventure compared with the drudgery of routine work at police headquarters. He took the wheel of the car as March shifted his seat. "Where to, sir?"

"I want you to help me look for a tall dark man, probably between thirty and forty, and, if Miss Munro is correct, a stranger to this district, or at all events to this village. If he doesn't live here, he must have arrived somehow. He is unlikely to have been in the place long before the time of his self-appointed rendezvous. Know anything about the bus service here? . . . Good man," he added as Norman produced a local time-table from his pocket.

"There's a late bus twice a week, sir, on Mondays and Thursdays—that's to enable the local people to get back from the cinema. Other days the last bus from Heathmere gets in at six-fifteen."

"That would be broad daylight, and give him nearly three hours to wait. Any other direction he could come from by bus?"

"Not on a Friday, sir. There are special Saturday buses to other places, but having a railway station Grassmere has to put up with rather a poor bus service."

"We'll make the station our first port of call then. It seems our best bid."

Norman let in the clutch. "I think you're right, sir. In any case he couldn't have got away by bus that night and nothing was seen of a car or cycle. Of course, there was the storm to reckon with."

"Did you get Miss Munro's information taped on the plan?" March inquired.

"I did, sir. Measured the ground to within a couple of inches, I reckon. It seems Miss Munro was pretty accurate. She places the body a couple of yards nearer the stile than Dr. Leigh did, with his pen-knife."

"I have a high opinion of Miss Munro as a witness. Unfortunately she fainted at the critical moment, or she would have been able to tell us, no doubt, which way the fellow made off. Leigh says Seely fell in a slightly hunched position, so he wouldn't have stretched the full five foot odd of his height. Well, Norman, we've got the right time, and the right spot, and now we want the right man, eh?"

They pulled up at the station and March told Norman to report to the Superintendent by telephone and ask him to arrange to have King sent home, while he pursued his inquiries among the railway officials. The man who had been on duty at the barrier when the eight-thirty-five came in on the Friday night was soon located. He remembered taking Seely's ticket and Seely had asked him when he gave it up if there was any chance of a taxi.

"I told him I was afraid not, sir. There ain't only the one car here, and I'd seen that waiting to take a party to Barton. They was first off the platform too; must have driven off before Seely spoke to me."

"How many in the party?"

"Man and woman, sir."

"Did you know them by sight?"

"Yes, sir, at least I knew the man; he often travels on the line. I reckon the woman was his missus."

"Know his name?"

"Mr. Robertson, he was; he runs a private school at Barton."

"Can you describe him?"

"Well, I dunno, sir. I reckon he's about forty, a bit on the stout side, light hair and moustache."

"Thank you. Mr. Seely started walking home at once when you told him there was no chance of a taxi, did he?"

"Almost at once, sir. He seemed a bit disappointed and asked if there was any chance of the car coming back. I told him not a hope, sir; it had to go all the way to Barton,

4

and I know Bob Ford, the driver; getting on in years, he is—he wouldn't go out twice on a night like that. I told Mr. Seely there was another gent inquiring for the car if it did come back and I told him the same as I told Mr. Seely."

"What about this other gentleman?"

"Never seen him before, sir. He came off the platform with Mr. Robertson and I thought he belonged to his party, till he asked about the taxi. "

"Could you describe him?"

"Well, sir, the station lights aren't none too good and there was a goodish few come off the last down train. He was a biggish chap, sir, wearing a raincoat same as everyone else and he had his hat jammed down over his face. I didn't hardly see what he was like to look at."

"Fair or dark?"

"That I never noticed, sir."

"Notice the colour of his raincoat?"

"I think it was light brown, sir."

"What became of him?"

"He passed through the barrier, and I never saw him no more. I went off duty as soon as I'd seen the last passengers through."

"You say there were a fair number of passengers. How many do you mean by that?"

"Goodish number for here, sir. It's pretty quiet as a rule, but that's the last London train in, and we generally has about a dozen passengers off it. I reckon there was ten or twelve that night."

"Any other strangers?"

"Most of them I knew by sight, sir, if not by name."

"No one else inquired for a taxi on a night like that?"

"They hadn't none of them far to go, sir, excepting Mr. Robertson. There was several from the new houses just outside the station, and a couple of commercials putting up at the station hotel. They was asking for a porter to carry their bags across."

"Had the second man who asked for a taxi any luggage?"

"No, sir, nothing."

"Did you get any idea of his age?"

"He was a young fellow, sir, not much above thirty."

"When you described him as biggish, did you mean he was tall—or fat?"

"He wasn't fat, sir. No—he was a biggish chap—tall and broad shouldered. Fine-looking chap, from what I could see of him."

"Right. Well, he left the barrier ahead of Mr. Seely and disappeared?"

"That's right, sir."

March elicited the information that Seely, the Robertson couple, and the unknown young man, had travelled first class from London. The rest of the half-dozen or so passengers had travelled third. The unknown first-class passenger had given up a single ticket. With indefatigable patience the Chief Inspector interviewed the handful of railway employees who had been on duty on the Friday night. A porter had seen the tall stranger get out of a first-class carriage, but could give no better description of him than the ticket collector. He had inquired whether he had any luggage, the young man said he had not, and Robertson had asked the porter to carry a heavy parcel out to the car. The young man had got out of the same compartment as the Robertsons; Seely had been alone in the carriage next door. There were no other first-class carriages on the train.

The ticket collector who had relieved the man March had first spoken to was, however, more helpful. The next train to London stopped at Grassmere station at nine-twelve, and left two minutes later. No one had boarded the train except a tall young man in a mackintosh. He had been dripping wet, and had shown a single first-class ticket to Bogmore—the next station the train stopped at up the line. "Twenty minutes' run," the ticket collector said. "And the only stop between here and London. It's a fast train after Bogmore."

"And the last up train that night?"

"No, sir, there's one more—the eleven-five—but no one boarded it that night except one of our own officials who was going to London for the week-end."

Asked to describe the young man, the railwayman proved remarkably observant.

"I'd say he was thirty-four or five, sir. Pleasant-looking, well-educated chap. He had a grey hat squashed well on his head and it was dripping on to his shoulders. Height? I'd say close on six foot. Didn't see his hair, but his eyes was dark. . . . No, he didn't seem out of breath, but he seemed in a hurry to get aboard the train."

The man at the booking office recalled issuing a single ticket to Bogmore, but had no recollection of the face of the purchaser. The voice was an educated voice. The ticket had been purchased just before the train was due in.

March went across to the hotel, a hideous new building behind the station, and obtained the names and addresses of the two commercial travellers who had slept there on Friday night. Both were known to the manageress, and she explained that they only slept there because the Heathmere hotels were so crowded. They had left for Heathmere early on the Saturday morning.

Eventually all the passengers who had arrived by the eight-thirty-five on Friday night were accounted for. There were only five third-class passengers in addition to the commercial travellers. Two of them, who had some distance to walk, had sheltered for an hour in the hotel, and had seen nothing of March's quarry. The other three had made a dash for their homes near the station. The first lived just outside the station and had passed no one. The other two were next door neighbours who always went up to London together for the day on Fridays on business. They both remembered overtaking a tall man in a raincoat as they ran for shelter. He was walking in the direction of Pillar-box Lane.

March asked whether the stranger could have been Seely. He could not, they both asserted, first because they both knew Seely well by sight, and secondly because he was a much taller man than Seely.

"What pace was he walking?"

"Very fast," one of the men replied. "But my friend and I were running. We had only a couple of hundred yards to go; he looked set for a good tramp. We felt sorry for the poor devil; he'd be drenched in five minutes in that downpour."

"We wondered if we ought to offer him shelter," the other man put in. "But he could have sheltered at the station or the hotel; he looked as though he had to get somewhere—so we left him."

It was well on in the afternoon when March recollected that they had had no lunch.

"Feeling famished?" he asked his companion.

"I hadn't noticed it, sir; I've been so interested following the trail. But since you mention it, I could do with a bite."

"So could I. What's our best chance?"

"I expect the station hotel could knock us up a meal, sir."

The station hotel provided cold meat and potatoes, washed down with rather dubious beer. After the meal March demanded black coffee. They sat in a heavily netted window and smoked their pipes.

"We'll have to see these Robertsons of Barton, Norman. Travelling in the same carriage as the young man we're after, they ought to be able to describe him pretty well."

"I gather he trailed Seely from London, sir. But I wonder he didn't try to get a carriage to himself."

"He may have meant to do so. But it looks as if he were faced with the choice of either sitting with Seely, or the Robertsons. Naturally he would avoid Seely. There may have been other first-class passengers earlier on."

"That train only stops at Bogmore. It's the best down train of the day. I wonder why he booked back only as far as Bogmore."

"So do I. I think the chances are that he is a London man, and comes into Seely's life that end and not here. Perhaps the storm upset his calculations. He couldn't make much pace on foot, and that train was his only chance of getting away from the district quickly. He may have thought to change at Bogmore would baffle us if we began to get interested in him. If he had been more of a nonentity in appearance, a man arriving from London might not have been connected with a man returning to another destination, whereas the other half of a return ticket is a complete giveaway."

They knocked out the ashes of their pipes and returned to the chase.

16

PETER surveyed his breakfast with a shudder. It was true he had overslept and kept it waiting, but surely someone could have covered the bacon which was almost hidden by grease. Nor had he any use for fried potatoes at breakfast. He removed the plate to the sideboard and attacked some limp toast. Food was going to be a serious problem if the case was a protracted one. He could not reckon on getting dinner in Heathmere more than twice a week; there were only two late buses. He must look up the trains; it was intolerable not to have one decent meal a day—not that the food in Heathmere had been anything to boast about, but it was at least eatable.

Still feeling crotchety, he set about his inquiries in the village. He must report some activity to the Chief Inspector, but his real object was to learn something about Mrs. Ling. In less than an hour he had amassed quite a dossier of information, and finding a cottage which displayed a sign advertising teas, he went inside and persuaded a young woman to make a pot then and there, although she told him they did not usually serve anyone until the afternoon.

Munching a biscuit, Peter used all the information he had collected about Ling's wife to construct a mental picture of her. He saw her as a fair-haired fluffy little creature of twenty-five or six. Rather kittenish and perhaps a bit nervous, and inclined to worry about her husband and the farm. Not much time to take part in village life, though she sang occasionally at parish concerts. Well, well, thought Peter, it all depended on whether Seely liked 'em fair and kittenish, or whether there was perhaps some other link between him and Cairn Farm. Unfortunately no one seemed to know where Mrs. Ling was staying. She had not mentioned that she was thinking of taking a holiday when she had attended a meeting of the Women's Institute on Thursday afternoon. One woman ventured the opinion that Mrs. Ling would not stop away more than a few nights at such a busy time of year. Peter was convinced that Ling himself had told him his wife was away for the week-end. On the strength of that he determined to call at the farm again after lunch. It was a very long week-end which lasted beyond Tuesday afternoon, he told himself.

On his way to the Buffalo he telephoned from the post-office to police headquarters at Heathmere. He might as well remind March of his existence; if they had kept in closer touch the day before, the Chief Inspector might have been saved from making a heinous error, though Peter admitted it would have been hard to prevent him taking King into custody without showing his own hand—which he was not yet prepared to do. Finding that March had actually been in Grassmere without calling on his sergeant, and was still out in a police car with Inspector Norman, Peter rang off in some dudgeon. The Chief ought at least to keep him apprised of developments his end. It was outrageous to expect a man of his mental ability to waste his time poking in and out of cottages in search of information which might be out of date before it was reported. Well, if March could play a lone hand, so could he. The next effort to establish contact should come from the Chief Inspector himself.

After lunch Peter smoked a pipe on the bench outside the Buffalo. He was glad to escape from the stuffy gloom of the thatched inn. He considered asking permission to transfer himself to the pub by the station which he had heard was a much more modern building and was actually spoken of as the Station Hotel, though whether this was more than a courtesy title Peter doubted. He would not approach Cairn Farm for an hour or so; he did not want to risk finding Ivan Ling having a late lunch.

After a refreshing nap he set off at last in better spirits. If Mrs. Ling were still away he felt sure he could fool old Hannah and obtain entry to the house on some pretext or other. No doubt Mrs. Ling had written to tell her husband of her safe arrival; to obtain the address by stratagem would be a definite coup and enable him to take the next step forward. He repeated the whole process of patrolling the area round the farm to ensure himself that Ivan was not in sight of the building, approached the front door and rang the bell. Receiving no answer, he tried the handle and found the door locked. He went round to the back door and obtained the same result. A note on the window ledge demanded two loaves of bread when the baker called. Peter clucked his tongue in annoyance. Hannah was evidently out for the afternoon.

All at once as he stood ruefully surveying the deserted farm, his expression changed. This was the very opportunity he needed! Hannah might have been awkward, but now all he had to do was to find some means of getting inside the house. Ten minutes or so in undisturbed privacy and it would be unlucky indeed if he could not find some clue to Mrs. Ling's whereabouts. He prospected for an open window and, finding none, examined the locks on the doors. They were old-fashioned locks which required large keys to unfasten them. There was probably a key concealed somewhere to enable whichever of the absentees returned first to enter. Peter poked around, lifting scrapers and stones outside both doors until eventually he found a key under the back door mat. In a moment he had opened the door and passed through the kitchen to the little sitting-room where Ivan had entertained him on Sunday. He began a rapid search for a letter or post card addressed to Ivan Ling.

" 'Everything's coming my way'!" he exclaimed in triumph under his breath when he discovered a plain stamped post card inside the blotter on the writing-desk containing precisely the information he wanted. It was addressed to Ivan Ling and signed Ann; it stated that the writer had arrived safely, and proposed to return the following Saturday if she could be spared so long. The weather was glorious; she was enjoying her holiday and already feeling better for it. The address was 17, The Parade, Leigh-on-Sea, and the date the previous day. Ling had evidently received the card that morning.

4*

Peter took out his note-book and quickly copied the address. He replaced the card and, humming Jack Hulbert's appropriate song, returned to the kitchen. There he stood still as a statue while the blood rushed to his face. He heard a firm tread on the path outside. Someone was approaching the back door. Praying that it might be only the baker he retreated on tiptoe to the hall and listened.

The back door opened and now someone else was singing to replace the song which had died in Peter's throat. The song was "Let me like a soldier fall", the voice a pleasant baritone—the voice of Ivan Ling.

Panic stricken, Peter bolted up the staircase. He could not be caught by Ling snooping about in his house. He must conceal himself until the man went out to work again. He darted into the first room he came to; mercifully the door was half open. He saw that he had entered the Lings' bedroom; blue-quilted twin beds took up the greater part of its space. There was nowhere to hide except under a bed; Peter dived for the nearest and was relieved to find that he was concealed from the door. He lay with his heart thumping against his ribs, trying to control his agitation so as to listen. . . . Ling was moving about downstairs. . . . It was all right; he had probably only come home for something he had forgotten. He would be gone in a few minutes. And then Peter remembered that he had left the key in the back door. . . .

Damn the fellow! Why couldn't he stop that infernal song and get back to his work? Was he searching for an intruder or had he attributed the open door to Hannah's carelessness? Oh, hell, he was coming up the stairs, still singing, curse him!

" 'Let me like a soldier——' " the voice broke off. Peter quaked and waited.

"You may as well come out of hiding, Cowie, wherever you are. I saw you enter the house and I know damned well you didn't come out."

Better be caught in the open than under the bed, thought Peter. It was foul luck, but the game was up. He must put a brave face on disaster. He crawled out and emerged sheepishly on to the landing. Ling surveyed him as though he were a worm.

"Come downstairs. I want a word with you."

Peter followed meekly to the sitting-room.

"Now then," began Ling, without inviting him to sit down. "Just what the hell are you playing at?"

Peter prayed for inspiration. The truth was too compromising to admit.

"I sprained an ankle walking over rough ground and I thought you wouldn't mind if I came in and rested a few minutes."

"Under my bed?"

"No, no. I was resting downstairs and when I heard you coming I stupidly thought you might misunderstand my presence."

"Tell that to your grandmother! Look here, Cowie, I know all about you. You came here on Sunday masquerading as a reporter——"

"It was you who mentioned the word reporter."

"I give you that, but you didn't deny it. Since then I have discovered your real name and occupation. You came snooping around here yesterday badgering Hannah Green for information she couldn't give you. To-day you reconnoitred to make sure I was out and then broke into my house. I saw you from a shed, so you needn't cook up any more lies. I demand an explanation."

"I admit I have been unorthodox, Ling. But the most successful detectives often use unorthodox methods."

"What the hell are you trying to detect here?"

"Several more or less routine matters. I was given the assignment of canvassing the entire village in search of anyone who was out in the storm on Friday night."

"Does that necessitate breaking into unoccupied houses and hiding under beds?"

"Of course not." Peter was recovering his dignity by degrees. "In most cases the information is given readily. But you know you told me you were not out in the storm and also that you hardly knew Seely——"

"And you got a different impression from Hannah. If

you had produced your police card on Sunday I would have
answered any questions you put as far as I was able. As it
is I told you the truth though I saw no reason to volunteer
information to a reporter. I told you I was under cover
during the storm. I was—either here, or up at the cowhouse. Perhaps you think from what Hannah said that I
quarrelled recently with Seely. Seely had a paddock at the
back of Beech House and he had let the grass get into poor
condition. He said he couldn't get a man to cut it. He
wanted me to have the grass cut and taken away right in
the middle of the harvest; he offered the crop as fodder in
return for having the job done. I told him it was impossible.
I'm not short of pasture here, but I am short of labour.
Instead of dropping the matter, he called to see me about
it and took a very high hand. I had not time to spare to
stroke his feathers, and to stop him pestering me in future
I refused as bluntly as possible. We had a few words; Seely
blustered as though he were the lord of the manor addressing a serf, and I told him to clear out. So there's your
quarrel, Detective-Sergeant Cowie! Make what you like
of it. And now you can clear out—unless you'd like me to
send for an ambulance to take you to hospital to have your
ankle seen to. And if I see you on my land again, you'll
leave it in a condition in which you really will need an
ambulance."

Peter saw that there was nothing for it but to retreat in
good order. Brains, he told himself, cannot compete with
brawn in a trial of physical strength. He must remove himself as far as possible from the reach of Ling's arm in order
to be free to set his wits to work on a plan to encompass
the downfall of the temporarily victorious farmer. He
turned and stalked out of the room and out of the house.
He stalked faster and faster until he almost ran up the lane,
and did not pause until he reached the sanctuary of the
Buffalo Inn.

17

NORMAN kept off the main roads on the drive to Barton. By making a detour which lost little time, he contrived to pass through the two most picturesque villages the county possessed. March was enchanted, and vowed he would take a sketching holiday the following summer and billet himself in the district.

The Robertsons' school was a cheerful white house with large windows. If James Robertson was disappointed to find his caller was not a prospective parent, he concealed the fact nobly. He read the card March offered him, then scrutinized the Chief Inspector's face, apparently welcoming the opportunity of seeing for himself what a Scotland Yard official really looked like. Perhaps he contemplated giving a talk on police methods to his young charges.

March explained his business briefly. "We are anxious to get in touch with a young man who travelled by the train reaching Grassmere at eight-thirty-five last Friday," he concluded. "I believe he travelled in your carriage."

"There was a young man in our carriage, certainly. I went up for the day to do some school shopping. As the term began the following Monday, I took my wife with me; it was our last chance of a day out together for three months. It is fortunate for you that I did; she is so much more observant than I am. We caught the train by rather a narrow margin. One of the first-class carriages was full, so we got into the other. There was only one man in it, sitting in a corner smoking. He's the fellow you mean, I expect, but after the first glance at him, I scarcely noticed him again. He was buried in a book, and I passed the time doing a crossword puzzle. But if you and your friend will come into the next room my wife will tell you what you want to know and give you a cup of tea at the same time."

Having introduced the two detectives to his wife, Robertson excused himself on the grounds that he had to preside over the boys' tea. Mrs. Robertson was plump and animated, and perhaps from constant contact with children, March thought, infused all her remarks with a rather forced heartiness.

Indeed, yes, she remembered the young man; he had looked a little disappointed when he found he was not going to have the carriage to himself, but he had got up and put some of her parcels on the rack for her. He hadn't seemed inclined to talk, however. She had made some remark out of civility, but he had lapsed into silence after a conventional reply.

"So I sat opposite him and knitted," she explained. "My husband sat in the other corner on my side. We both prefer sitting with our backs to the engine, so much less draughty, we find it."

March asked if it weren't rather odd that one first-class carriage should have filled right up leaving the other nearly empty until the last minute. "People generally spread out and make for the corners," he observed.

"Yes, we were lucky. But there was a party of Army officers in uniform in the next coach and they all got out at Bogmore; there is a training camp at Bogmore, you know."

"That explains it. Could you describe this young man, Mrs. Robertson?"

"I should think I could for I'd nothing else to do but watch him the whole journey. Of course, I didn't let him notice I was doing it, but I thought him such an exceptionally nice-looking young man. . . . Particulars? . . . Well, he had dark colouring, clean-cut features, and rather a worried expression. He was reading a book but I am sure he was really thinking something out—he scarcely ever turned a page. He was wearing a dark suit, very well cut, and his mackintosh was folded up on the top of his suitcase just above his head."

"Suitcase? You're sure he had a suitcase?"

"There's no doubt about it at all. I looked at the case to see if I could discover his name, but, as I've said, it was hidden by the raincoat. But when the train stopped at Bogmore, he moved the coat and took the suitcase down. He got out on to the platform and I thought he was leaving the train and had forgotten his mackintosh and hat. I called after him, but he thanked me and said he was coming back. He came back a minute later without the case and sat down again. I supposed he had left it in the cloakroom. But I had had a good view of it when he took it off the rack. It was marked with the initials D.G. in white letters; the case itself was dark brown leather, not new but very good quality—pre-war, I should say."

March exchanged glances with Norman who had nearly upset his tea-cup in his excitement.

"I never met a more observant and lucid witness," March told Mrs. Robertson.

She laughed a hearty laugh. "I have to be observant in my work. When Mrs. White asks me whether Bobby has been having second helpings this term, or Mrs. Blake wants to know if Claud has been less greedy over his sweets, I should look silly if I said I hadn't noticed. When you have to have the case-history of twenty small boys at your fingertips, it becomes second nature to store up little details in your mind."

"It's an amazing piece of luck for us to have met you," the Chief Inspector declared. "I suppose I need not insult you by asking whether you could identify this young man if you saw him again."

Mrs. Robertson was confident that she would know her travelling companion anywhere.

"I should like to buy that woman a new hat!" March exclaimed as he climbed into the car.

"Bribery and corruption, sir," laughed Norman. "But she certainly knows what she's seen and what she hasn't seen, which is more than most people do."

"Initials D.G.—that will give John Derwent something to get his teeth into. See if you can find a call-box, Norman; I'd like to pass the information to him right away."

Norman drove to Barton post-office, and March emerged after five minutes' absence nodding his satisfaction. "Lucky,

I just caught him preparing a report for me. He's going to start this instant looking for a D.G. among Seely's circle of acquaintances. Derwent's a fast worker; he's hopeful of getting down here to-morrow night with some news. He's been on the case all day, and he's established Seely's movements on the day of his death. He doesn't seem to have done anything out of the way. He spent a couple of hours at the offices of *Intelligentsia* in the morning, lunched with the editor and the literary critic, attended a staff conference in the afternoon, and later called on Parry and Garle, the publishers, who were to have brought out a volume of essays by him next spring. He had a drink and a sandwich at his club alone, and took a taxi to the station. After that we know his movements this end."

Bruce Norton rubbed his hands together approvingly when he heard March's story that evening. "It will take some of the sting out of the crime if it proves not to have been committed by a local man," he said. "The publicity will switch from here to London."

"It's a bit early to use the word 'proves', Bruce. There's nothing at present to show any link between Seely and the dark stranger in the next carriage. If Derwent can find one —well, I wouldn't care to be in D.G.'s shoes, whoever he is. He will have to explain what he was doing wandering in the rain at Grassmere on Friday night between eight-thirty-five and nine-twelve, and he will have to face an identification parade with Miss Munro as star selector."

"This looks like being a woman's case, Chris."

"It does, God bless 'em! I don't know where we should have been without Miss Munro and Mrs. Robertson."

"I can't quite follow that suitcase business. Why didn't the fellow park it in the cloakroom at Grassmere?"

"At a guess, I'd say he didn't intend returning by train from here at all. His objective was evidently Bogmore, where he must have planned to sleep on Friday night. That would be to explain his absence from his home address at the time of the crime. Even if it were part of his plan to catch the nine-fourteen, he saved his time by not having to get his case from the cloakroom and made it less likely he would be noticed at the station. As it happened, owing to the paucity of local passengers, he was noticed. He wouldn't have known that, nor reckoned on the storm soaking him so that he became conspicuous. We didn't get that storm till later in London, though it threatened us all the afternoon."

Norton suggested rather wistfully that if Chris were stopping in that evening, they might have a game of chess. "Like old times," he said. "You were always too good for me, but I used to look forward to our games. There's no one round here to play with. It's a pity—a game takes one's mind off things."

Chris laughed. "Things like young women novelists who fall into ditches and sit on the fact that they've witnessed a murder for four days and tall dark strangers who get lost in the rain! Don't look so pathetic, Bruce. I'm pining for a game myself. Just give me five minutes to ring up the police at Bogmore. I must institute some inquiries there; Derwent will have his hands full looking for D.G. in London."

"By the way, Chris, your sergeant rang up this morning."

"Anything to report?"

"Nothing. I told him to ring up again at nine o'clock to-morrow morning."

"Good. I'll send him over to Bogmore. No harm in setting the ball rolling to-night though."

Bruce took his chess board from a cupboard and dusted it tenderly. It was a long time since it had seen service. Smiling contentedly, he began to arrange the pieces.

18

PETER was in a quandary. He frowned fiercely and ruffled his sleek hair with agitated fingers. But without result; his was not a problem that could be solved by brainwork, at least not without time, and something had to be done at once.

The Chief Inspector had made, or was in the course of making, another blunder. Peter had gasped when he received his instructions on the telephone, telling him to proceed to Bogmore on the next train in quest of a man whose initials were assumed to be D.G. The description which followed fitted Ivan Ling with such precision that it might have been designed for him—as of course it was— by Miss Munro. But Ivan Ling could not be the D.G. of the train journey, and therefore there must have been a tall dark man who for some reason travelled first class to Grassmere on the night in question. It was March's pigeon to discover why. But he had chosen to drag Peter into the inquiry, thereby putting a spoke in his wheel and preventing him carrying out his own more urgent plans. It would have been a perfect day to go to Leigh-on-Sea; the last day of the brief fine spell according to the weather forecast. Peter had planned the trip overnight, assuming that the Chief Inspector would leave him to complete his nebulous inquiries in the village. He had hoped by the evening to be able to report to March that he had solved the crime; his slight unorthodoxy in going to Leigh without instructions would be commended as an act of resource and initiative, and his reputation as a wily and astute investigator would be established beyond doubt.

Now he must either waste his precious time at Bogmore, or spring his surprise on March prematurely. The latter course was distasteful, both because the coup would be robbed of its dramatic effect, and also because his rather sordid adventure at Cairn Farm would have to come out, without any compensating glory to atone for it. Bogmore was perhaps the lesser evil, but none the less it was a damnable waste of time and energy. Peter gave a final scowl at his reflection in the mirror, brushed his hair and adjusted his tie, and set off to catch the train.

On the journey he took out his note-book and sketched out his case against Ivan Ling. He covered a page with neat annotations.

(1) The name Ling fits Seely's dying accusation.

(2) Ling lied about the extent of his acquaintance with Seely and later was forced to admit that he quarrelled with deceased two days before his death.

(3) He also lied about his movements at the time of the crime. It was impossible for him to have got as wet as Hannah Green asserts he did in the short walk between the farm and the cowhouse.

(4) Ling's appearance fits Miss Munro's description of the man she saw stab Seely.

The last item gave Peter a good deal of anxious thought. Miss Munro had not recognized Seely's assailant, yet he was a man who lived within half a mile of her cottage. Well, these country people did not seem to be particularly matey from what he had gathered. It was possible Miss Munro had never spoken to Ling; she was a writer and no doubt spent most of her time in her cottage and garden. It was scarcely possible that she had never seen him. But a flashlight view of a man such as she had obtained left the matter in the air. He would have to see her and obtain details of her exact impression of the murderer before he could satisfy himself on that point. He might be able to manage it on his return that evening. His spirits began to rise, for it struck him that if a little judicious prodding of Jessica Munro's memory enabled her to identify Seely's attacker as Ling, his journey to Leigh would be unnecessary.

He thought of his humiliation at the farm, and how he would turn the tables on Ivan Ling when he brought the crime home to him. It was exasperating to be flatly disbelieved when one told a lie—not a very good lie, perhaps, but a naturally truthful person cannot lie well on the spur of the moment. It was one of the injustices of life that superiority in height and weight should have the advantage over superiority in brain power when it came to a showdown. Peter was of average height but of light build. Ling must be as near six foot as made no matter. Damn it, thought Peter, staring gloomily at the flat scudding landscape, he had practically risked his life to lay hands on Ann Ling's address, and now March's interference prevented him from turning the risk to account.

Bogmore was an uninspiring little town, low lying, straggling, inadequately equipped to carry the traffic which passed through it. Peter made contact with the local police, found that they had done very little towards tracing the mysterious D.G., and wearily set about covering the ground himself. D.G. had apparently made no impression on the cloakroom attendant when he deposited his suitcase. A case had been handed in by a passenger who might have come off the London train and reboarded it; the attendant had not noticed whether he had actually done so. Nor did he now recall the initials on the case; he had too much stuff passing through his hands to remember such details. Anyhow, the case had been reclaimed before he went off duty, he supposed by the person who deposited it; he had produced the cloakroom ticket and that was all that concerned the authorities. Peter obtained from this nonchalant witness the approximate time when the ticket had been presented and found that it fitted the time of the arrival of the "up" train concerned on Friday night, and let it go at that. It was, however, the extent of his success at Bogmore. There had been a party of soldiers returning to camp on the same train and none of the railway officials appeared to have noticed a tall dark civilian in the crowd. It took Peter several hours to round up all the taxi-drivers who had been at the station to meet the train. Not one had driven anyone answering to the description Peter gave to his destination. Whatever had become of D.G. it was clear he had not engaged a taxi. Peter thought he might have gone on to London by the next train, but if he had done so no one had noticed him, and in any case the need for a suitcase was obscure unless he had stayed the night at Bogmore.

Peter returned to Grassmere feeling that so far as that day's work was concerned his abilities had been given no scope. Any fool could question railway officials and taxi-drivers, and perform other routine duties of a like nature. March ought to get the Heathmere police to devil for him, and let Peter save his energies for the more tricky lines of investigation. He arrived at the Buffalo in a peevish mood; he had had to wait over an hour for a train; it had begun to drizzle on the journey and he had no overcoat. He demanded a late tea, changed into dry clothes, and lit the gas-fire in the room in which his meal was served. He determined that before telephoning to March to report the negative results of his mission he would call on Jessica Munro at Cairn Cottage. He might then have something positive to tell the Chief Inspector which would redeem his comparative failure at Bogmore.

Jess was sitting in premature twilight doing nothing at all when she was startled by the sound of the door bell. She had been doing nothing all day, not with the conscious joy of well-earned relaxation, but with the clogging lethargy of being unable to find anything to do that was worth doing. The creeping dusk was depressing, but it was too much trouble to turn on the light. Equally it was too much trouble to turn on the wireless; the *Radio Times* was lost amidst a sea of papers and she hated listening at random. The world was a half-toned no-man's-land, in which one remained just wakeful enough to be aware that it was a foul world in which a man might stab another in the back, and a grim world in which human bloodhounds trailed the killer for days or weeks, or months, so that the primitive demand for an eye for an eye and a tooth for a tooth might be satisfied.

The bell brought Jess unwillingly to her feet. It scarcely ever rang because it was so embedded in creepers that visitors tired of searching for it and hammered on the knocker. Expecting that the Chief Inspector had returned to summon her to an identity parade and recoiling at the prospect, she crossed the hall and opened the door. It was a relief to find a stranger, a fair young man huddled in a mackintosh, who looked as forlorn as she felt herself.

Peter divested himself of his wet coat and Jess turned on the light and the electric fire, and produced some sherry. They raised their glasses and smiled vaguely at one another like a couple of children uncertainly making friends. Peter had not yet explained his errand.

"You know, I've been dying to meet you," he said, warming to the fact that it was remarkably good sherry. "I called on Sunday but you were in bed; it was a terrible disappointment, though luckily only a temporary one. And now I have crossed the threshold, you are so utterly different from what I expected."

"Oh!—expected from what?"

"From your books. Your style is so mature I thought you would be much older."

"I am thirty-two—and I feel very much more at the moment."

"But that is a mere baby where art is concerned. One must live before one can write."

"I have lived—quite a bit. Yes, I suppose you are right; it does help one indirectly, though I never deliberately write about my own experiences."

"I just can't believe that someone as young as you wrote *Good-bye To-morrow*. How did you know what the old people felt like?"

"Well, one has parents and grandparents. You might as well ask how a woman can imagine how a man thinks, or the other way round. Oddly enough, all except a very few writers who specialize in children, are bad at writing about them, and yet everyone who writes has been a child."

Peter nodded sagely as he allowed his glass to be refilled. "I'm sure you have a great future before you," he said.

"I don't know. Anything which depends on mood and atmosphere is bound to be precarious. If I find myself writing badly I shall stop, and take up something else. I'd rather not write at all than pot boil."

Over his third glass of sherry Peter said, "I'm afraid it has to come out, Miss Munro. I'm connected with the police—in fact I am assisting Chief Inspector March who called to see you yesterday."

Jess finished her sherry and refilled the glass. "I was afraid it was so. I didn't see who else would be likely to call on a wet evening. Don't tell me I have to attend an identity parade to-morrow?"

"I don't know anything about that—it's the Chief Inspector's pigeon. I don't think he has anyone for you to identify yet. No—I'm working on a line of my own and I'm hoping you can help me."

"How?"

"I'm sorry to have to introduce what must be for you an unwelcome subject. And I must be careful not to lead you. Could you just imagine that this is a game, and we're not talking about real people at all?"

"It's rather difficult."

"I know, but I want to make it easy for you. It would be too bad to upset your work."

"I'm not writing anything at present. Still, go ahead. I'll try and make believe if you do."

"Splendid. Well, there's a village which we'll call Grass for short. People in Grass are rather spiky; they don't fraternize much even with their neighbours."

"They do in the village. You must remember—if you're thinking of me—I'm not a typical villager. It's quite true I hardly know anyone. Mrs. Bradshaw, my daily woman, is about my best friend."

"I thought it might be like that. Well, there's a dreamy young woman living in Grass, then, and one night she has a really bad dream. There were two men in this dream and afterwards it is tremendously important for her to remember what one of them looked like. She thinks he was a stranger, but might she be mistaken?"

"You mean might he be a neighbour? And she is so frightened by the dream she didn't know him?" Jess screwed up her eyes and bit her fingers like a puzzled child. "I can't play this game any more. You're thinking of Mr.

Ling, the man at the farm down the lane; there isn't anybody else. . . ."

"Was it Ling?"

"I can't say no—or yes. His wife called here soon after I came and I went once to the farm to see her; he wasn't at home. She and I had nothing in common; neither of us made any further move. I've never spoken to him, but I've seen him about, of course. But not indoors and not at close quarters. He's just a figure to me; a tall dark man in breeches—nothing more. There was something vaguely familiar about the—you know who I mean; I told Mr. March so. But that is as far as I can go."

"Have you seen Mr. Ling since Friday night?"

"I've not been out to see anyone, except to the village to telephone and to the top of the lane in the police car."

"If you saw Mr. Ling at close quarters, you might know . . . ?"

"I'm afraid I might."

"I know it's perfectly damnable for you. But it's going to be worse than that for someone—if the Chief Inspector makes a mistake. Mrs. Ling is away but you don't know that. Could you call at the farm to-morrow and ask to see her, some time when Ling will be at home?"

"He's out all day."

"Yes, but in the evening . . ."

"If it wasn't wet I would go now. I won't be able to sleep a wink till I settle things one way or the other in my own mind. I wish you hadn't put the idea in my head. And I hope he's not the man. Oh, but he can't be! I don't see what harm Mr. Seely could have done him."

"Never mind about that—that's our funeral. Your concern is purely with the matter of identification. And don't forget, if we can lay hands on the right man, it may save other people a lot of suffering."

"Oh, I know that. I felt terribly guilty about the Kings. But I wish there didn't have to be a murder in one's own lane. . . ."

Peter was on his feet thanking Jess for her hospitality.

"I'll call round to-morrow evening then, latish—to give you time. . . ."

"Yes, not too early," agreed Jess. But any time, she thought, would be too early if the news she had to give was the wrong news.

19

"ONE up to me," thought Peter as he retreated through the rain. He called at the post-office and telephoned Norton's house; no doubt March would be safely under cover awaiting the fruits of other people's labours.

As soon as he heard the Chief Inspector's voice at the other end of the line, Peter began to describe his activities at Bogmore, but March cut him short.

"I've been waiting for you to report, Cowie, to tell you we want you here. Derwent has news for us—I gather it is important; he sent a message to say he is coming to Heathmere to-night. He's on his way by train now. The idea is to hold a conference at Mr. Norton's house after dinner among the lot of us. Get a meal somewhere and jump on to the next bus. . . . Never mind about the return journey; we'll get hold of a police car."

Peter rang off and almost stamped his foot with annoyance. So Derwent was coming down to steal his thunder, no doubt with some fantastic story about the mysterious D.G. Well, two could play at that game. He would let Derwent make a fool of himself and then spill his own story. He couldn't afford now to wait another twenty-four hours for Jessica Munro to provide the final chapter. There was a bus to Heathmere due in ten minutes; he would reverse March's instructions and have a meal at the other end.

At the Deputy Chief Constable's house he found Norton, March and Norman, sitting round the oval mahogany table in the dining-room, awaiting the arrival of John Derwent, who, the Chief Inspector told him, would be with them any minute now. The room was bright with polished wood and burnished brass; the curtains and carpet were of deep russet and a bowl of yellow chrysanthemums adorned the table. There was also beer, Peter noted with satisfaction, which they were to drink from pewter tankards. It was very suburban, but on a sopping wet night even suburban comfort was not to be despised.

He sat down and told March about his abortive inquiries at Bogmore. He had just finished when Norton's housekeeper showed John Derwent into the room.

Derwent was about the same height as Peter and of similar build, but in other respects could hardly have been less like his junior colleague. He was dark and wiry; a bundle of nerves and energy. His hair was permanently rumpled and his curious slaty blue eyes were never at rest. He precipitated himself into the chair next to March as soon as he had been introduced to Norton and the young Heathmere Inspector, and taking in his surroundings with a sweep of his keen eyes, demanded, "Are we all set, sir? Can I shoot?"

"Go ahead, John," said March, picking up a pencil.

"Right. Well, I scouted round from when I got your message yesterday till midnight, and again to-day up to the last minute before my train left. I've written a report in the train, so I won't tell you now how I got my information. I'll confine myself to summarizing what it adds up to. The only D.G. I can trace who had any connection with Ambrose Seely is a man called Derek Garle. The connection so far is the weakest link in the chain. Garle is thirty-four, and fits the description you gave me perfectly in height and colouring. I lunched at the next table to him in a small restaurant to-day. Garle works in his cousin's office at Parry and Garle's, the publishers; Rupert Garle is the Garle of the partnership. Derek in his spare time—and Rupert sees to it, I am informed, that he isn't overworked at the office—is a playwright. His first full-length play *The Eiderdown* was produced at the *Fantasy* last winter. It was a flop—only ran a fortnight. He is having his new play produced at the same theatre next month. Derek Garle lives alone in a tiny studio flat in South Kensington; gets his own breakfast and has his other meals out. The man in the flat below told me he was away last week-end—that is on Friday, Saturday and Sunday nights. He was back in the office as usual on Monday morning. No one knows where he slept on those nights, and following your instructions I didn't approach Garle directly. The only connection I can trace between Seely and Garle is that Parry and Garle were to have published Seely's book, and that Derek Garle was present when Seely called to see his cousin on Friday afternoon. Seely may have mentioned the train he was catching in Derek's presence. I couldn't get any further in that direction without showing my hand to the Garle cousins. And I couldn't search Derek's flat for a suitcase without a warrant. On the strength of Garle's resemblance to the man in the train, and of his absence from his flat on Friday night, I think I ought to have a warrant to-morrow, sir. I can enter while he's out and still keep him in the dark about our suspicions."

"I'll fix that on the telephone. You've done amazingly well in the short time at your disposal, John."

"There's more to come," said Derwent, concealing his elation—if he felt any. "Derek Garle was married two years ago to the novelist, Jessica Munro. They separated last year; hence Derek's solitary bachelor existence."

"Good God!" exclaimed March. "It's impossible, Derwent; I can't believe that!"

Derwent looked mystified. "I've seen the notice in the file of *The Times*, sir. The fellow in the flat below Garle's told me about the separation. He's a novelist and knows Jessica Munro fairly well—and Derek slightly. I pretended to be an old friend of Garle's who had lost touch with him for several years."

"Well, I'm damned!"

"You know best, but I don't see why, sir."

"You will in a minute. Jessica Munro lives close to the spot where Seely was attacked. She is the young woman whose name I didn't mention on the telephone who claims to have witnessed the attack. I thought she was unmarried."

"Holy smoke!" groaned Derwent, and pushed his fingers through his hair till it stood up like a dark halo.

"What d'you make of it, Bruce?" asked March.

"I'm dumbfounded. I hope your team won't produce any more shocks; they're bad for my constitution."

Peter put his knuckles to his lips to conceal a smile. He would hold his hand a little longer, and even decoy his rival deeper into the wood.

"Miss Munro passes as a single woman in Grassmere," Norman remarked diffidently, as though afraid of speaking out of his turn. "There couldn't be another Jessica Munro, I suppose?"

"Not if your Miss Munro is the novelist."

"She certainly is," put in Peter in a detached voice. "I gathered that much in the course of my inquiries in the village. By the way, I think I can suggest another link between the late Mr. Seely, in his guise of *Ambrosia* of *Intelligentsia*, and Derek Garle. I was at the first night of *The Eiderdown*: it was crude and badly cast, but it had verve. Seely tore it to shreds in his critique; some people thought he killed the play."

"Give me time to think!" exclaimed March. "We seem to be leaving solid ground and floating off into a dream, eh, Bruce? Garle protects his new venture from Seely's destructive pen by assassinating the critic! We'll have to get back to earth again before we lose our sense of proportion."

"What about some beer?" suggested Bruce. "See to it, Norman, will you? I hope you won't crush me in the presence of these youngsters, Chris, but to my humble intelligence, it appears that Derek Garle being Jessica Munro's husband lets him out. She must have recognized her own husband if he were the man she saw, and from what you say of her, she's the last woman to betray him, even if they had quarrelled. She could have cleared King quite easily without giving a precise description of the attacker."

"She could," March agreed. "And no doubt would— if she had recognized her husband. I'll give you that, but I won't concede that it was impossible, in the very strange circumstances of that Friday night, for her to have failed to recognize Garle. She admits that the dark stranger was vaguely familiar. Remember that she would suppose him to be in London and that she fainted shortly after the fatal blow was struck. The marvel is that she retained any coherent picture to pass on to us. We can't exclude improbabilities from our theory of the crime. All we can do, when faced with a choice, is to follow up the lesser of two improbabilities first. It seems to me less improbable that Jessica Munro did not recognize her husband, than that Derek Garle should have been wandering about in the storm at Grassmere for no apparent reason, at the very moment when his double—or near double—was plunging a knife into Seely's back at the corner of Cairn Lane. I am excluding all question of motive for the present and considering only physical facts. I am also assuming that with the help of Mrs. Robertson we shall identify Garle as the man in the train, without any help from Jessica Munro. The identification parade will not now take place. Jessica Munro can't be forced to give evidence against her husband. If he's brought to trial no doubt the defence will try to get her to swear that he was not the man she saw. Altogether we're faced with a very pretty problem."

"I should say with a first-class headache," amended Bruce. "But I take your point about the unlikelihood of two men answering to the same distinctive description being on the scene at the time of the murder, Chris."

Peter took a long pull at his tankard and cleared his throat. He felt like an actor who has just heard the voice of the call-boy. He looked round the circle of thoughtful faces before he spoke, and fixed his eyes on March who was sitting opposite him and was just then in the act of lighting a cigarette.

"I don't think the possibility of Garle having a double—or rather of there being someone like enough to Garle to answer to the same elementary description—can be ruled out, sir."

"Eh, Peter! What are you sitting on?"

Peter held the stage for half an hour. It was his moment of triumph; no one interrupted him, and no one stirred. He had as hushed an audience as if he were delivering a Hamlet soliloquy. He omitted no detail of his recent discoveries and adventures except the episode of the bed at the farm. He left the circumstances of his discovery by Ivan Ling undefined; otherwise his narrative was faithful to fact. When he finished speaking he dropped his eyes modestly, waiting for applause.

There was a moment's stunned silence. Then March spoke. "In future, Cowie, make your report from day to day. Otherwise you break the liaison of the team. But you have done an excellent piece of work. I retract what I said a few minutes ago. From all the facts we have at present there *were* two men abroad on Friday night, both of whom look like the man Jessica Munro described, and both of whom could have been on the right spot at the right time. They may be quite unlike close up but superficially they share certain qualities which we know Seely's murderer to have possessed."

"And we still have our headache!" said Norton. "How are we going to eliminate one of these fellows, Chris?"

Peter looked critically across at the Chief Inspector. He had flushed at what he interpreted as a public reprimand, and puffed himself out like a pouter pigeon at the commendation which had followed. He was still very red and still puffed up. He watched March impatiently. Would the fellow realize that his course was as clear as daylight?

"Elimination," said March slowly, puffing out a cloud of smoke and lazily watching it curl upwards, "is the easiest part of our task. The hardest will be to complete the case against the man we can't eliminate. Thanks to the good spadework Derwent and Cowie have put in, our course is clear."

"Thank God he isn't as obtuse as I feared," thought Peter.

Bruce asked March to outline his plans.

"One thing is obvious," March said. "There must be

no interference with the arrangement Cowie has made with Miss Munro. All right, Peter, you can come off your tenterhooks! We'll mark time at Grassmere until we hear the young woman's verdict. Ling mustn't know there's any special purpose in her visit; she mustn't know her report may affect Garle. Now as to Garle; I think it quite likely Mrs. Robertson would be able to identify him from a good photograph. Derwent will search his flat to-morrow; he may be able to find one that he could borrow without Garle missing it. If so, we'll rush it over to Barton to-morrow afternoon."

"If not, there was a photograph of him in one of the society papers when his play was produced," volunteered Peter.

"Good; you can hunt that up if you need a second string, John. Anyhow, off you go to London by the first train to-morrow, and back you come as soon as you've done your job. By the way, Bruce, I don't want to keep you up all night, but I've no idea where Derwent is to sleep and I want to get Cowie back to Grassmere."

"John can have my ditch with pleasure," said Peter bitterly. "I should be quite as comfortable on the floor."

"No good, I'm afraid," objected Norton. "The early train doesn't stop at Grassmere; it's a fast one. I wish I had another room, Chris; the hotels are packed and it's too late to hope for a bed in any of them to-night."

"We have a spare room at home, sir," Norman said shyly. "I could take Inspector Derwent back with me and see him off in the morning."

"Splendid, Norman," agreed Bruce. "Call in at police headquarters on your way and get the sergeant to send a car for Cowie. It can run you two home first, if you like. Derwent must be tired."

Peter went to the door and announced that the rain had almost stopped. He would go with the other two and take the car on; it would save the driver's time.

When the three young men had said their farewells and departed, Bruce looked at his friend. "Just the same, Chris,

I'm glad it's more your headache than mine. It is, isn't it?"

"If you say so," laughed March. "I don't propose to let it break my sleep though. We may have a lull here to-morrow, but I sense stormy days ahead."

20

JESS looked anxiously out of her window directly she woke the next morning. She had slept badly, and her head ached, and she wanted to know the worst quickly. It was cloudy, but not raining; there was a drying wind; that meant that Ivan Ling would be out until sunset making the most of the favourable weather, and she would not be able to get her ordeal over for at least twelve hours. With a leaden depression she went back to bed. There was no point in making the day longer by getting up before her usual time; it would drag intolerably in any case. She half wished that she had told Peter Cowie that she was certain Ling was not the man she had seen, but she knew that even if she had lied to someone else, she would have had to see Ling and answer the question he had raised for her own peace of mind. One could not live with these morbid doubts and fears for another night, remembering even in one's sleep that one had suddenly been given power of life or death over a fellow creature. Oh, but it was unthinkable that she should exercise such power except to save the quarry from the hunters! Whatever the conclusion she reached, there was only one answer she could give the police. She strove to persuade herself she could find sanctuary within the cloisters of her imagination; she would build a wall and shut out the truth even from herself. She had her life before her, barren without Derek, but still life—so long as she could write. Surely in losing Derek she had paid her debt to fate if there had to be payment; it was a high price for the small sum of happiness that lay behind her. She had a right now to live in at least a negative state of peace, so that she might use her one talent. Loaded with the burden of a fellow creature's death, how would she ever enjoy again the rapture of building words into a pattern?

"And that one Talent which is death to hid,
    Lodg'd with me useless. . . ."

But Milton had not recovered his sight. . . . Human
beings, it seemed, had no absolute rights, only such relative
rights as they could establish for themselves against the
rest of humanity. And to retain even those each succeeding
generation paid a price in blood. "Life, liberty and
estate. . . ." If she said the word they would take away
Ivan Ling's liberty and his life. She would not say the
word. . . .

Mrs. Bradshaw's infallible cheerfulness grated on Jess.
With all her protestations of horror and condemnation of
the wickedness of the crime, she was enjoying the fact that
there had been a murder in the village. It coloured her
drab life, no doubt, and gave the villagers something to talk
about as a relief from local gossip; the detailed symptoms
of their various illnesses; the Rector's sermon; quarrels
between neighbours and the endless "what I said to her
and what she said to me" which floated from one back door
to another.

"I've scrubbed out the kitching this morning, miss,"
Mrs. Bradshaw informed her. "Friday's my day really, but
I done it a day early. I seen Mrs. King last night and
she says as they're burying Mr. Seely to-morrow morning.
I thought you wouldn't mind if I didn't come along till
the afternoon; I wouldn't wish to miss the funeral."

Jess controlled a desire to shudder. "You needn't come
to-morrow at all. I can manage quite well and I've nothing
to do now I've finished my book."

"You ain't fit for much yet, miss. You still look washed
out after that chill you took. I reckon you ought to go
along to the doctor and ask him to give you a nice strong
tonic. And I reckon I'll pop round for an hour after I've
had my dinner; then I can tell you all about the funeral,
unless may be you're going yourself."

"No, I'm not going."

"I dessay you're wise. They say it always rains in Grassmere for a funeral and it wouldn't do for you to take

another cold. Poured cats and dogs for my poor father's funeral, it did. As bad as it did last Friday night, I reckon, only there wasn't no thunder. My poor mother took a fever and it carried her off in a fortnight. They say one funeral makes another. . . ."

Jess forbore to inquire whether it had poured at Mrs. Bradshaw's mother's funeral, and whether the cycle of death had continued. She put an end to the woman's cheerful recapitulation of past tragedies by saying she would go for a little stroll in the lane to shake off her headache.

Automatically she turned to the left and walked as far as the gate opening on the track which led to Cairn Farm. She saw Hannah Green beating mats in the yard; of Ivan Ling there was no sign. She envied the Hannah Greens and Mrs. Bradshaws of the world who go on beating mats and scrubbing kitchens even though the skies fall. She went back to the cottage and tried to kill the rest of the morning by reading the newspaper, came across a paragraph headed "Grassmere Murder—the police investigating the murder of Ambrose Seely, well-known dramatic critic . . ." threw down the paper and went into the garden. She must become a Mrs. Bradshaw for the rest of the day and find something to do with her hands. She found a hoe and began to weed the path. . . .

As the light began to fail, Jess set out again for Cairn Farm. In half an hour she would know the truth, and if she could honestly acquit Ivan Ling her mind would be at rest. She began to walk quickly—almost to run. No, that would not do; one does not run when one is merely going to invite a neighbour to tea. She forced herself to proceed at a natural pace, through the farm gates and down the dirty track. As she approached the yard Ivan Ling came out of a shed, saw her and came to meet her. He said "Good evening" with an inquiring smile.

Jess returned the greeting. "Is your wife at home?" she asked.

"I'm afraid she isn't. As a matter of fact she's away for a few days staying with her mother."

"Oh, I'm so sorry to miss her. I ought to have been to see her before, but I've been so busy I let it slide. I was going to ask her to come and have tea with me on Sunday."

"I expect she will be glad to come. She'll be back on Saturday evening; I'll give her the message."

Jess hesitated. She could not see the young man's face clearly in the dusk which was deepened by the shadow of the farm buildings, but he did not seem to be going to ask her into the house. "Thank you," she said, "I'll expect her about four o'clock unless I hear to the contrary." Ivan remained silent and she turned reluctantly to go. He began to accompany her towards the gate, then hesitated in his turn.

"Would you care to come inside, Miss Munro? I was just going in for a drink myself. I'm afraid I've nothing to offer you except beer or whisky."

"I should love some beer—that is, if you're not so tired you just want to flop into a corner by yourself."

"Not at all. Come along in."

Ivan showed Jess into the sitting-room, turned the light on and went in search of beer. "Now," thought Jess, "when he comes back I shall see him under the light and I shall know. He'll have to put the beer on this table and he'll sit in that chair. . . . Here he comes—in two minutes I shall know."

Ivan came in with the beer and followed the programme Jess had outlined for him faithfully. The light fell on his face as he filled her glass. It was serene and tranquil; the face of a man who has done his day's work well and is looking forward to his rest. Immediately Jess knew her mistake . . . she could not pass judgment on Ling while he wore that air of serene repose. His height and colouring were the same as the murderer's, but something was lacking. She could not tell how he would look if his features were distorted by effort—and effort to accomplish an evil purpose. She had deceived herself and misled the police and come on a fruitless errand.

Ivan was asking her politely how she liked Grassmere. He was an interesting-looking young man, she thought, as she framed her conventional reply; if she could get to know him she would have more in common with him than with his wife, she was sure. He was nearer her own age and he looked as though he must have intellectual interests. She sounded him on that point as soon as she could escape from the exchange of banalities. He gave her a cigarette, asked permission to smoke his pipe, and embarked on a modest little sketch of his career and his thwarted ambitions.

"However, I dare say I'm a better farmer than journalist," he concluded with a smile.

"Do you have any time now for writing?"

"Oh yes, in the winter evenings, plenty. The only trouble is one gets sleepy being in the open air all day; one's inclined to doze over a fire with a pipe. Appalling, isn't it, at the age of thirty-one! But this winter I'm going to fight the tendency to grow into a cabbage. I wrote a few short stories last winter—I had two accepted, as a matter of fact. I'm going to stick at it this winter and try to produce enough for a volume of short stories. I met Rupert Garle years ago when I was on the staff of *Intelligentsia* and I thought of sending them to him. Rather a pompous chap, but his firm do publish that kind of stuff. I'm afraid I'm boring you. . . ."

"On the contrary," said Jess, who had bent her face over her glass to conceal the fact that she had reddened at the mention of the name Garle. "It's nice to find I have a fellow-writer for a neighbour. Perhaps you'll lend me some of your stories to read some day? But now I really ought to be going. Thank you so much for the beer."

Ivan accompanied her as far as the gate leading to the lane. As they neared it he said diffidently, "I shall be going to Mr. Seely's funeral to-morrow, Miss Munro. I feel I ought to as he was such a near neighbour. I shall be taking the car, so if you wish to go, I could pick you up. I'm afraid it's going to rain, according to the weather forecast."

"Thank you; it's very thoughtful of you. But I don't think I shall go. I've only just recovered from a chill, you see, and I don't feel quite up to it."

"Oh, I see," said Ivan quickly. "I didn't mean to suggest,

of course, that there was the least obligation on you to turn up, as Seely's neighbour. I just thought it would be a pity if you walked when the car was available. By the way, please let me know any time you want a lift to Heathmere. I go in about twice a week."

Jess thanked him again and assured him she would take advantage of the offer. It was deep twilight when they separated at the gate and Ivan's face as he smiled his good night was no more than a blurred patch of colour under the shadowing blackness of his thick hair.

"I shall never know for certain now," thought Jess, as she hurried towards the cottage.

She had forgotten all about Peter Cowie until she found him waiting patiently on her doorstep.

21

"I THOUGHT you wouldn't be long," said Peter. "I didn't come to meet you, because I didn't want to queer your pitch."

"Come in," said Jess, and thought how wooden her voice sounded. She led the way to the sitting-room and went through all the actions appropriate to the occasion, turning on the lights and the fire, and producing drinks in the same lifeless way. As she handed Peter his glass, she said:

"There wasn't any pitch to queer."

Peter looked aghast. "You mean . . . ?"

"I know no more than I did last night. I thought I should be able to decide at once, but I talked to Mr. Ling for about twenty minutes in a strong light and I was completely baffled."

"Oh God!" said Peter.

Jessica grew angry. "I did my best and it wasn't my fault that Mr. Ling, smiling and talking small talk, didn't look like a man in the act of killing another. You can't expect me to break my heart because I've fallen down over this test. In any case it was a foul thing to have to do—to lie one's way into a man's house in order to decide whether he ought to go to the gallows or not. Mr. Ling is a good farmer and a more productive member of society than Mr. Seely. I'm glad I'm not in a position to deliver him up to justice."

Peter gaped. "If that is your last word I ought to go. I have to catch the last bus to Heathmere."

Jess did not relent. "You can tell Mr. March I found I was mistaken about my ability to identify Mr. Seely's attacker. That means I shan't be any use if he decides to hold an identification parade later—but he'll see that for himself, no doubt."

Peter put down his glass and, rising unsteadily to his feet, mumbled his farewell and let himself out of the house. Unless he was mistaken, Miss Munro was on the verge of becoming hysterical and he had no time to cope with an hysterical woman if he were to catch the bus. He felt utterly deflated and in no shape to sprint to the bus-stop. His house of cards had collapsed and he could only curse his folly in putting his faith in a woman. Jessica Munro didn't want to identify Ling and so she had taken care to give a non-committal verdict. Well, it was the Chief Inspector's job to bring her to her senses.

At the Deputy Chief Constable's house he found the same assembly—with the exception of Derwent, who was absent —sitting in exactly the same surroundings. March was holding forth but broke off on Peter's entry.

"How about it, Peter?" he asked.

"Afraid it was a washout, sir. Miss Munro turned sentimental and hysterical and blathered about Ling being a better citizen than Seely." He recounted the details of his brief interview with the novelist.

"Then she has neither cleared Ling nor incriminated him," observed March. "Don't look so dejected, Peter, I wondered if she were perhaps a shade rash in claiming she would know Seely's attacker again the moment she saw him. If I saw a murder by the light of a flash of lightning, I wouldn't care to swear that I could reconstruct it perfectly afterwards. By the way, I should imagine the incident itself is unique; I don't recall coming across anything to equal it in the history of crime. We'll let Miss Munro take a back seat for a little while; she may be able to help us again later. Now, this is what we've accomplished this end. Derwent visited Garle's flat and found the initialled suitcase; there was also a fawn raincoat hanging in the lobby. He got a photograph from an old *Tatler* and came straight down here with it. I took it over to Barton and Mrs. Robertson declared positively that it was her travelling companion. Her husband backed her up. Since then one railway official has picked out the photograph from a collection of half a dozen as being that of the man

5*

he saw last Friday night and another also selected it, but said he couldn't swear to it in court. So we know that Derek Garle came down here by the same train as Seely last Friday. John has gone back to London to help keep a cautious watch on Garle until I can interview him. I shall have to put him to the test to-morrow to see whether he can account for his movements on Friday night."

"Then you're no longer interested in Ling," Peter said disconsolately. "In spite of his name rhyming with the sound all the witnesses heard Seely utter when he was dying."

"My dear boy, I'm vitally interested in Ling. I propose to ask him to account for his movements too. In fact, as he is in the locality, I shall see him before I go up to London."

"There's one point that strikes me, Chris," put in Bruce Norton. "If Ling's story is true, that he spent the critical time in his cowhouse, he can't have an alibi."

Chris grinned. "No, I realize that cows are dumb, Bruce. But there is something to be learned from the way a man tells his story. And then this alleged quarrel he had with Seely will have to be gone into."

"Garle won't have an alibi, either, sir," said Norman. "Unless he was seen again after those fellows passed him leaving the station."

"True, Norman," agreed March. "But I'm not so much banking on one of these two producing an alibi—though I confess it would be a pleasant surprise if he did—as on digging up some positive evidence against one of them."

"Well, I don't see how the deuce you're going to do it, Chris," said Norton. "Is there anything more you want to discuss to-night, or do you think we might pack up and have a game of chess? I'm hoping—though I'm not over-sanguine—that I may have my revenge for the beating you gave me the other night. There's a late bus Cowie can catch and I dare say Norman would be glad to have a spot of home life."

"All right," March agreed. "I don't think there's any profit in talking any more until I've seen Garle and Ling.

By this time to-morrow we ought to have got somewhere."

"Let's meet here again at the same time to-morrow night, then. I'll get the chess board out."

Outside in the road, Peter said to Norman, "Feel like going to a cinema? It's much too early for that bus; I don't know what your boss expects me to do, turning me out into the street because he wants to play chess. I feel I'd like to do something to take my mind off this damned case, anyway. If March doesn't pull up his socks we shall be dawdling around here till Christmas. It's all very well for him eating his head off at Norton's, but I'm on a diet of husks, and sleeping in a damp ditch as well."

"You look pretty fit on it," laughed Norman. "And I don't think your chap's the type to let the grass grow under his feet. Yes, I'd love to see a film. Let's take a trolley bus up to the Majestic, shall we?"

Peter agreed and they made for the bus-stop, the young sergeant continuing his grousing on the way. "I don't know what more March wants," he complained. "I'll bet he couldn't have landed a simpler case. Somebody actually *saw* the murder committed. Pity it was a woman, but you can't have everything. As he admitted, the case is unique."

"He was referring to the flash of lightning," Norman protested. "It's not unique for a murder to be witnessed. I read up an old case where four people—it may have been more, I forget the exact details—saw a man attacked in his own house and no one was ever convicted."

Peter snorted. "I don't believe it!"

"It's a real case, believe it or not, Cowie. The murderer rushed into the victim's house with a gun. The victim's wife and daughter and two—if not more—servants all had a good view of him. There was a struggle and someone got the fellow's gun away from him. The daughter and the servants fled out of the house for help. But the attacker also had a knife and he stabbed the householder in the presence of his wife and got clean away before help arrived. The case was rather like this one in some ways, now I come to recall it. Two men were subsequently arrested and brought to trial one at a time in due course. Each had some grudge against the dead man; one was a cousin whom he hadn't deigned apparently to acknowledge as a relative. The other was an old employee whom he had sacked for some reason. And these two independent suspects were so much alike in build and features that the murdered man's wife picked out first one and then the other as the assailant at separate identification parades. Each was acquitted in turn and the case was dropped."

"Suffering snakes!" exclaimed Peter. "You give me the willies. I hope to heaven this isn't a murder film you're taking me to!"

"Oh no, it's a comedy. But I'll get that book again from the library and you shall read the case for yourself."

"Heaven forbid!" said Peter as he boarded the bus.

Left to herself, Jess found to her chagrin that her outburst had left her trembling all over. She did not in the least regret it, but it was mortifying not to be able to speak one's mind without shaking like a jelly over it. She reached out a hand to refill the glass and found that the scene around her was beginning to grow blurred. In a minute she was crying helplessly, without even the will power to search for a handkerchief. She waited limply for the spasm to pass. But her loss of control had a cumulative effect; each involuntary sob seemed to tear her heart-strings and self-pity produced another. It was a vicious circle; she sobbed because she was weak and she grew weaker because she continued to sob. She remembered that she had eaten very little lunch and no supper; the suspense had killed her appetite. She must pull herself together and prepare a meal. She needed someone to give her a good shaking; one could not shake oneself.

It was five minutes before she was able to dry her eyes and stumble out to the kitchen. There, as she fried a chop and made some strong coffee—carefully avoiding catching sight of her face in the mirror over the dresser, lest the sight should make her want to weep again—she took counsel with herself. She had never been addicted to tears; the rot had set in quite recently, ever since—yes, ever since last

Friday. Something must be done about it before she degenerated into a chronic weeper. She felt intensely tired and floppy too, and she had not slept properly for a week. Mrs. Bradshaw was perfectly right; she ought to see the doctor and get a tonic; something to put some stiffening into her. She would go up to the surgery to-morrow evening; there wasn't a surgery on Saturday so it would have to be to-morrow. She vowed she would not put it off over the week-end. With this firm resolution she picked up the tray and carried it to the sitting-room.

22

THE obsequies of the late Ambrose Seely were cloaked by a heavy autumn mist which turned imperceptibly to fine rain as the coffin was lowered into the grave. The crowd of villagers turned up their coat collars, shivered and stared, their eyes smarting in the foggy gloom. Ivan Ling did not stare with the rest but stood on the fringe of the assembly with his eyes fixed upon a patch of luxuriant grass. . . . "Earth to earth, ashes to ashes, dust to dust; in sure and certain hope. . . ." Ivan's lips moved as though perhaps he were repeating the familiar words to himself. When the last words had been spoken and the watchers on the outer ring began to dodge forward to secure their turn for a close up view, Ivan slipped quietly away to his car.

When he reached home he saw that another car was standing in his yard with two occupants; a young man at the wheel and an older man with a distinguished-looking face by his side. Ivan scrambled out of his car and went across to speak to them.

"Were you waiting to see me?"

The older man replied. "We were. I am Chief Inspector March—perhaps you would like to see my card?" He fumbled in his pocket.

"Don't trouble," said Ivan. "I have heard your name in connection with the Seely case. As a matter of fact I have just come back from Seely's funeral. If you'll wait a minute I'll open up the house; my housekeeper was at the funeral and she wished to see some friends before returning home."

Ivan went round to the back of the farm and presently appeared at the front door and signed to his visitors to enter. Norman, as he sat down next to the Chief Inspector, watched Ling's face intently. He noticed its superficial resemblance to Garle's photograph; the dark clinging hair and the clean-cut outline of the jaw. He noticed also the dissimilarities. Ivan looked younger, although Garle's photograph had been taken a year ago. His ears—and Norman was trained to notice the distinctive properties of ears—were considerably larger and flatter. Garle's photograph indicated a more fully developed personality than Ling as yet possessed. If one could see the two men side by side, Norman thought, the differences would probably greatly outweigh the resemblances.

Ling seemed completely at his ease. He had taken off his raincoat, which Norman had noticed was of the popular buff colour in which at the moment the police were interested, and was leaning forward in his chair waiting for the Chief Inspector to reveal his business.

"I want to make my position clear, Mr. Ling," March began, "and, what is more important, I want to make your position clear. You were a near neighbour of Seely's, as distances go in the country. From information received, I believe you were not at home on the night of the crime. I should like to take a voluntary statement from you covering the extent of your acquaintance with Seely and your movements on the night of his death. On the other hand, you are under no obligation to make any statement, nor to answer any questions I put to you. Before you decide what you wish to do, consider the fact that anything you choose to say will be taken down in writing and may, if it proves relevant, be used later in evidence."

Ling smiled and showed very white well-shaped teeth. He looked like a film star, Norman thought, though he was completely unselfconscious. "Your manner of conducting an investigation is remarkably unlike that of your young colleague, Sergeant Cowie," he observed.

March nodded. "I know about that. Cowie is very young, and has yet to learn his job. I'm sorry for any inconvenience he caused you."

"It was rather amusing really, though I nearly let myself in for a charge of assault at the time. However, that is all over and done with. I should like to make a full statement, Chief Inspector, if you think it necessary. But I believe it will save your time if I deal first with the second of your points—my movements last Friday night."

"Certainly," agreed March. "Take this down, Norman. Perhaps you could speak at dictation speed, Ling; it may save a good deal of checking and correcting later on."

"Right, Mr. March," said Ivan. "We've had one of our cows a bit off colour for the last ten days. I didn't send for the vet because my herdsman, an old man named Wade, is an absolute wizard with cows; he has acquired a kind of natural lore from long experience. I was leaving him really to doctor Primrose—the cow—but I didn't think the old chap—sorry, Inspector—amend that to Wade, will you?— I didn't think Wade would turn out in the storm on Friday night, and at the same time I thought someone ought to take a look at Primrose because she had been fairly bad that morning. So I decided to go up to the cowhouse— about five minutes' walk—myself. I set out some time after half-past eight, I can't tell you when to a minute. Primrose seemed better, but glad to receive a visit. She's almost human—Primrose is—but don't put that in the statement, Norman. I shouldn't have stayed with her more than a few minutes, but the rain came down like hell—I mean, it came on much more heavily, so I decided to stop under cover until it slackened. I was still sheltering there when, to my surprise, old Wade turned up in his oilskins and waterboots. He was most indignant to find I hadn't reckoned on his seeing Primrose in such weather. It would take more than a thunderstorm to keep him from doing his job, he said. He looked her over and said she was doing fine. We were talking together when there came an appalling flash of forked lightning; we saw it through the window; my cowhouse is very modern, by the way, and has scientific ventilation, electric light and a cement floor. The lightning jagged right across the sky and the thunder deafened us. We waited until the rain slacked off and then separated and made for home. Wade lives over on the road close by where the old Beech House drive comes out, I should tell you. It would take him quarter of an hour to get home, the pace he walks. I believe I was home by half-past nine, but I'm not certain of the times either way. My wife, who was working herself up for fear I should catch cold or be struck by lightning, told me I'd been gone nearly an hour."

"Take Wade's address, Norman," said March, and waited for Ling to dictate it. "You've been rather a cuckoo, haven't you, Ling?" he went on. "If you had given this information to my sergeant, you would have saved your time and ours. That flash of lightning is the crucial point. It struck Beech House, and we know Beech House was struck at five minutes to nine. From other information we have, if Wade was with you at that particular moment, it doesn't matter where you were the rest of the time."

"I didn't feel inclined to tell your sergeant anything. First he masqueraded as a newspaper reporter and then he hid under my bed."

March laughed heartily. "He hadn't told me that, but I still think you were foolish, because you did yourself much more harm than you did him. One thing I should like to know, being a curious creature by nature, and that is how you managed to get so wet as you did, if you were only in the open for ten minutes?"

"It wasn't difficult to get wet that night, I can assure you. True, I wasn't out then in the worst of the deluge. But I had been out before supper, and my raincoat was sodden when I put it on again to go to the cowhouse."

"I see. And there was nothing in that dispute you had with Seely?"

"I gave Sergeant Cowie a true account of the incident."

"Thank you. We'll pack up now then and call on Wade. Will he be at home?"

"Yes, I sent him home after he'd done his work before breakfast. There's nothing much he can do till feeding time comes round again and he had no wish to go to the funeral. He said he'd buried three wives in his time and the only funeral he means to go to in future is his own."

"He sounds a character. Come on, Norman. We shall get your statement typed, Ling. You may as well sign it to complete our records."

"Delighted," agreed Ivan, leading the way to the door.

He smiled farewell to the two policemen, not exactly a mocking farewell, Norman thought, but it was plain that the young farmer was feeling quite pleased with himself and realized that he had scored off the unorthodox Cowie.

"Poor old Peter!" sighed March as they drove away. "I can't help feeling a twinge of compassion for him. He was so very clever-clever, and his original tactics landed him just where such tactics generally land a policeman—outside a detective novel."

"Inside one," observed Norman, "he would have discovered a vital clue to Ling's guilt, and have emerged as the Yard's coming sleuth. Anyway, I'm glad he didn't. Ling seems a nice quiet chap, with a sense of humour."

"Yes, and he could, of course, have charged Cowie for searching his house without a warrant. There really was not enough evidence against Ling to justify proceeding without one."

"And yet you cautioned him, sir."

"Yes, Norman, because at the ripe age of forty-three, I've learnt the wisdom of being prepared for all eventualities—as they say. If I hadn't cautioned Ling and he had made any damaging admissions, I should have been in the soup."

Old Wade was smoking an ancient pipe in his snug kitchen. He received the strangers with the inborn courtesy of the old countryman, showing neither surprise, embarrassment, servility nor familiarity. He set chairs for them and asked what he might do for them, as though he received strange guests every day of the week. March sighed at the reflection that Wade was a relic of an ancient breed that was slowly dying out. Another generation or so and gone would be the pure dialect and with it the smell and the smack of the soil. Feasting his eyes on the gnarled dignity of the face and his ears on the soft, slow speech, he encouraged Wade to tell his story.

The old man gave his age as eighty-three. He had just missed compulsory education, left school at the age of eleven on his father's death, and worked on the land ever since. He had married for the first time at nineteen, reared nine children, the eldest of whom—his widowed daughter—was over sixty and kept house for her father. Of course Wade only worked short hours now; the master wouldn't let him do more than he felt able. He spoke with proprietary affection of Ling. On the night of the storm he had gone out to have a look at Primrose—it was half-past eight by his grandfather clock when he set off. Weather had never "done him no harm"; man and boy he had never stopped indoors for rain or snow. He had found Mr. Ling in the cowshed. When the storm burst right over their heads he had said to the master that he "reckoned as that lightning had struck suthing". He didn't stop above a half-hour in the cowshed, Primrose was doing well, and man and boy he had been early to rise and early to bed. He wasn't going to change his habits now. He and the master had left the shed together; the worst of the storm was over then.

March got to his feet and with a word of thanks handed the old man a ten-shilling note. Wade made no move to take it. He didn't take money except he earned it. He had a good pension and he reckoned he had earned that. He was a radical, always had been and always would be, and there wasn't anyone to compare with Mr. Gladstone, but the labour folk had increased his pension, and they were "better than they danged tories any day". Mr. Ling paid him well for what he did; he didn't want for anything. The Chief Inspector shook his hand and asked him what tobacco he smoked. Wade named his brand and agreed that a bit extra wouldn't come amiss though he lacked for nothing. Finally March induced him to accept the tip for extra smokes, the old man remarking that it would last him to the day of his death and maybe leave a bit over.

"I hope not," said March. "You look well set for a century."

"We've missed the train, sir," said Norman, as he pressed the self-starter.

"I know, Norman. I couldn't hurry the old man. What time is the next train?"

"Nothing from Grassmere till the three o'clock. I think

I'd better run you over to Bogmore. I don't know what you'll catch, but there's a better service there."

"Step on it then. I want to catch Garle at his office. He has become the focal point of the investigation now."

"I was glad I didn't have to take Wade's dialect down. I don't know how you understood all he said."

"It took some doing. But you gathered that he confirmed Ling's story and that was all that really mattered. Incidentally, Ling is the second candidate Jessica Munro has eliminated, indirectly, in this case—by giving us the exact moment of the attack on Seely. I wasn't far out when I told her she had made it virtually certain that Seely's murderer would be brought to justice, though if I had known her husband was implicated I would have held my peace."

"I don't think I ever heard of such a complicated mix-up, sir. We didn't think either Ling or Garle would have an alibi. Suppose we were wrong about Garle too?"

"Ah, then I shall have to put on my thinking cap, Norman. So far I've left most of the work to other people. I'm a timid prophet, and I don't bet, but if I did I would lay heavy odds against Garle joining King and Ling in the ranks of the 'elsewheres'. And, by the way, on your drive back through Grassmere, you'd better look up Cowie and tell him to inquire from the station outwards for anyone who saw a tall stranger in the storm on Friday night. He'll be getting into more mischief if I don't keep him occupied."

There was a London train due in twelve minutes. Norman promised to meet the eight-thirty-five at Grassmere that evening, wished the Chief Inspector a profitable journey and set off home.

23

MARCH took a taxi and drove to Scotland Yard, picked up John Derwent, and changing into a police car, directed the driver to go to Parry and Garle's offices at Ludgate Hill. On the way he told Derwent the position with regard to Ling.

"Poor old Peter!" Derwent exclaimed, grinning broadly.

"Exactly what I said, but it won't do the young jackass any harm. What's been going on this end?"

"Nothing much. Garle has been putting in his usual hours at the office, and taking his meals at his customary haunts. Sergeant Cooper is keeping a weather eye on him to-day; I thought he might grow too familiar with my uncommon physiognomy. Cooper looks like a demobbed chap from overseas taking a peep at dear old London. I dunno where he gets his deep tan from unless he uses ultra-violet rays."

The bronzed young man in a smart new civvy suit appeared to be queuing for a bus, but he detached himself from the queue when the police car drew up twenty yards from the publisher's office.

"Garle has been back from lunch about three quarters of an hour, sir. Got a cigarette on you, Derwent?"

"Dammit, I gave you a packet this morning, you old cadger. Here you are; don't take more than one; you'll run me short."

"Go and sit in the car, Cooper. You'll look less conspicuous there than if you spend the afternoon missing buses, and I shall know where you are if I want you. Come on, John."

A call at the inquiry office produced the information that Mr. Derek Garle had a small room opening out of Mr. Rupert Garle's office on the second floor. The informer inquired whether March had an appointment. March did not produce his card, but asked if Mr. Derek Garle was disengaged at the moment. Hearing that there was no one with either of the Garles, he said that he would announce himself. This was apparently an unheard-of procedure, but the Chief Inspector waved aside all counter-suggestions and approached Rupert Garle's office with Derwent in his wake.

Their knock was answered by a bass shout, and they entered to find a rather portly, florid man, with startling auburn hair, which could with advantage have been denuded of a couple of inches of its growth, regarding them with outraged eyes. March took Rupert Garle to be a man of about his own age, and judged from his complexion that he did himself over well for one who leads a sedentary life.

A torrent of expostulation poured from the publisher's lips. He was unaccustomed to being interrupted at his work, and could not imagine what the deuce his office was thinking about to allow such an incident to occur. March let him exhaust a little of his spare energy and then, without speaking, produced his card.

Rupert stared at it with incredulity.

" 'Chief Inspector March', eh? I think you must have come to the wrong address. This is Parry and Garle's, the publishers." His tone indicated that his firm had no dealings with the police.

March assured him that he had read the name of the firm on the door plate. "You have a cousin working here, I believe—Mr. Derek Garle? I should like to see him at once if you will kindly arrange it."

Rupert looked stupefied. "My cousin works next door. I'll see if he is disengaged."

He stalked heavily towards the inner room and closed the door behind him. March set it ajar, saw that there was no second exit, and waited. Soon Rupert came puffing out again. "You may go in," he said with all the dignity he could muster, and returned to his own desk.

Derek Garle had risen from his seat and was standing with his back to a small high window. He looked strained, Derwent thought, or perhaps only tired—it was difficult to tell. He spoke quickly with a studied jocularity that was rather embarrassing.

"My cousin tells me you are police officials. As I don't drive a car, we wondered what you wanted here."

"I have no concern with traffic regulations," March told him. "I work under the Assistant Commissioner for Crime."

"I see, or rather I don't see, but please sit down. Perhaps you will lighten my darkness?"

March sat at the desk. There was no other chair in the room except an arm-chair in the corner. Garle pushed this forward for Derwent, and fetched a small cane chair for himself from the next room. He placed this on the far side of the desk and disposed himself awkwardly upon it, for it was much too small for a man of his height. The preliminaries concluded, he looked at the Chief Inspector, his arched black eyebrows expressing his demand for information.

"You knew the late Ambrose Seely?" March began.

"I did, slightly."

"When did you last see him?"

"A week ago to-day. He called here during the afternoon and discussed the plans for his volume of essays with my cousin and myself."

"Was that the last time you saw him?"

"Yes."

"About what time?"

"He had a cup of tea with us next door and left about half-past four."

"From that point, Garle, I want to proceed to other questions, the nature of which is such that, before I put them, I ought to warn you that you can, if you wish, refuse to give me an answer. If you prefer to answer, my colleague here will make a note of what you say. In that case we shall regard your statement as voluntary, and it will be valid as evidence——"

"But I've no idea what you're getting at! Evidence of what?"

"You read the newspapers, I expect?"

"Oh, I know Seely was murdered, of course."

"And you know no doubt that murder leads to a police investigation?"

"I saw in the papers that you were in charge of the case. But where do I come in?"

"That is for you to tell me, Mr. Garle. Do you wish to volunteer information or not?"

"I've volunteered the little I know about Seely."

"We shall see. After Seely left here, at about four-thirty, how did you pass the rest of the day?"

"I left the office myself about half an hour later. I had arranged with my cousin to be away for the week-end."

"Describe everything you did precisely, please."

"I'd brought my week-end case up here with me. I was going to Bogmore by the seven-fifteen to stay with a friend —Hugh Sydney, of 24 Station Road, Bogmore. I collected my case and went out and had a proper tea—we hadn't had anything but a biscuit to eat here—and I expected to be late for dinner. I caught the train and spent the week-end with my friend. I was back at the usual time on Monday morning."

"After an uneventful week-end?"

"Yes, it was much like any other week-end in the country."

"What class did you travel?"

"First class: I wanted to read in the train."

"Did you see Mr. Seely on the train?"

"No, I didn't. Was he on that train?"

"He was. However you didn't see him and you got out at Bogmore. What time was that?"

"We got in at eight-fifteen. Sydney's house is close to the station so I didn't take a taxi. At least I thought from the address that it would be close to the station—I hadn't stayed with him before. Actually it was farther than I expected—about quarter of an hour's walk, carrying a fairly heavy case."

"So you reached Mr. Sydney's house at half-past eight?"

"Thereabouts, I suppose."

"No doubt he will know what time you arrived?"

"I'm sure he will."

"Who else was present?"

"No one. Sydney is unmarried and it was his cook's evening out. She had left us a cold supper and gone off to the pictures."

"Now, Garle, I want you to look at this photograph. Have you seen it before?"

Derek Garle, who had been giving his answers promptly and confidently, held out his hand for the cutting with a jaunty gesture, but turned very white when he beheld his own features.

"Of course I've seen it, seeing that I posed for it," he said, and seemed to have trouble in controlling his breathing. "But how did you get hold of it?"

"I believe it was cut out of an old *Tatler*. You agree it is a good likeness, Garle?"

"As far as one can judge one's own picture, I don't think it is bad."

"It was good enough anyhow, Garle, for two people who travelled in the same first-class compartment with you on Friday night to recognize it as a photograph of their travelling companion. They are both prepared to state on oath that you travelled with them as far as Grassmere."

Garle said nothing but turned the square of paper over and over with his fingers as though he would like to tear it to shreds. Against his dark hair his skin seemed bleached to the colour of the white blotting-paper on the desk beneath his elbow. As Derwent had stopped writing and March was as immobile as a statue, there was silence in the room for the space of several minutes. Then Garle put the photograph down on the desk, sat back and folded his arms.

"And if I deny that I travelled to Grassmere?"

"Do you wish to deny it?"

"I wish to adhere to what I have already said. Sydney can testify that I was at his house before eight-thirty-five."

"What is the significance of the time eight-thirty-five?"

"Well, isn't that the time the train reached Grassmere?"

"Possibly it is, but what did that matter to you if you were getting out before Grassmere?"

"It didn't matter to me, but I saw what time it was due

at the next station when I looked out my train to Bogmore. There's nothing incredible in that, surely?"

"No, Garle, I can accept the fact that you might conceivably note the time a train was due at a little wayside station, even if you had no intention of travelling to that station. But other statements you have made are not credible."

"In God's name, why not? You mean you take the word of two people who never saw me in their lives before, before the word of a man who has known me for fifteen years."

"Perhaps it is because he has known you for fifteen years that he is willing to perjure himself for you. I haven't, of course, seen him yet, but I suspect you have persuaded him to give you an alibi for last Friday night. But the alibi is useless to you."

"But I don't need an alibi! Can't I travel on the same train as Seely—I accept your statement that he was on that train—without needing an alibi for the time of his murder? I didn't meet Seely more than about a dozen times, and on the last few occasions my cousin was present at our meetings."

"I want to leave the question of how well you knew Seely alone for the present, Garle, and return to the subject of your movements on Friday night. Do you deny that you left a suitcase marked with the initials D.G. in the cloakroom at Bogmore station at about eight-fifteen and picked it up about an hour and a quarter later?"

"What the hell——? Of course I didn't. Do you suppose I'm the only chap in England whose initials are D.G.?"

March ignored the question. "And that having deposited the case, you boarded the train again, and left it at Grassmere station, where you gave up your ticket and inquired if there were a taxi available? Also that you went back to Bogmore by the nine-fourteen train, having got extremely wet during your stay in Grassmere?"

Garle jerked himself out of his minute chair and knocked it over backwards in the process. He went over to the window and threw up the bottom half so quickly that he had his head outside before Derwent leapt to his side and grabbed his coat. At a nod from March, Derwent hauled Garle back into the room and closed the window.

"I was only getting some air," Derek protested. "I think, Chief Inspector, I shall take advantage of the option to remain silent. There seems to be either an amazing case of mistaken identity, or else a colossal conspiracy on foot against me. In either case it will take a lawyer to unravel it."

"As you like, Garle. But you have said so much that is in direct contradiction to reliable information I have received that it will be necessary for me to take you into custody. Arrangements will be made for you to communicate with your solicitor."

Derek leaned against the wall and closed his eyes. Derwent stood at his side watching him suspiciously. But the young man made no further move towards the window. When he opened his eyes he seemed to have regained some degree of composure. He shrugged his shoulders and addressed March.

"What is the procedure?"

"The Inspector will accompany you while you collect your belongings. We have a car outside. Technically, you will merely be detained while we investigate your statement. It will be typed and brought to you for signature some time this evening. Unless you are charged with a definite crime within twenty-four hours, you will be released."

"I thank you, sir," said Derek ironically. Derwent accompanied him through Rupert Garle's office, and the publisher, having failed to halt the procession, collared March who was bringing up the rear and began to bluster.

"The best thing you can do," March told him firmly, "is to take a grip on yourself and get busy on Derek Garle's behalf. Telephone his solicitor and ask him to get in touch with this telephone number as soon as possible."

"Grip of myself!" echoed the scandalized Rupert. But he sat down at his desk and reached for the telephone.

24

MARCH travelled to Bogmore by the now much publicized seven-fifteen train and alighted at the station an hour later. Recalling Garle's statement that Sydney's house was fifteen minutes' walk from the station, he hailed a taxi and gave the address. That part of Garle's unreliable story would no doubt prove true. He was curious to discover what sort of man this Hugh Sydney was; a man willing, it seemed, to run very heavy risks on behalf of an old friend. Sydney must surely be a man of enough education to know that he would lay himself open to a more serious charge than that of perjury if he persisted to the end in sheltering a criminal. The short run up the hill along the narrow station road did not give March time for further reflection, though he calculated that a man on foot, carrying a suitcase, might well take quarter of an hour to cover the distance.

The bell at 24 Station Road, a semi-detached brick house, which lacked distinctive characteristics, was answered promptly by a grey-haired woman—no doubt the cook who had conveniently taken her evening off the previous Friday, but this Friday was evidently on duty. This circumstance savoured of premeditation on Sydney's part as well as Garle's and March determined as he was invited to enter a small front sitting-room, that he would handle the owner of the house with the utmost discretion. The room was empty, and, saying that she would fetch Mr. Sydney, who was upstairs, the woman asked as an afterthought what name she should give. The Chief Inspector gave his name as Mr. March and made no mention of his occupation.

He had to wait ten minutes for the occupier of the house to appear, and he looked round the room to see what clues it gave to the character of Hugh Sydney. He seemed to be a man of some taste for the room contained the minimum of furniture, and so looked larger than it was. And the furniture was so good that it redeemed the otherwise villaish character of the room. Two large leather-covered arm-chairs and a narrow oak table pushed into the window recess, were all the contents of the room which took up any appreciable space. The floor was completely covered by a dull patterned Indian carpet and dull red curtains of heavy velour were drawn across the window. In one corner, beside the open fire, stood a small writing-desk, and the other was filled by a glass-panelled book-case. The only pictures were two original water-colours by a Dutch artist. Sydney could not be hard up, or he would sell these and realize a small fortune. It was incongruous that he dwelt in such inartistic, almost sordid, surroundings. If Hugh had not precipitated himself by his rash bargain with Garle into the midst of a criminal investigation, March felt that he would have been keenly interested in learning his history for its own sake.

March stood up when he heard steps approaching and was standing with his back to the fire when the door was thrown open. He had hard work to maintain his poker face, for he had expected to see a man of Derek Garle's age. Instead there entered a slight, fragile-looking man of about sixty, with curly grey hair and small pointed beard. A small grey moustache curled upwards and disclosed a little bow-shaped mouth.

"Mr. Sydney?" asked March.

Sydney bowed with old-fashioned courtesy. "You have the advantage of me, sir."

March held out his card. Sydney took his spectacles from his pocket and put them on, before he scrutinized it. "I am honoured to meet you," he said, returning the card to its owner. "Pray be seated. I must apologize for my discourtesy in keeping you waiting. I was developing some negatives in my dark room upstairs and they would have been spoilt had I come down sooner."

"You are acquainted, I believe, with Mr. Derek Garle," March began, feeling a strong inclination to adopt his companion's mode of speech.

"Indeed I am. Derek Garle is my godson."

"That is rather strange, sir. I understood from Mr. Garle that you had known him for fifteen years only. He would have been nineteen when you met him in that case."

"That is perfectly correct. I first saw my godson in 1932, when I retired from my post in India. I was in the Indian Educational Service and retired somewhat prematurely for reasons of health. I need not trouble you with details of my career. No doubt it is my godson, not my humble self, in whom you are interested."

"Primarily, yes," agreed March. "Derek Garle spent last week-end here with you, I believe?"

"He did. I hesitated to invite him here, because there is little amusement for a young man in Bogmore. But it was the only way in which I could see anything of him. I so seldom go to London these days."

"Quite so. Was the invitation of long standing?"

"The invitation to visit me here was, I think, given some months ago. I left him to propose the date himself, as I am always here, while he is a busy man. He selected last week-end two or three weeks ago."

"Did he say what train he would arrive by?"

"He was uncertain what time he would be able to leave his office. He asked me not to wait dinner for him if he should be delayed."

"And what time did he actually arrive?"

"He was here soon after half-past eight."

"*Soon* after? How soon, sir?"

"Oh, very soon, I believe. Perhaps even a minute or two before. I was sorry I had not recommended him to take a taxi-cab. He was carrying rather a heavy case, and, as no doubt you noticed, the road is uphill."

"Mr. Sydney, this is all very perplexing. Are you ready to swear that Garle was here at all events by quarter to nine and that he did not arrive much later, say, at about ten minutes to ten?"

"Well, as a matter of fact, I never swear. It may seem fastidious to you, but I have made a practice for years now

of avoiding oaths. It arose from an incident when I was a
young man, when I quite inadvertently gave false testi-
mony. I won't trouble you with the details, but I learnt the
lesson that one is seldom in a position to trust one's senses
sufficiently to take an oath on their evidence."

"But you would have to take an oath in a court of
law."

"I should add a rider to the effect that the truth of my
evidence was subject to the fallibility of my senses."

March sighed. He was tired after his long day, and
regretted that the law forbade him to take this courteous
gentleman by the shoulders and shake a straightforward
answer out of him.

"Very well, do you maintain that, according to the
evidence of your fallible senses, Garle was here in this
house at this time last week?"

"He was as much here as you are here now."

March switched to another tack. "I believe your cook
was out last Friday evening? Is that her usual evening
out?"

"She is usually out on Saturday night. Last week she
kindly altered her arrangements to suit my convenience.
I had invited a friend to dinner on Saturday to meet my
godson—Augustus Flemming, the curate at St. Jude's; a
charming young man. I thought Derek would appreciate
meeting someone of his own age."

The Chief Inspector consulted his wrist watch. It was
five minutes to nine and he had telephoned for Norman
to meet him at Bogmore station with a car at nine o'clock.
He asked Sydney whether he might see his cook for a
moment. Sydney insisted on summoning the woman to
the sitting-room, saying that he himself would slip up to
the dark room and have a look at his negatives.

The cook, who seemed a sensible woman, a little taken
aback at being questioned by a police officer, could tell
March nothing except that she had changed her evening
out in order to be at home to cook the dinner on Saturday
night and had returned about half-past ten on Friday to
find Mr. Garle and Mr. Sydney together in the sitting-

room. Two people had eaten the cold meal she had pre-pared, judging from the plates which had been used.

March did a little quick thinking. "Had they had coffee after the meal?" he asked.

"Yes, sir. When I go out I leave the coffee ready on the gas stove for Mr. Sydney to heat up. He generally pours it straight into his cup, but of course, seeing that he had company, I left the coffee pot out."

"What kind of coffee pot?"

"An old silver one, sir. It doesn't pour very well, but I broke the china one last time the curate came to dinner; knocked it accidentally as I was drying it."

"Did you clear away the things on the dinner table directly you got home?"

"Oh yes, sir. I washed up before I went to bed."

"What about that coffee pot? Was it cold?"

"Why no, sir, it was still warm, and there was a nice drop of coffee left in it. I heated it up with some milk and drank it myself."

"Thank you. I won't disturb Mr. Sydney again, if you'll tell him I've left to keep an appointment."

"Very good, sir."

The faithful Norman was waiting outside the station, and whatever curiosity he felt about March's visit to Bogmore, he did not ask to be enlightened on the homeward drive. The Chief Inspector did not reveal his news until they arrived at Norton's house.

Bruce Norton was eager for information, but he insisted on Chris having some food before he related his experiences. Over a cup of coffee by a snug fire, March at last relieved the tension by addressing Peter, who was sitting in a corner with something of an air of a bored child at a party.

"Get anything, Peter?"

"Damn all, sir, except wet feet."

"I'm not surprised. Norman has told you about Ling, Bruce, I expect?"

"He has; it's the London end we're all bristling to hear about, and why you mysteriously demanded to be dug out of a hole like Bogmore."

March told his story concisely and effectively. The audience, except Peter, who glowered in his dark corner, sat up and registered surprise and satisfaction.

"Looks like you're on the last lap," commented Bruce.

"I wouldn't say that yet; it takes the devil of a time sometimes to complete a case. But I've pulled all the strings I can get hold of to speed things up. I've co-opted half the department; Derwent is standing by to see Garle when his solicitor turns up, with a sergeant in tow. Two other fellows under Derwent's supervision are making intensive inquiries into both Seely's and Garle's careers. There must be something more to it than pique at an adverse dramatic criticism. The A.C. must wonder what we're doing this end."

"Wearing our shoes out tramping the highways," put in Peter.

"Cheer up, Peter. I've a better job for you to-morrow. Hunt up one Augustus Flemming, curate of St. Jude's, Bogmore, and ask him just what he knows about an eccentric gentleman named Hugh Sydney."

"Oh Lord," grumbled Peter. "I dislike curates."

"And he probably dislikes detective sergeants, but no doubt he will have the courtesy to conceal the fact."

The telephone rang and Bruce, after answering it, called March to take the call. "It's Derwent on the line," he told him.

The Chief Inspector had a long talk with his assistant, and at once relayed the gist of it to Norton. "Garle's solicitor had left London for the week-end. Garle refused to see his partner or anyone else, so he is dashing back to town immediately. Personal friend of Derek's, apparently. I hope he isn't another eccentric godfather! I've told John to go to bed and get some sleep; I don't think he's had more than a dozen hours in bed since this case started. I've also told him to get on to the India Office to-morrow and find out what they know about Sydney. I can't do any more till I have Derwent's report; it's not much use even thinking until I know what line Garle's solicitor advises him to take. Like a game of chess, Bruce?"

Bruce beamed his answer and made at once for the cupboard containing the chess board. Peter said he would make for the last train and try to get a few hours' sleep in his "ditch". Norman stayed behind to consult Norton in some matter and March followed the sulky young sergeant out into the hall.

Peter struggled into his mackintosh, still damp with exposure to rain and fog. March gave him a hand and Peter suddenly began to speak quickly and indistinctly. "Other fools seem to get away with it all right," he said. "I must be the wrong sort of fool, I suppose. I think I'd better go in for commercial travelling; I believe I could make good in that line."

March patted his damp shoulder. "You'll make good in the C.I.D., Peter, if you'll profit by your failures. I had some terrific flops in my early days. Our job isn't a hundred per cent success, you know, and never will be so long as criminals have wits to fool us with."

"I'd like to wring Ling's bloody neck," said Peter feelingly.

"It's much more likely he will wring yours! You'd better skip now or you'll miss the train. See what you can do with Mr. Flemming to-morrow and report on the 'phone as early as you can. Good night."

"Good night, sir," said Peter. March was not a bad old chap, he thought, as he boarded a bus. Evidently he did not want to lose the services of his new sergeant. Perhaps he had the brains to realize that the present case had not so far given his assistant scope for exploiting his flair for deduction to the best advantage. Some knotty problem might still crop up in which, by a flash of intuition, he might hit on a solution while the Chief Inspector himself remained baffled.

25

UNDETERRED by the fog, Jess set out for the doctor's house a little before seven. Surgery hours were from six to seven and she timed her arrival so as to be the last patient, and thus avoid sitting in a crowd in the waiting-room. Her scheme worked nicely; as she arrived the last remaining patient passed through the door into the surgery. He would probably be there about ten minutes, just time to smoke a cigarette. Eyeing the soiled magazines on the table before her with distaste, she lit up and waited. Of all depressing places on earth, she thought, a doctor's waiting-room headed the list. This one was stuffy, the chairs were hard, and the wallpaper hideous. The atmosphere, full no doubt of germs exhaled by the previous occupants, was enough to make you ill, even if you felt quite well when you entered. She opened a window and let the mist seep through the aperture. It was better to be chilly than asphyxiated.

She finished her cigarette, and lit another. The man was taking a long time, perhaps he was having a thorough overhaul and she would have to wait half an hour. Why couldn't they put some current periodicals on the table?— Miss Leigh ought to see to that—one couldn't expect old Dr. Tom to bother. Some flowers would be refreshing too, only they wouldn't last very long in such a fug. She heard someone approaching the inner door and hurriedly crushed out her cigarette. The patient was coming out at last, saying something about calling again in a week as he opened the door. Jess hurried to take his place, almost jostling past him in her eagerness to get her interview over. She closed the door after her, and looked across at the desk. . . . It was not Dr. Tom, but—Good God! . . . It was . . . the room began to grow black and, clutching at nothing, Jess felt herself first stagger and then fall. But she did not reach the ground, and she did not quite lose touch with her surroundings. She knew that she was caught and lifted on to a couch, arranged in a most uncomfortable position, with her back supported and her head bent down, and after a short lapse of time given something bitter and stinging to drink.

She opened her eyes, shivered and half closed them again. Better not look again until she felt stronger. . . .

"That was a most dramatic entrance," said a pleasant, low-pitched voice close to her ear. "It looks as though you have come to the right place, doesn't it?"

"No, I . . . I thought Dr. Tom was here."

"My uncle is on holiday."

"I knew, but I had forgotten. Or I thought he would be back; I'm not sure which."

"He won't be back for another week."

"Was that poison I drank just now?"

"Well, not in the usual sense of the term. It would be if you had a very concentrated dose. So would a lot of drugs in common use, you know. It was just a pick-me-up and your colour is coming back already. Try sitting up; I think you will be more comfortable. That's better. Now, you had better tell me about yourself. How long have you been feeling under the weather?"

"About a week."

"What has been troubling you?"

"Everything. I can't sleep, don't want to eat, and I keep on crying."

"Do you do any sort of brain work?"

"Yes, I write books."

"What about a holiday?"

"I've been resting for a week. That is, not doing any writing."

"That's not much use unless you go away."

"I don't want to go away; there's nowhere to go, for one thing. If I could sleep I should be all right at home."

"You mean you want a narcotic. It ought not to be necessary at your age. It would be better to discover the cause of your sleeplessness and eliminate it."

"I am thirty-two."

"Yes, but you don't want to take to narcotics yet, if you can avoid it. Are you married or single?"

"Both. I mean, I am married, but not living with my husband."

"Well, that may have something to do with your nervous condition. How long have you been separated? Or are you divorced?"

"Oh no. We separated a year ago."

"Did you leave him?"

"No, he left me. At least, he didn't actually do that. I suppose it would be more correct to say that he asked me to leave him."

"Against your inclinations?"

"Completely."

"What went wrong between you? Sex?"

"Not as far as I know. It was a mystery to me."

"Then it's no use thinking of a reconciliation as an immediate solution to your problem?"

"We never quarrelled. I can't force myself on him, can I?"

"No; it wouldn't help you either to go back to him if he didn't wish it. We'd better leave him out of it for the present. I think I'd better send you home now and come and overhaul you to-morrow morning. Where do you live?"

"Cairn Cottage, Cairn Lane."

"Will it be all right if I call about noon? I'd like you to stay in bed."

"Yes, it will be all right."

"Very well, I'll come along about midday then. But it's rather far for you to walk. I'd better run you home; the surgery is over."

"No, please don't. I want some air. I'd much rather walk."

"Are you sure? You can rest here for a bit if you like."

"No, I'd rather go straight back, thank you. Oh, my name is Miss Munro—that is—it's my own name and I always use it here."

"Miss Munro. I'll write it down. Cairn Cottage—that's

at the bottom of Cairn Lane, isn't it? I haven't been down as far as that but I shall find it all right. Good evening."

"Good evening," said Jess, passing through the door which Leigh held open for her and out into the thickening mist. She opened her mouth and gulped in the wet air. Her legs were tingling from the effects of the draught she had drunk, and her body was so light she felt as if she were floating along, and could continue to float along indefinitely, as she had done on the night on which she had first seen Jerome Leigh.

Jerome Leigh . . . who had thrust a knife into Ambrose Seely's back. She would be alone with him in the cottage at noon to-morrow; Mrs. Bradshaw would have finished her work and gone home. In the power of a murderer, who, if he knew it, was in her power. Without her, the police could never, never get him, because she had misled them with a description which did not fit Leigh. He was tall, and looked about thirty-five or six; that was all right. But he was not dark—or not nearly so dark as she had declared. His hair was a non-committal shade of brown, neither dark nor fair, or perhaps a little more nearly dark than fair. It did not matter; she had described Seely's assailant as having black hair, and so long as she kept silent Leigh was as safe as could be. It must have been the rain which had soaked his head and made it look black; he must have been waiting some time in the open—no, of course, he had walked from wherever he had left his car. And gone back to the car and driven along to pick Seely up while she had been in the ditch.

She had known the moment she saw him sitting at his desk. She hadn't needed to see the look of evil purpose on his face, the absence of which on Ling's had made her doubt her ability to identify the murderer in normal circumstances. It had been just as she had imagined at first; if she ever saw the face of Seely's killer again, she would recognize it beyond shadow of doubt. Like Cæsar she could say—"I came. I saw——" But who had conquered? Why had she not said she would wait and see old Dr. Leigh when he came home? Why had she told

Jerome Leigh all about her symptoms, and the failure of her marriage? Why had she allowed him to make an appointment to see her the following day? She could not have done these things if she had meant at some future time to betray him to the police. Power of death was also power of life.

When she reached home she lit a coal fire; it would be more companionable than electricity and the mist had crept into the house. If she were to remain in bed the next morning until midday, there was no point in going to bed early that night. She sat for hours by the fire scarcely moving, telling herself that the dream she had been living in for the past week was real and that there would be no awakening from it. She would live all her life in the knowledge that she had shielded a murderer; technically, she supposed she was now a criminal herself. She had a vague notion that in law she was giving aid to Leigh by the mere fact she knew what he had done. Concealment of such knowledge probably made her an accessory after the fact. It was as though she and Leigh were now in a conspiracy together, though only one of the parties to the bond knew of its existence. But the bond would hold after he had left Grassmere—in a week's time, he had said. And he would return next summer when Dr. Tom took his holiday; perhaps he would even take over the practice when the old man retired.

Staying up till midnight had a beneficial effect, for after an hour or two Jess slept soundly until she was awakened by Mrs. Bradshaw with the cup of tea which was her Saturday morning treat. Mrs. Bradshaw puffed in and told Jess she was looking a better colour. "Looked like a ghost, you 'ave, this parst week, miss. I reckon now you've maybe turned the corner."

"I took your advice, Mrs. Bradshaw, and went to see the doctor last night."

"That was right sensible of you. Winter's coming on and you oughter build up your strength. The young doctor is a rare clever 'un, Bert says. He won't say a word against old Dr. Tom, having bin on his panel ever since Lloyd

George took and started the panel, wot some thought was a rare nuisance at the time, but Bert was allers for it, but he do say the young doctor knows more what's going on than the old 'un, as is only natural."

"I'm glad your husband thinks well of Dr. Jerome Leigh, because he's coming to examine me this morning."

Mrs. Bradshaw beamed approval. "I'll bring you up a nice bit of breakfast soon as I've given the sitting-room a good do."

After breakfast Jess dozed again. She had a lot of sleep to make up and, having begun to sleep again, she seemed able to doze at will. When Mrs. Bradshaw departed, she had a bath and went back to bed. He would be here in half an hour now.

She threw on a wrap and went downstairs to let Jerome Leigh in as soon as she heard his knock.

"None the worse for last night?" he asked, pulling up a chair to the bedside.

"I feel better. I slept quite well last night."

"Do you often faint like that?"

"I didn't quite faint. I knew what you were doing all the time. I used to faint quite a lot some years ago, but I thought I had shaken off the habit, until last week. I had rather a shock on the Friday night and I really did go off properly that time."

"Well, let's have your pyjama coat off. I'll find out whether there is any physical cause for the habit."

Jess threw her lemon-coloured silk jacket on to a chair and shut her eyes. Her heart began to beat quickly and she wondered whether Leigh would suppose that was its normal pace. He sounded her heart and lungs and retrieved her jacket.

"There's nothing wrong with your heart," he said. He looked at her eyes and gums, and opened the case he had placed on the table. "I'm going to take a drop of blood from your finger; it won't hurt."

He walked over to the window and stood with his back to the room. "Well, Miss Munro," he said as he returned to the bed, "you are a little bit anæmic and a course of iron tablets won't do you any harm. Otherwise, you don't need any medicine. From what you told me about yourself last night, I should suggest you don't begin writing again for six weeks or so, and that in the meantime you get all the fresh air and mild exercise you can. No need to walk more than a few miles a day for a start. Ever had any artificial sunlight treatment?"

Jess shook her head.

"Come to the surgery about the same time on Monday and I'll start you on a course. My uncle will be back at the end of the week and I'll arrange for him to continue it."

"Oh," said Jess, without weighing her words. "You mean I shall only have the treatment once a week."

"Oh no, you will have it three times a week, and the dosage will be gradually increased."

He picked up his case, said good morning and went out. Jess cursed herself for a fool in having betrayed her wish to see Jerome Leigh as often as possible during the last week of his stay. But he seemed completely professional and detached. He probably had not read her mind at all. She would just have one cigarette before she dressed, and after lunch she would go for a walk; the sun was fighting its way through the mist; it was going to be a glorious afternoon. She stretched out a hand for her cigarette case. Fifty-five hours to go before seven o'clock on Monday evening.

26

MARCH was with Norton at police headquarters when he received John Derwent's report by telephone. He relayed the gist of it to the Deputy Chief Constable.

Derek Garle's solicitor, in response to his client's SOS, had managed to travel across country by car and train so as to reach London in the small hours of the morning. He was a young man, no older than Derek himself, and perhaps hardly experienced enough for the responsibility which devolved on him, but Garle's faith in him was complete. After an hour's consultation, Garle had expressed a wish to revoke his previous statement and make a fresh one. Derwent had taken it and was having a copy sent to March at once.

"What is Garle's story now?" Bruce asked sceptically. "I suppose he has hatched another fictitious yarn to cover the points where the old one broke down."

March was looking thoughtful. "Oddly enough, the amended statement has the elements of plausibility. Derwent is convinced the earnest young lawyer believes in it; otherwise he would have played for safety, and advised Garle to keep silent and wait and see whether he was charged. I believe that is what an expert in criminal procedure would have done; put the onus on us of making out a *prima facie* case against Garle. However, here is his story. He now declares that he travelled to Grassmere on the Friday night with the intention of seeing his wife. He planned to have about a couple of hours with her, and return to Bogmore by the eleven-five. He did not want his proposed visit known, so he said nothing to anyone about it, and left Sydney with the impression that he might be delayed in London. For the same reason he deliberately avoided Seely in the train. That story explains the depositing of the suitcase at Bogmore, which he now admits.

"So far so good. He had not seen his wife for a year, and he had private business to discuss with her. He had not warned her he was coming. Well, I think we can let that pass too. He says he did not definitely make up his mind to combine the Grassmere with the Bogmore visit until rather late in the day and he did not want to tie himself to keeping an appointment in case he changed his mind. But now we come to the reason why he never reached Cairn Cottage and I leave you to judge its credulity. The train ran into the storm during the last part of the journey and Garle hoped to get a taxi at Grassmere. Failing in this, he set out on foot. The rain became heavier and the lightning was alarming. After five minutes' walking he concluded that it was too bad to continue. He claims to have stood for some time partially sheltered by the lee of a wall. While he waited, Seely passed him. Garle then returned to the station and sheltered in the waiting-room. The place was empty; he did not speak to anyone until he took his ticket for the nine-fourteen to Bogmore. He knew there was a train at that time, because he had made a complete list of the trains in both directions, and it was the possibility of getting back to Bogmore without much delay which prompted him to turn back in face of the exceptionally bad weather."

Bruce considered the matter for a moment. "The story *would* be fairly credible, in my opinion, if he had told it in the first instance. As it is, it strikes one as having been concocted only because we proved he actually came to Grassmere."

"Yes, there is that. When I saw him yesterday, he was still trying to keep his wife's name out of the business. She was living at Grassmere, he said, under her maiden name, and he did not want to disclose that she was married, or start any gossip about her in the papers. He did not know that we were already aware that Jessica Munro was his wife."

"Suppose we accept his new story. What then?"

"We can accept it as the original reason for his plan to come to Grassmere, without accepting it *in toto*. It does nothing at all towards giving him an alibi for five minutes to nine because he was not seen at the station until just before nine-twelve."

"You mean he may not have planned the murder until he reached Grassmere?"

"No, I don't mean that, Bruce. The carving-knife rules the notion out altogether. The attack on Seely must have been planned not later than Friday afternoon when Seely was with the Garles in their office. Derwent had the wit to ask Garle how he knew the way to Cairn Cottage. He set out from the station, you remember, without asking the way; we thought that queer at the time. Garle replied that he did not need to ask the way because Seely, in his presence, had asked his cousin to come to Beech House for the day one Sunday. Rupert had fixed on to-morrow, as it happens. Seely gave him exact instructions as to how to reach the house from the station, mentioning Cairn Lane, of course. Garle had his wife's address; Cairn Cottage, Cairn Lane."

"That was a pretty damning admission for him to make. It suggests that he made up his mind then and there to waylay Seely, procured a knife, dodged Seely on the journey, carried out his project and just caught the next train to Bogmore."

"It does suggest that, but Garle had to explain how he knew the way somehow. That part of his story has been confirmed by Rupert Garle. Derwent is after evidence of Derek procuring the knife. If he gets it, Garle is finished. But I doubt if he will get it to-day, and Derek must either be charged or released by this evening."

"Released and shadowed, I suppose?"

"That goes without saying. But we'll go all out to avoid having to release him. Cowie hasn't reported yet; no doubt he is still seeking Mr. Augustus Flemming. I shan't wait to hear from him, Bruce. I'll go over straight away and see Miss Munro again. There are several things I want to say to that young woman."

Norman drove the Chief Inspector over to Grassmere. A car already stood outside the gate of Cairn Cottage.

"That's the doctor's car," Norman asserted. "I'll drive on, sir, and turn at the bottom of the lane."

March reached the door just as Jerome Leigh was emerging. "Hullo," said the doctor, "I've been wondering how you were progressing."

"Not too badly. I hope Miss Munro is not ill?"

"Do you want to see her?"

"That is why I am here."

"She is well enough to see you, but she is not dressed yet."

"Police are like doctors; they have entrée to bedrooms in the course of their work. Where is her room?"

"Facing you at the top of the stairs. But wait a minute, Chief Inspector. I have an interest in this case, you know. I've heard no more since I saw you except that King was detained and released. What's going on?"

"Come and sit in your car, Leigh. I can spare five minutes, but I won't talk on Miss Munro's doorstep."

March spent fifteen minutes with the doctor and gave him a confidential account of the present state of the investigations.

"Were you aware Miss Munro was married?" he asked Leigh.

"I never met Miss Munro before last night, when she consulted me professionally. She did tell me she was married, but I should not have disclosed the fact, of course. She did not mention her husband's name. Apart from my interest in the case, I am glad you took me into your confidence, March. I have to treat Miss Munro for a nervous condition and it isn't very easy when I know so little about her. No doubt the shock she had on the night of the crime has contributed to her illness. But I cannot believe that she would describe her husband to the police."

"We think she did not actually recognize him."

"What is Garle like to look at?"

"About your height, possibly a year or two younger, and very much darker."

"I am thirty-seven."

"In that case he is three years younger than you. His

hair is as near black as human hair ever is, and he is a good-looking chap."

"Had he any motive for killing Seely?"

"If he killed him, presumably he had. We are still working on that angle. But his opportunity was perfect."

"I did not meet him, and I suppose he would have made straight for the station."

"I think he would have kept off the road as long as possible. The stile to Beech House was near at hand. He could work his way back to the road across the meadow."

"No doubt. Look here, March, this rather changes my view of the best treatment for Miss Munro. These artistic women react badly to shocks, and she has had one severe shock already. As a doctor, I ought to press her to get away from Grassmere at once."

"As a policeman I could not agree to that. She *saw* Seely murdered, remember. She must stay on the spot for the present. And if she went to the Hebrides, nothing could spare her the shock of her husband's arrest and trial—if it comes to that."

"Is it imperative for you to see her this morning?"

"What is the use of putting it off?"

"I said she was well enough to see you, but I did not anticipate the nature of your visit. If you give her another shock now, I can't be responsible for the consequences."

"No one would require that you should be responsible, Leigh. A lot of people are having unpleasant shocks over this case. Mrs. King has had a very bad twenty-four hours. Another young man, not unlike Garle in appearance, was unjustly harassed for a day or two. I shan't rush at Miss Munro and tell her that her husband is a murderer. If you like you can be present at the interview, although I think that would serve to give her the impression that something alarming is going to break."

"I dare say it would. I'll leave you to it then, but don't say I didn't warn you. And if you want a medical opinion, I don't think it at all unlikely that Miss Munro has embroidered the incident of Friday night out of all relation to fact. She has an exceptionally fertile imagination, and

I doubt if she could really have seen the details of the crime."

"She was extremely convincing. I took her to the spot and she indicated where Seely fell when he was stabbed. Her location was within a couple of yards of your own."

"Mine was absolutely correct; I put my pen-knife in the ground before I moved Seely."

"An error of two yards is very slight, Leigh. I formed a high opinion of Miss Munro's powers of observation. Far from imagining that she could identify Seely's killer, I believe she would have been devoutly thankful to have washed her hands of the whole affair. It isn't pleasant for anyone—let alone a particularly sensitive woman—to know they have the power to bring a man to justice."

"She can't be made to give evidence against her husband."

"I am aware of that. I'm sorry our interests pull in opposite directions, Leigh. But I must get on with my job now."

Leigh made no reply. March climbed out of the car and watched the doctor drive up the lane.

27

JESS was dressed when March finally knocked at the door. She was in the kitchen wrestling with the problem of lunch. She looked surprised to see the Chief Inspector and asked him to wait in the sitting-room while she turned the gas off. She came back, still in her cooking overall, and sat by the open window.

"I called for several reasons, Miss Munro," March began in a quiet, reassuring voice. "First, I wanted to thank you for seeing Mr. Ling on Thursday evening. I can tell you now that at the time of the attack on Mr. Seely, Ling was in his cowhouse with one of his workmen."

"So it didn't matter . . . ?"

"No, your uncertainty was of no consequence. Seely's attacker must have been some other man of about Ling's height. . . . Miss Munro, it has come to our knowledge that your married name is Mrs. Garle. Jessica Munro is your pen-name, I suppose?"

Jess had jumped at the mention of her marriage. She looked inquiringly at March. "I didn't want my real name known here. At least Jessica Munro was my real name; I haven't given out here that I am married for private reasons."

"That is no concern of ours. But were you, I wonder, expecting a visit from your husband last week—on the Friday night?"

"Oh, no, I wasn't. I hadn't heard a word from Derek for a year, since we separated, in fact. I hoped he might write to me, but he didn't."

"Would you have been surprised if he had come to see you without letting you know beforehand?"

"Yes, I think so, very surprised—and glad. But he didn't come, Mr. March! Why do we have to talk about such things now?"

"I'm afraid, Miss Munro, we have to talk about some things which we should both be glad to avoid discussing, if it were possible. Your husband *was* in Grassmere on that Friday night, although he did not call to see you."

"Derek in Grassmere! Oh no, it is impossible. He would have come to see me. It was our wedding anniversary."

"He has admitted that he came to Grassmere by the train which arrived at eight-thirty-five."

"Admitted! But why should Derek admit anything? People only admit detrimental facts. . . . Oh, no, no, no! I see you are trying to accuse him of attacking Mr. Seely! Do you think I wouldn't recognize my own husband, if I saw him? The man in the lane was not my husband, Mr. March; I swear he was not Derek."

"Your husband resembles the man you described, Miss Munro. And at first sight he is not unlike Ivan Ling. You told me there was something vaguely familiar about Seely's assailant, if you remember."

"I am certain the man was *not* my husband. But why was my husband here?"

"He says he was coming to see you, but turned back on account of the storm."

"Why did he want to see me? To suggest a reconciliation?"

"He has not disclosed the purpose of his visit."

"He hasn't been arrested, has he?"

"No. You are sure to hear it, so I will tell you that he has been detained in London for questioning. He is being advised by a lawyer. There is nothing you can do at present, but you know, no doubt, that a woman is not a competent witness against her husband, except in certain cases, and this is not one of the exceptions."

"I know all about that. I shall give my evidence for the defence. But people will know I should be bound to take that line anyhow, so I suppose it will be worth very little."

"I wouldn't look ahead too far. The situation changes from day to day. I fear my advice will sound ironical to you, but I would suggest that you try to concern yourself with immediate plans. I am afraid you are not very well, and I don't like the idea of your being alone here for the week-end. Could you get a friend to keep you company, perhaps? Or can I be any use in telephoning a message for you?"

"No—thank you. I should be poor company for anyone, and I would rather be by myself."

"Won't you think that over? Perhaps I could send someone; the clergyman here—or his wife—to help you make plans?"

"He isn't married. And I implore you not to send him here. It's grotesque! First you suggest I have accused my husband of murder, and then you want to send the rector to see me. What for? Do you think I feel like singing hymns?"

"It must seem grotesque," said March patiently. "But I hardly know what else to suggest."

"Don't suggest anything. The best thing you can do is to go."

March got to his feet. It was no use saying any more and he left the room with only a word of farewell which Jess ignored. She watched him go and then got up and began to walk up and down the room until she finally came to rest by the window. She stared out into the little garden, seeing nothing. Grotesque! It was fabulous! No one could possibly have been faced with such a dilemma since the world began. The one thing she had longed for for the last year had happened; Derek had wanted to see her. And she had to learn about it in such a way that the knowledge was hell instead of heaven . . . to have described Seely's murderer as so like Derek that she had endangered his life . . . to be unable to save him without betraying Jerome Leigh, and unable to save Leigh without sacrificing Derek. No, it was absurd, there must be a way out. What was the use of having brains if she could not outwit March and his henchmen? She held the trump card, because she alone had seen the murderer. She would find some way of saving them both. . . . She would need strength if she were to keep a

clear head and use her brains, she reflected. She would
have a good lunch, and go out for a walk as though nothing
had happened; as though the world had not become a
madhouse, presenting her with an impossible choice and
forcing her to use every resource she had to defeat the ends
of justice. There was one crumb of comfort, she thought,
as she relit the gas and set her tray. Henceforth she would
be bound by no rules; whatever way of escape presented
itself to her, she would jettison all conscientious scruples
and take it. No one could be expected to play for such high
stakes and keep their hands clean.

She ate with steady determination, thinking quite coolly
and clearly as she chewed her food. Jerome Leigh was a
little like Derek; it was the indefinable likeness between
them which had made Seely's attacker seem familiar. But
it was not the kind of likeness the police would detect in a
hundred years. It was not based on similarity of feature
at all. It was impossible to analyse it; it was probably only
because she knew Derek so well and had been thinking
about him all day that she had noticed it. The gracefulness
of the leap from behind the tree, the quick backward jerk of
the head, as the arm was raised to strike the blow, the long
slender hand in which the blade had flashed in the flood
light of the storm; all these things had been reminiscent of
Derek, but to anyone but his wife would have meant
nothing. That was the strength of her defence of Leigh.
And if Leigh, who was guilty, could be defended, surely it
would be easy to save Derek, who was innocent.

When March returned to Heathmere he found Peter
waiting to make his report. He had struck up quite a
friendship with Augustus Flemming, who was the nicest
curate he had ever come across—in fact, not a bit like a
curate.

March smiled. "Let's hope he is able to return the com-
pliment and say you are not a bit like a detective."

"I'll bet he is. Well, he sees a good deal of Sydney and
thinks the poor beggar is slightly touched, though quite an
amiable kind of chap apart from that. Flemming had

heard from Sydney himself that he was invalided out of the
I.E.S. after having severe sunstroke, but he says no doubt
you can get direct information on that point."

"Thanks, Peter. Well, don't blow up, but while you've
been gone, we've heard that Garle has admitted his visit to
Grassmere—but that does not mean that your journey was
wasted. I don't know until I get Derwent's written report
what explanation Garle gave of the faking of the Bogmore
alibi. Now, look here, Peter, you're a person of resource.
As soon as you have had lunch—oh, you've had it, have
you?—wise creature—well, go along now to Cairn Cottage,
will you, and cook up some excuse for seeing Miss Munro.
Don't discuss the case with her; I just want to know that
she is all right. Tell her you're off duty and at a loose end
—anything you like."

"Leave it to me, sir. I haven't had an afternoon off
since we came down here. I'll take her for a walk and
ask myself back to tea. Of course, a car would be
better."

"What about it, Norton?"

"Cowie can have my car for a few hours. I shan't want
it till to-night."

Peter drove off in fine fettle. The sun was in great form
and so was he. A dash round the country in the Deputy
Chief Constable's comfortable saloon would be a welcome
change from wearing out his shoe-leather in muddy lanes.
He honked unnecessarily in his exuberance as he disappeared and March smiled at Norton.

"Someone is pleased with the way things are going, anyhow. I only hope Miss Munro will play ball."

"Aren't you pleased, Chris?"

"Not altogether. I have an uneasy suspicion that things
are not quite what they appear to be on the surface. Apart
from that, Miss Munro is a clever young woman. I've no
doubt she's hatching up some plot to bring me down with
a humpty-dumpty crash. I hope Peter will put her off
her game with his chatter."

"It would take more than a clever young woman to bring
you down."

"I'm hoping so. But the trouble is if I am to keep on my feet I shall have to bring her down."

"Not turning chivalrous, are you, Chris?"

"Far from it. I'm wondering where detection ends and something else begins—what, I don't quite know. It may be I shan't reach the bottom of this case by orthodox methods."

"You want some food, old chap. I've been waiting lunch for half an hour. No use exercising your grey matter on an empty stomach."

Norton led the way to the dining-room and March trailed behind him still lost in thought.

28

"It's that damned carving-knife that's holding me up," John Derwent explained, pushing his fingers through his hair, and finally grasping a stray lock and giving it an exasperated tug.

"Don't pull all your hair out, John," March said. "You won't be such an ornament to the force if you go prematurely bald."

"I don't feel particularly decorative this morning. It doesn't appear to suit me to spend the whole night in bed. I was cursing in my sleep because the A.C. would have Garle sent home last night. I think he ought to have been charged and remanded."

"The A.C. consulted me on the telephone. I agreed that it would be wiser not to charge Garle for a day or two, until we get one piece of good, solid, tangible evidence— the sort a jury can get its teeth into. Sydney, from your report and Peter's interview with the curate, is a harmless case of mental derangement. We shall never prove that Garle fixed up his alibi with him before the news of the murder broke that week-end. If Sydney were a competent witness, it would smooth our path. But he ain't, and that's that. Connect Garle with the acquisition of a stout carving-knife, John, and I'll pack my bag and return to London."

"I wonder you don't in any case. The interest has shifted to London since we got on to Garle."

"Not altogether. Miss Munro and other potentially valuable witnesses are here. Peter, bless the boy, is not as competent to work on his own here as you are to carry on in London."

"Well, about the knife, sir. It isn't a match with any of the cutlery in Garle's flat—not that that is much to go by. But it is certain Garle did not acquire that knife on his way to the station on the Friday evening. He left the office in the company of Rupert Garle's secretary, a young woman of about twenty-five, attractive-looking wench——"

"Never mind her looks. What's her evidence?"

"But her looks are evidence, sir. Garle's a bit struck on her, I should say. She also had that week-end off and they went out and had tea together at Fuller's in the Strand and lingered till it was time to catch their respective trains. We found the waitress and checked that. Garle then called a taxi and they went to the station together. They were both going from Waterloo, but his train went first. She saw him off, Cooper checked that, and there again her appearance is relevant, sir."

"Rub it in, John. Why?"

"Because she is a striking-looking blonde. She was hatless and wearing an emerald green coat."

"Blondes are two a penny. But go on."

"Well, Cooper picked up their taxi-driver and he was struck by the girl, anyway. Says he thought she and the chap with her were engaged. Cooper picked her up again at Waterloo. She met a girl friend who was going away with her for the week-end there. The girl tactfully left her to see Derek off and waited for her on their platform. Derek's beauty is called Sheila, and she tells me she held his raincoat while he put his case on the rack, and is certain there was nothing in the pockets. I reckon he couldn't have got that knife out of the case at Bogmore and transferred it to his raincoat pocket under the watchful eye of Mrs. Robertson. So what?"

"I don't know, John. It would be better for Garle perhaps if Sheila was not emotionally interested in him. Still, she is useful. For if Garle did not acquire the knife after he saw Seely in the office on Friday afternoon, he must have planned the murder earlier. And I don't see how he knew Seely would be on that train."

"Except that Seely was in touch with the Garles about his book, and invariably did catch that train on Friday evenings. I'm thinking this way, sir. It wasn't a new knife, and it doesn't seem possible for Garle to have acquired a second-hand one—or any other—*en route* to the station. Could he have had the knife, with the blade suitably sheathed, on his person somehow? It's too big for a pocket, but say, tied round him under his waistcoat."

"It would be uncomfortable, but it could be done."

Peter breezed into Norton's sitting-room, where the dialogue was in progress, looking exceedingly pleased with himself.

"I saw Mr. Norton in the garden, sir, and he told me to come right in. What's John been up to?"

"He brought Garle's statement down himself to save time. How is Miss Munro?"

"Bearing up fine, sir. We did about a hundred and twenty miles in Mr. Norton's car, yesterday, and she asked me back to supper. It was quite a treat to talk to someone with a brain for a change—such a rare experience—present company excepted, of course. I did most of the talking but Jess is such an intelligent listener——"

"If she was listening," March commented dryly. "And not working out a means of sending me home with a flea in my ear."

"She wasn't the least distrait, I assure you. She said she had been quite absorbed in my conversation."

"You didn't mention the case, I hope?"

"Lord, no. I talked about Aristotle and his views on the importance of a good plot; I think her plots are her weak point, but I didn't say so, naturally. But I think it sank in. And I got on to political philosophy and explained the idealist doctrine of the general will, and the influence of idealism on the Fascist state—she seemed rather vague about that. I touched on Marx too——"

"And on Peter Cowie, no doubt."

Peter looked hurt. "When one is talking to a sympathetic soul there is no need of personalities. I didn't finish my exposition of dialectical materialism, and we're going to thresh it out when I go to supper to-night. She makes quite delicious little continental dishes; a nice change from the dog's food at the Buffalo. You can manage without me here this evening, I hope?"

"I hope so," said March with becoming gravity.

After Derwent had returned to London, March asked Norton whether he was dead set on his Sunday afternoon's rest.

"Not in the middle of a case," Norton declared. "What do you want to do?"

"I've been re-reading all my notes on the case. I don't want to mark time here while Derwent keeps on at the Garle angle in London. When we were at Beech House it was clear that King wanted to prevent his wife from talking to us freely. That was explicable enough if King were guilty. But it has occurred to me that there may be some other explanation."

"I don't see what bearing anything Mrs. King says can have on Garle."

"But Garle isn't in the bag yet. Can you drive me over to Beech House? Sibyl King won't be so nervous now she knows her husband is no longer under suspicion, and I might profit from a talk with her."

"As you like, of course. How would it be for me to get King to show me round the garden while you exercise your charms on the fair Sibyl? Seely had quite a nice bit of garden there, only he couldn't get the labour to keep it up properly."

"That will suit me fine."

King was delighted to show the Deputy Chief Constable over the garden. He had been putting in a bit of work on it himself during the past week, he said. He couldn't do any heavy work such as digging, but he had been sweeping leaves and tidying up.

March sat in the kitchen with Sibyl King. He lost no time in getting to the point.

"I believe, Mrs. King, that you might have talked more freely to me the other day, if you hadn't been afraid of saying something that might harm your husband. You had a nasty scare, I know, when we took him away to the police station. It's always hard on a wife when her man gets into trouble. Now, there is another married man under suspicion, and it will be hard on his wife if he charged with Mr. Seely's murder. I want you to tell me now whether there is any information which you kept back because you were in fear for your husband's safety?"

"Is it Mr. Ling you're speaking of, sir?"

"No, it is not Mr. Ling. It is no one you know. Just an unknown man, but he is married."

"George wouldn't like me to tell you, sir. There was something I didn't mention. If I had told you, I don't believe you would have taken George away at all. I'd made up my mind to come and see you on the very afternoon that George came home. He said it's always safest not to talk to the police; let them find things out for themselves, that's his idea."

"The way the police find things out generally is by talking to people, Mrs. King. We can't read thoughts, you know. It isn't fair to this other man for you to keep anything to yourself. Suppose some other woman knew something that might have cleared George when he was in trouble and she refused to talk. What would you have thought of that?"

"I should have thought bad of her, sir."

"I should think so. I'll tell you something else, Mrs. King, in confidence. There was a woman who came forward and gave evidence which cleared your husband, and it is this woman's husband who is in trouble now."

"Fancy that, it's like a book! It was no married man that killed Mr. Seely, sir, I can tell you that."

"Tell me all you know."

"Oh, sir, I hardly like to. I promised George, and then I wouldn't wish this man punished for killing Mr. Seely. Mr. Seely wasn't a good man, sir. His kind are best dead and buried."

Sibyl was on the point of tears.

"Don't upset yourself, please, Mrs. King. We knew Mr. Seely was not a man of good character where women are concerned. And it may help you if I tell you I'm fairly sure I know who stabbed him, though I don't yet know why. Young Dr. Leigh called to see Mr. Seely the day before his death, didn't he?"

"He did, sir," Sibyl whispered. "Mr. Seely sent for him to come."

"And your husband was away that day. What happened?"

"They quarrelled dreadful, sir. I heard them in the kitchen. I ran out to the hall, being frightened, George being away and all, and I heard the doctor say he'd see Mr. Seely dead and in hell before he would treat him as a patient, and he wondered he had the something nerve to send for him. Terrible language he used, sir, and he passed me in the hall without seeing me as he went out of the house. His face was black with rage, sir; I never saw a living face like it in all my life. I told George and he said the doctor would have no chance with the police if I was to tell what I heard and when a man is fighting for his life he ought to have a fair chance. My husband talks a lot about fair play, sir; I suppose it is because he was always playing games when he was a young man."

"Maybe," said March absently.

He rejoined Bruce Norton and expressed a wish not to talk until they reached home. Then he telephoned to John Derwent before he lit his pipe and prepared to enlighten his friend.

"I've told John to intensify that research into Seely's past, and to go back as far even as his first marriage and its tragic sequel. I'm afraid even John can't work miracles. But he must get what I want by the end of the week. Have you got a couple of fellows who look inconspicuous in plain clothes, Bruce? Norman's no use; he's been seen about with me too much."

"Good Lord! whatever for?"

"I'm sorry to tell you that Jerome Leigh will have to be shadowed night and day during the rest of his stay at Grassmere—until we put the bracelets on him."

"Chris! You're raving mad!"

"On the contrary, it is Leigh who is mad. No, not technically, of course. But he has acted like a madman in killing a man he had threatened within twenty-four hours of his death."

"But, my dear chap, Seely was stabbed at eight-fifty-five——"

"I know, I know. But who said Jerome Leigh's car was parked by the side of the lane at that moment? Jerome Leigh. It was parked—not on the grass verge, but the other side of the gate, with the lights off. Leigh arranged to see that sick baby so as to have an excuse to be on the road. The child was not critically ill. Anyhow he could have gone out earlier; his surgery finishes soon after seven and I doubt whether any patients turned up in that storm. Leigh waited for Seely, stabbed him, and returned to his car while Miss Munro lay unconscious in the ditch. Luckily for the young woman, he had not seen her. He drove on to the corner and picked Seely up, carefully placing his pen-knife at a spot which showed that his headlights would just have picked the body up. According to Miss Munro's estimate, Leigh would not have seen Seely if he had driven past without stopping. Leigh knew well enough that Seely would not recover when he took him to hospital. He took care to step behind his head when Seely recovered consciousness and to hear a sound which did not implicate anyone of his name. Like normally truthful people, he told no unnecessary lies. He did not even deny having met Seely before. He simply said he did not meet Seely at all when he was locum here last year. When I met him outside Cairn Cottage yesterday, I took him into my confidence. He immediately tried to prevent me from seeing Jessica Munro and to throw doubt on the value of her evidence. I have turned my mind towards Leigh several times before; there were several curious points about his discovery of the injured man which drew my attention. But he seemed ruled out by Jessica Munro's description of a man whose hair was nearly jet black."

"Well, he hasn't changed the colour of his hair, Chris."

"No, but the rain did! Leigh never wears a hat. He walked along in the rain in the worst of the downpour, and stood for some time waiting under a dripping tree. What does your hair look like when you've just had a shampoo, Bruce? And you are much fairer than Leigh."

"Good God, Chris! This will break poor old Dr. Tom's heart."

March seemed quite unmoved. "Leigh knows he's in danger, Bruce. You ought to fix up to have him kept under observation at once."

"So is Miss Munro, it seems to me. Why hasn't she betrayed Leigh?"

"Perhaps because she is a woman. Perhaps she has fallen for his *beaux yeux*, which, if he hadn't killed Seely, would have been the best thing she could have done, since her husband seems to be getting off with a lovely blonde. I believe our clever Jess is hoping to save both Leigh and her husband. But I can't stop to work things out now, Bruce. You arrange for Leigh to be shadowed and I'll arrange additional protection for Jessica Munro. Peter can watch her by day. But now that Leigh has professional entrée to her house, that isn't enough. Hurry up with that telephone; I want to make a call myself."

"I don't think we've taken any chances," March said later to Norton. "Young Cooper is coming down on the next train and will put up at the Station Hotel at Grassmere. He won't let Leigh enter Cairn Cottage after dark. How about your fellows? Are they reliable?"

"Norman has recommended the best men available. Two on duty all day and one to watch the doctor's house at night. That's six fellows' time you're taking up, Chris. We're working them in six-hour shifts. I hope to glory we don't have another murder."

"We may, if we don't protect Miss Munro adequately. I shall keep an eye on her myself from a distance; I shall have time to burn till I hear from John again."

"She ought to be safe enough in that case," vowed Bruce with an attempt at levity. But he fell to brooding over the sorrow about to strike his old friend Tom Leigh, and March, who suffered from no sentimental handicap, beat him three times at chess in the course of an hour.

29

JOHN DERWENT needed no spur to incite him to increased
activity. He had already discovered that Ambrose Seely
had married for the first time, in 1931, a girl of name of
Delia Martin. He rang up the young detective constable
who had been working under his directions on that line of
research and asked him to come round to his rooms forth-
with. Sighing at the encroachment on his free time, the
young man took a bus and went.

"Hullo, Sam," said Derwent. "Haven't you any more
news for me, yet? Gosh—you young chaps are slow!"

"I was up late last night," the indignant youth protested.
"I had to go to Acton on some fool's errand. I found out
that Delia Martin's mother is still living. Here is her address
—somewhere out beyond Golders Green station. I was
going to call on her first thing to-morrow morning."

"To-morrow morning! What's the use of that? The
Chief Inspector is sitting on the line waiting for news right
now, you booby."

"Well, I thought I was off duty, but I'll go along and
see her this evening, if you like."

"No, I'll go myself. Everything else seems to be petering
out; this seems our best line now."

"But the girl has been dead fourteen years."

"I know she has, but the circumstances of her death
were unusual. When you get a murder, motive unknown,
there's some sense in seeing whether it links up with any
other unusual circumstance in the deceased's life. And
remember this, you sleepy owl, when you start on a murder
hunt, you don't know who the murderer is, but—unless
you're damned unlucky—the corpse has already been
identified. So you're sure of something to begin with."

Sam grinned. "You're not thinking this Delia girl was
murdered, are you?"

"Not legally murdered, no. But Seely was a complete swine in his dealings with women. A girl of twenty-one doesn't take her life without some cause."

John sent Sam home with instructions to get up some energy for the morrow and, after drinking a cup of tea, set off for Golders Green. There he met with a check, for the little house which corresponded with the address Sam had given him was locked up and uninhabited. John inquired of neighbours and found at last a woman who knew Mrs. Martin. The latter, she said, had gone into the country for the week-end. She believed she was visiting her married daughter but could not say where the daughter lived. John frowned and asked when Mrs. Martin would be back.

"Some time to-morrow, I am sure, because she promised to come in after supper and make a four at bridge. We have a little private club which meets on Monday evenings and to-morrow it is my turn to be hostess."

Derwent made valiant endeavours to trace someone who knew Mrs. Martin's week-end address, but by dusk had to admit himself beaten. He went scowling home to supper. Nothing to be done before the next day; the lazy Sam would have got there just as quickly.

By nine o'clock the next morning he was on Mrs. Martin's doorstep, though he knew very well she was unlikely to return from the country for several hours. An hour later Sam joined him in response to a telephone message to the Yard.

"What's the game now?" he asked.

"Wander about up and down this road, Sam, and tell me as soon as anyone enters this house. I've got some paper work to do, and I'm going along to the Public Library round the corner to do it. If you haven't communicated with me by noon, I'll relieve you and you can go and feed."

"Okay," said Sam. "Don't be late because I had a bad egg for breakfast. I could do with some 'levenses."

"You'll damn well have to do without them. 'Make not thy belly thy god', you young pig. Keep your eyes open all the time, Sam."

"You bet I will. You don't think I want to decorate this road any longer than I can help, do you?"

Sam was, however, still decorating the road when the young Inspector returned at noon.

"Say, boss, there's no sense in expecting this dame to get back from a holiday before tea-time," he protested. "I'll lay you any odds you like she'll come tripping home in time to boil the kettle at five o'clock."

"If she does, she'll find you here," returned Derwent implacably. "There's a Lyons just beyond the Library. Get back inside the hour, or everything will be off before I get there."

Sam was acutely bored during the long hours from one o'clock onwards when he patrolled the road alone. Derwent had made no mention of relieving him for tea; the old lady might not turn up until nightfall, and then most likely nothing would come of the Inspector's interview with her. This vigil was worse than being on a beat; at least you knew then when you were due to be relieved. The Inspector was a ruddy slave-driver, although one had to admit he worked like a coolie himself, didn't put on any side and never shunned the dirty jobs that came his way. Most of the greenhorns at the Yard liked working with Derwent, although he never seemed to expect them to claim any time off. Four hours he'd been tramping about this ruddy street, and not a sign of his quarry. A clock in the distance was striking five.

"Jimini!" exclaimed Sam to himself as a taxi grated round the corner. "Timed it to a second, I did." He had been wrong about the old lady though. A smartly dressed woman paid off the taxi and went into the house carrying a light week-end case. She didn't look more than fifty; must be fifty-five at least though, if she were Delia Martin's mother. The case had borne the initials Y.M., so she was pretty certain to be a Martin anyhow. Sam trotted off to the Public Library.

"What did I tell you, boss?" he said to Derwent. "The dame is boiling the kettle right now. Youngish-looking woman, very chic and elegant, but her initials are Y.M.

If you hurry up you'll be in time for a cup of tea, which is just what I'm needing."

"You can have tea and pack up, Sam. I shan't need you again this evening. Oh, before you feed, ring up Chief Inspector March, will you? Tell him I hope to make a report between six and seven, if he could make it convenient to be on the end of the line. Even if I draw blank I'll report just the same."

Sam shot into the nearest call-box and John went to call on Delia Martin's mother.

Jess was listening to Peter with half her attention, and devising means of getting rid of him with the other half. It was after six and she must make herself look attractive before she went to Leigh's surgery for her sun-bath.

"Listen, Peter, I can't ask you to supper to-night. I've got a date and I don't know what time I'll be back. Come to-morrow and I'll make you another mushroom omelette."

Peter's face fell. "You shouldn't talk about having dates, Jess. You're not the modern type, and it doesn't suit you."

"Oh, it's just a silly habit. Actually, it isn't a date at all. I just meant that I have to go out. Finish your sherry, there's a lamb, and skedaddle. I want to change my frock."

"I like that dusky red. If you want to appeal, I should stop as you are. But far be it from me to outstay my welcome. Can't you tell me who he is? I've not noticed any eligible males in this cockeyed village. Don't tell me you're playing fast and loose with the handsome Ivan Ling! You can break his heart if you like; I owe the chap a grudge and a policeman can't settle his private scores."

"Of course it's not Ivan Ling. His wife is home, anyway; she came to tea with me yesterday. You landed me into that, but she's rather a nice girl when you get to know her, but very, very young—about your age."

"I," said Peter with dignity, "am twenty-six, but age, my dear Jess, is not purely a matter of years. Who is the chap then?"

"Peter, you are a pest. I've told you there is no chap in the case. If you must know, I'm going to see the doctor and I don't want to be late. Let yourself out, will you?"

Peter drifted to the door. "Why shouldn't I stay and escort you to the village?" he demanded.

"Oh, all right, but I shall be quite half an hour, I warn you."

Peter refilled his glass and turned on the radio. He was not sure that March would approve of Jess going to see Leigh, but he did not quite see how he could prevent her. He had stuck to her like a leech all day, and Cooper was to keep watch outside her house from nine o'clock onwards. Two stout fellows were shadowing Leigh, but Peter hardly supposed that they would interfere with patients attending his surgery. Norton and March had taken elaborate precautions to insure that Leigh should not decamp, and that Jess should not be molested, but it seemed to Peter that between them they had bungled the affair. It was for him to devise some means of retrieving the situation; he had felt all along that the opportunity to use his brains would occur sooner or later. But at present the way seemed slightly obscure. His grey matter did not function with quite the celerity he had learnt to expect of it. Perhaps he had drunk rather too much sherry. Oh well, there was time yet for inspiration to visit him. The tighter the corner, the more merit in negotiating it successfully. His head would feel clearer when he got out into the open air. What a hell of a time Jess was! Not a date, by heaven! She was taking much more trouble to get herself up for the murdering doctor than she had for Peter. He threw away his cigarette and turned off the radio. The music made it difficult to think. . . .

Jess came in in a black frock with a short tight-fitting buff coat over it. She wore no make-up, but her face was flushed and her eyes sparkled. Peter saw that she looked at herself in the glass over the fireplace. He made no comment on her appearance but followed her silently into the lane, for once in his life at a loss for conversation. Jess was speechless too as they fell into step and tramped towards the village.

When they reached the corner of the lane Peter said

desperately that he was afraid it was going to be foggy again. There was in fact a slight mist gathering above the surface of the meadows. Wouldn't it be wiser for Jess to return home and postpone her visit to the doctor until the following day?

"Oh, it's only a country mist," said Jess. "It's often like this in the evenings here. The grassland is cool, you see, and as soon as the sun goes the moisture in the air begins to condense. It's too early in the year for a real fog."

"I should like to know what it was we had on Friday night then. I was out in the thick of it, and I know I got unpleasantly wet."

"It was nothing to what we get here in the late autumn —or did last year, and I think it was characteristic of these low-lying grassy regions. I love our mists; they shut Grassmere in so that it seems to be a little island of refuge. My brain always works well when I get that feeling that nature is protecting me from interruption. I hope the mist thickens later on."

"I'm sure it will. I do think you ought to go home, Jess."

"Don't fuss, Peter; you're behaving like a grandmother to-night."

"I could leave a message at Dr. Leigh's for you."

"And tell him I am afraid to go out because there's a few feet of mist in the meadows! Look, it's almost clear in the village. I should think your wife will have a poor time if you're as nervous as this at the age of twenty-six."

"I'm nervous on your account, not mine. You need someone to take care of you, Jess."

"I'm not a young girl, you silly boy. I can take care of myself. What do you suppose is going to happen to me? That I shall be attacked and raped on the way home?"

"Don't joke, Jess. I was never more serious in my life. I think it is dangerous for you to go on. Won't you turn back now, just to please me? I think I'm slightly psychic, and I have a presentiment of evil."

"Nonsense! One would never go anywhere if one were

guided by other people's presentiments. Have you never read the story of the man who was superstitious, and it took him about two hours to get from his home to the next street dodging ladders and chasing after black cats and piebald ponies? Well, here we are, anyhow. There's not the slightest sense in my turning back now, because if it turned really foggy, Dr. Leigh would take me home in his car. Thank you for coming with me. Good night."

Peter watched Jess walk up the drive to old Dr. Leigh's rambling house with a troubled mind. A woman came out of the gate and he asked her whether there were any other patients waiting in the surgery. She was the last but one, she told him, until the young lady who had just gone in arrived. There wouldn't be any more to-night; it was after seven. Peter was cheered by the information that Jess would have to wait a little while before seeing Leigh. He looked round for signs of the two men detailed to keep the doctor's house under observation. They were not in evidence, but that, no doubt, was part of the arrangement. The question was, how was he to establish contact with them?

He prowled around the untidy garden, with its unmown lawns and unswept paths. There were plenty of shrubs to shelter a watcher, but Peter found no trace of one as he flitted from one patch of shadow to another. He went round to the back of the house where the garage door was standing open. There was not a soul to be seen. He poked into tool-houses and wood-sheds. At last, anxious and disappointed, he returned to the front of the house, keeping out of sight on a path bordered with shrubs. He peered over the bushes, and saw a man come out of the door, with a white bandage over his forehead, turn up his collar and make for the front gate. Peter made for the road, reaching it by a gap in the fence, and ran towards the post-office. He went straight into the telephone booth and rang up Bruce Norton's house.

"Number engaged," came the brisk voice of the operator.

"Listen," said Peter urgently. "I am a police officer and this is urgent. Can you clear the line?"

"The number you want is taking a call from Golders Green; the inquirer was a police officer and we cleared the line for him."

"Damn!" said Peter. "Ring this number then as soon as he rings off. Grassmere 01."

"Grassmere 01. Ring off, please."

Peter replaced the receiver and waited.

30

ALONE in the waiting-room Jess sat down and lit a cigarette. She heard a faint murmur of voices from behind the inner door. She hoped the patient was not one of those cases which require minute examination; she was impatient for the moment when she would cross the threshold of the inner sanctum again. This time she knew whom she would see behind the desk; there would be no need for her to faint. Instead her heart would beat with that fractional increase in pace which has stimulating rather than adverse consequences.

The same dirty magazines confronted Jess on the table but they no longer depressed her. There were two worlds now, one of which mattered while the other did not. The comfortless waiting-room belonged to the insignificant world; all that was vital lay beyond the closed door. It was strange, she reflected, how one's horizon could change overnight so that even the colour of one's thoughts was transformed. But perhaps it more easily happened when one has lived for a year with a memory than when the focal point of life is actively present. Poor Derek; why did he have to want to see her again just at the moment when she no longer needed him? At any time during the past year she could have welcomed him with tears of relief at the ending of a long barren interlude. Now she had not even attempted to think what she should say to him.

She hadn't had much time for thought the last three days, just when she had so much to think about. Peter had clung to her like a lost child; there was something both pathetic and companionable about Peter, but it was impossible to listen to his chatter and follow any consistent train of mental activity at the same time. Her plan for outwitting Mr. March had not materialized. Various desperate projects had half-shaped themselves in her mind, but she had abandoned them when she had heard from Derek's lawyer that her husband had been released. There was no need to do anything desperate at present. Derek might be able to clear himself without her intervention; if so, so much the better, since it was hard to devise effective intervention which would not implicate Jerome Leigh.

Derek himself had not written to her. No doubt he had been too shaken up by his experience, and too much occupied with the police and his solicitor to find an opportunity to explain why he had started off to see her on that Friday night. If all went well, he would probably write later in the week and suggest a meeting. There was no need to climb that fence until one came to it. She would be better prepared in a few days' time to frame her response to his overtures. . . .

The inner door opened and a young man with a bandage over one eye appeared on the threshold. Behind him stood Jerome Leigh. The young man vanished through the outer door. The doctor called, "Come in, Miss Munro," and turned back into the surgery. As Jess entered he was pulling the curtains across the windows. The lights were already on.

"My uncle's lamp is the old-fashioned carbon arc type," he explained. "Actually I believe they are more effective than the modern bulb lamps, though not so convenient to use. He does not use it often enough to employ a nurse to give the treatments. The patients are mostly children with a tendency to rickets, and so on. I shall only give you a few minutes' exposure this evening. Take off your things and lie on the couch."

Jess slipped off her frock and vest and stood up in a pair of lemon-coloured silk panties. Her smooth skin began to feel rather cold and creepy.

"Put these on," said Leigh, handing her a pair of goggles. "The room will soon warm up when I switch the lamp on. Lie this way, facing it, first, will you?"

Jess obeyed instructions and Leigh switched on the lamp, which spluttered for a minute and then began to purr rhythmically. A warm glow banished Jess's feeling of chill instantly. She breathed deeply and contentedly, feeling ready to purr with the machine.

Jerome Leigh's quiet voice sounded from behind her head. "So you have not betrayed me to the police?"

A galvanic shock shattered the drowsiness which had been stealing upon Jess. She tore off the sun-glasses involuntarily and gasped.

Leigh turned off the lamp. "You mustn't do that, you know, while you are facing the light. You can begin with your back if you prefer it, but keep still or you will upset my timing. I am giving you six minutes each way."

"I must sit up," said Jess. "How did you know about what you said just now? No—I won't put those horrid things on again. I can't talk unless I can see your face."

"You'll catch cold like that. Put your coat on for a minute then. How did I know? Your friend Mr. March let me know on Friday."

"Oh! Well, he isn't my friend at all. Can't you turn some other kind of heat on? My legs are cold."

Leigh switched on a radiator.

"That's better. You know I don't think much of you as a doctor giving me a shock like that when you are supposed to be treating me for nerves."

"No? I can't understand why you came to me at all, knowing what you did."

"I came quite accidentally in the first place, expecting to see Dr. Tom. It was only then that I recognized you."

"I realize that. But you need not have stayed."

"Well, does it matter why I stayed?"

"I should, not unnaturally, like to know what your intentions are with regard to the police."

"I don't mean to give you away ever. I suppose you had some reason for what you did, though however strong your motive was I don't think you need have stabbed— have attacked him from behind. And I wish you wouldn't keep dodging behind my head now. It may be an idiosyncrasy, but I cannot talk to people when they're out of sight."

Leigh transferred himself to the foot of the couch and

sat on the edge of it. "Why are you shielding me, Miss Munro? And what will you do if it comes to a toss-up between your husband and me? . . . Yes, March told me who your husband is."

"Give me a cigarette and I'll explain. . . . Thank you. You can see I'm in a very difficult position, can't you?"

"I accept your statement, though I should not have expected you to hesitate a moment between your husband's safety and that of a stranger. Go on."

"I've been trying to think how to save you both—that sounds melodramatic, but it happens to be true—all the week-end. Actually, if my reasoning is correct, it is much easier to ensure your safety than Derek's. The police will never suspect you unless I make a move, whereas they are already on to Derek. At the moment, however, they have released Derek; I heard from his lawyer and he thinks they have not got a complete enough case against him to charge him. That gave me a chance to indulge my habit of procrastination and wait to see what the police do next. But you can rest assured that I mean to outwit the police somehow. I shall find some way of clearing Derek without involving you."

"You still have not told me why this passionate desire to save me?"

"I expect you would hardly believe me."

"You might try and see."

"If you will persist don't blame me if you are embarrassed."

"I never am embarrassed."

"Neither am I. One outgrows embarrassment after the age of thirty, I find. Naturally, I can't let any harm come to Derek—I couldn't even if he had killed Seely and I know he didn't. He is still my husband. I was and am very fond of him and I have been living for a year closeted with the memory of Derek at his best—before those horrible cousins of his entwined their tentacles round him and warped his mind. Never mind that—I can't explain his cousins now. But I suppose I'm not quite old enough to live only with a memory. This is where you determine not

7*

to be embarrassed, because I am almost entirely free from the usual female inhibitions. The first time I came here, even though I knew you had killed Seely, I was 'struck all of a heap', as they say. I felt I could be in love with you quite easily and naturally, though of course the beginning part of love is rather disturbing; I didn't go through that part with Derek, you see—he only grew on me gradually after I had married him."

"Why not have a little sunlight on your back? You can still see me if I sit here."

"Good heavens! I asked you not to be embarrassed, I know, but I did expect you to say something. I've never done a thing like this before. . . ."

"The eternal feminine!—you want to have it both ways. If I begin to talk, we should both be—if not embarrassed—at least not completely cool and detached."

"Turn the lamp on then. Do we have to be cool and detached?"

"Well, my life is at stake. What will you do if you can't save your husband without betraying me?"

"You mean you feel uneasy at being in my power? If it comes to that, I am in your power too. You could have some sort of accident with that lamp and electrocute me."

"I couldn't."

"Well, you could poison me with some medicine. I thought that drink you gave me on Friday was poison for a minute."

"Are you going to answer my question?"

"If I can. That lamp is getting too hot. I can't think if I feel sick."

"Move a little further from it. My question. . . ."

"I think if a person is prepared to lie on oath, provided their reputation is good, they can do almost anything. I could remember something fresh about that Friday night."

"Such as?"

"Oh, I don't know. What a pest you are! I can't think under a fire of questions. That lamp is getting too hot again."

"Turn and face it now, and put the glasses on."

"No, I will not be blindfolded again. If it comes to that, you don't trust me, so why should I trust you? You might do anything. . . ."

"If I meant to harm you, your eyes wouldn't help you much. My aunt and the maid are both out. We are quite alone here."

"You make me feel quite creepy. What are you doing?"

"Only moving the lamp a few inches farther back."

"I'd rather you stayed where I can see you. I'd sooner have my back burned than—— What was that noise?"

"I think a door creaked. The wind's getting up a little."

"It wasn't a door. It sounded like a footstep. Listen!"

The lamp purred softly. A faint shuffling sound outside the door mingled with its purring.

"Another patient perhaps——" began Leigh.

"No, Dr. Leigh, it isn't another patient."

March had turned the door handle so gently that he seemed to have floated into the room.

"Stand away from that couch, Leigh."

"Get out of here, March. If you want to see me, I'll talk to you elsewhere. You have no right to enter my surgery while I am engaged with a patient."

"I have a right to enter any room you are in, Leigh. I have a warrant for your arrest."

"Oh, no no!" cried Jess. "You are all wrong, Mr. March. Dr. Leigh wasn't the man I saw; he isn't even like him!"

"What is the charge?" asked Leigh.

"The charge is murder. The Deputy Chief Constable is outside. He will read it over to you."

"Not here—can't you see Miss Munro isn't dressed?"

"Come outside then. Miss Munro, I am sorry to have intruded in this way. If you will get ready, Sergeant Cowie is waiting to take you home."

31

JESS watched the two men leave the room in a daze. Leigh had left the sun-lamp burning. She got up mechanically and switched it off, then began to scramble into her clothes. Her brain started to function again. She thought suddenly of a way of clearing the doctor. She would remember before she fainted seeing Seely's attacker run off down the lane towards her cottage. Would that do? She had only been in the ditch for quarter of an hour, and Leigh had done a lot in that time; gone back to his car, driven it to the corner, picked Seely up and driven out of earshot. It seemed unnatural for him to begin running in the wrong direction when he was in a hurry to reach his car. It might do, or she might improve on the story later. At the worst, if Jerome Leigh were brought to trial, could he be convicted in the face of her evidence on oath that he was not the man she had seen stab Seely? She could exaggerate the assailant's dark hair now Derek was no longer in danger. She might even endow him with some distinctive mark, such as a facial scar—but that perhaps would be overdoing it.

In the waiting-room she found Peter.

"Thank God you're safe, Jess!"

"Safe? Of course I am."

"Not 'of course'! That brute might have murdered you. I dare say he would have done if I hadn't telephoned the Chief Inspector just in time."

"So it was you! But, Peter, what made you think there was any danger? And why does Mr. March suspect the doctor?"

"I'll tell you on the way home. We'd better start now; it's getting late."

They set off down the drive. "All the week-end," said Peter, "I've had orders to protect you at all costs and whatever the risk to myself. Imagine my horror when you walked right into the lion's den."

"Oh, cut it out, Peter. I wish I'd known you were paid to hang around my house till I could have screamed with boredom. I wouldn't have taken so much trouble making you omelettes."

"I didn't do it for money. You make me feel like a mercenary:

'Followed their mercenary calling,
And took their wages and are dead.' "

"Well, you're not dead, and don't quote Housman now or I shall scream. Get on with your explanation. I'm not going to ask you into the cottage, so be quick."

"I think you are very unkind. Leigh is a much bigger chap than I am, and I really did run a risk. Leigh killed Seely, you know, Jess. But of course, you know—you saw him do it."

"I did not. But go on."

"Well, I only know the bare outline. I walked to meet the car after telephoning, and March told me what had happened. He had just had a telephone report from one of our chaps in London who had seen the mother of Seely's first wife. John had a job to get the story; the woman didn't want to talk. And no wonder!"

"What has Seely's first wife to do with Dr. Leigh?"

"Everything. He was engaged to marry her when he was a medical student and she hardly out of the school-room. Leigh couldn't afford to marry until he was quali-fied, which meant several years' waiting. The girl was lovely and she met Seely and took his fancy. He induced her to chuck Leigh and marry him. Two years later she committed suicide. Seely was a sadistic brute; we'll draw a veil over that. She died fourteen years ago. That is all March had time to tell me in the car; Norton was driving like the wind. But before that March had told me what put him on to Leigh. The doctor met Seely again after all these years when he came here a few weeks ago to act as locum for his uncle. Seely had the nerve to call him in professionally one day when King was away. I doubt if Seely wanted medical advice. He wanted to gloat over Leigh and watch him squirm. But Leigh didn't squirm; he flatly refused to treat him and the two men had the hell of a set to. Sibyl King overheard the gist of it. The doctor waylaid Seely the next night and stabbed him in the back. Mrs. King, prompted by her husband, kept silence. King did not love Seely so well that he wanted to help to hang a man for doing him in. Sibyl might have continued to hold her peace, but March got suspicious and tackled her again. The second time he managed to get her story from her. Quite a number of little things also add up to complete the case against Dr. Leigh. I don't think it's much use for you to hold out on us, Jess. You mustn't risk being charged with perjury."

"Very interesting," said Jess dryly. "But there's nothing in your story to justify calling whoever killed Seely a brute. I should think he is well out of the way."

"Perhaps, but stabbing in the back is brutal."

"Not if it is quick. If you let a man see you while you torture him to death slowly, where is the mercy in that? Thank you for seeing me home, Peter."

"Can't I come in?"

"No, I'm afraid you can't. I want to be alone to-night."

"Very well, Jess. I can still come to supper to-morrow, can't I?"

"I wouldn't have asked you if I'd known why you were sticking to me so closely."

"But you're no longer in danger now that Leigh is in custody, so you see I really like being with you for your own sake."

"Very well, Peter. But don't turn up before seven. I must have some time for my own affairs the next few days. Good night."

Jess went straight to the kitchen resisting the temptation to sit down and let the conflicting emotions of the past hour battle within her. She fried an egg and bacon and made some coffee. She had told Jerome Leigh she loved him and he had been arrested a few minutes later for murder. Love and death—the two elemental facts of nature—had been intertwined in a kaleidoscopic pattern. Light and dark were strangely mingled; beauty and horror. The polite curtain which veils the naked facts of life had been drawn aside. She had seen behind it and Jerome Leigh had seen behind it too. Yet one still cooked eggs and bacon! Would they give Jerome a meal at the police station? Or would he go hungry and sleepless to bed?

She could not bother to take her meal to the sitting-room, but spread a cloth over the kitchen table and pulled up a hard chair—that same hard chair in which she had cried her eyes out for Derek ten days ago. She had no tears either for Derek or Jerome Leigh now. Her nerves were completely steady. She would not procrastinate another hour. Directly she had swallowed her meal she would write to Derek's lawyer and ask him to come down and see her, or make an appointment for her to see him in London. She must have expert advice as to her position as a potential witness in a murder trial.

She was writing her letter when she heard a knock on the door. Peter again, she supposed irritably, or possibly even Chief Inspector March. Why couldn't they leave her alone for one night at least? She went out to answer the door, determined to repel the intruder if possible.

The door stuck a little and she fell back as it came open with a jerk.

"Hullo Jess!"

"Derek! How on earth did you get here?"

"I came off the eight-thirty-five. Can I come in?"

"Of course. Have you had supper?"

"I had a snack at the station. I don't want anything else. Unless you've got a spot of coffee going?"

"I've only just had some myself. I'll have another cup with you. Take your coat off; I won't be a minute."

"There's a lot to say, Jess," said Derek, sipping his coffee. "I like this cottage. Have you been all right here?"

"In a way, yes. Does it matter?"

"I wanted to know. I couldn't start off talking about

myself without asking, could I? I should think it is better here for you than London—for your writing, I mean. You know you always complained of the wireless in the flat next door."

"And the baby up above and the man who snored down below. So it was out of consideration for my work that you sent me here! You'll be glad to know I have written two books since I migrated to the country."

"I know I behaved like a prig, Jess. Rupert dictated every word I said to you that night. I felt it was all quite out of harmony with my character."

"Why on earth didn't you just tell me in your own words that you didn't love me, and couldn't live with me any longer?"

"It wouldn't have been true. I did love you, but Rupert told me I loved art better. He was right that I didn't seem able to concentrate that year with you."

"Neither did I. It's not surprising the first year of marriage. You needn't look miserable, Derek. I understand much better now than I did then. You wanted to do two incompatible things at the same time——"

"Yes, yes, that was exactly it, Jess. I told Rupert you understood me better than anyone else ever could."

"Let's leave Rupert out of it. I think if you had waited, you would have settled down. After all, plenty of married men have got to the top in every form of art. We both made the same mistake in trying to write our masterpieces that year. We ought to have made it a sort of sabbatical year and set to work seriously the next year. Have you been able to work better since we parted.

"Perhaps. I hope my play is good. There won't be any Seely to wreck it this time anyway. But apart from writing, Jess, it has been plain hell. So much so that I——"

"Well?"

"You see, I had promised Rupert not to communicate with you for a year. But—I suppose it's the way I'm made, anyhow, I'm sure you will understand—I couldn't wait so long."

"But you did wait."

"That's just it, I didn't. That's why I'm here now. I kept my promise to Rupert, but I drifted into an affair with a girl at the office—Sheila Fayre, Rupert's secretary."

"I've seen her once or twice; she is a very pretty girl, I think."

"She is, isn't she? Rupert didn't mind that; he encouraged it. He thought Sheila was the kind of girl who would live with me without interfering with my work."

"So she is your mistress?"

"I don't like that word. Why should there be a special word for a woman who does that sort of thing and not for a man?"

"I can't imagine, but there is. We can't alter the dictionary now, Derek. I want to hear more."

"I'm trying to tell you. Sheila took the affair more seriously than I expected. She had never lived with a man before, and says she wouldn't have done it now but for the fact that I wasn't free to marry her. She has very high ideals, Jess."

"I'm sure she has, Derek. Why shouldn't she have? You don't think I'm condemning her for what she has been to you, do you? I don't think her conduct is any more incompatible with high ideals than your own."

"I'm afraid I misled her. She says nothing would induce her to come between a married couple and I kept her under the impression that you had run out on me."

"It doesn't matter. Let her go on thinking that. This is all quite funny!"

"Funny? I don't find it so. Why are you laughing?"

"Why, because when I heard you had come down here on our wedding anniversary, I thought it was to ask me to come back to you. Now I find it was to ask me to divorce you. It was an odd day to choose."

"Not at all. It was the first day I could come, because of my promise to Rupert."

"Oh damn Rupert. If I divorce you, Derek, it will be on one condition and one condition alone—that you don't let Rupert wreck your second marriage. You see, you are quite in my power. I'm getting used to having people in my power these days; I must have been born under some very peculiar star, I think. No promise, no divorce."

"Rupert won't interfere this time. He knows Sheila wants me to marry her. He practically gave me his blessing. He was surprised that Sheila wouldn't go on as we were, but after he had thought it over, he said it might work out quite well after all. You see, he has quite a false idea of Sheila. He thinks she is the kind of woman one can put out of one's mind when one isn't actually cohabiting with her, whereas you would be more important——"

"Thank you, you needn't dot the i's. Thank God you can admit that Rupert has false ideas about something. You shall have your divorce. I suppose you'll arrange it all so that Sheila is kept out of it."

"I shall, but oddly enough she says she doesn't mind being co-respondent. It's easier that way; judges are rather snuffy about hotel divorces now. But there's no need for you to worry about that, Jess. You've done your part in being so nice about it. You know, I shall always feel married to you in a way all my life. I shall never really forgive Rupert. If Sheila wasn't so completely different from you, I couldn't bear to marry her."

"Let's get this straight, Derek. You do want to marry her, I suppose?"

"I did an hour ago. Being with you has rather shaken me up."

"That will pass. One can't live with memories."

"That was what I found. But all the time——"

"For God's sake don't quote *Cynara*, Derek, or I shall shriek. Now that we've agreed on the divorce, I think we might talk about something else. I was going to ask you to stay the night, but obviously that wouldn't be wise now. What did you mean to do?"

"I thought of catching the eleven-five—the train I meant to go back on if I had got as far as here last time I came down. But I brought a case with me and left it at the hotel by the station. I can have a bed there if I miss the train. I think I will miss it, Jess; I don't want to leave you yet, and Rupert has given me the week off from the office, so

I needn't catch an early train in the morning. You don't mind my staying another hour or so, do you?"

"Stay as long as you like. Let's have some sherry. You'll have to open a new bottle; I finished the last before supper."

"Here's to you, Jess," said Derek, raising his glass.

32

"TALKING of my last trip down here, Jess," said Derek, after his second glass of sherry. "D'you know it damned nearly put a noose round my neck? Weren't you staggered to hear old Seely had been bumped off?"

"No, I wasn't surprised. I saw it happen."

"You—saw—it—happen! Have you doped this sherry, or have I gone mad? You saw Seely stabbed?"

"Indeed I did. It happened quite near here, you know. I was coming back from the post in the middle of the storm. The lightning flared up just as a man jumped out on Seely and stabbed him."

"Then—Good God!—then you knew I didn't do it!"

"Yes, I knew, and I told the police when I heard you had been detained, but they thought I was a prejudiced witness. You see, I had already described the man I saw as a stranger, but the description happened to fit you."

"Gosh—I've had a narrower squeak than I realized. Everything seemed against me, even without your description. I felt pretty blue when I sent for Harold Bryce, but he put new life into me. He advised me to admit that I had been coming to see you, and he got Sheila to tell the police we were hoping to get married, which rather robbed me of any motive. That didn't quite do the trick, so he got Sheila to make a confidential statement which was not to be used at all unless I was brought to trial, in which case it would be available as evidence for the defence."

"What was in it?"

"She swore she had spent the night with me at my flat on the Thursday before I came down here."

"And had she?"

"Yes. We could prove it too, because Lang, the fellow in the flat below mine, ran into her when she took the milk in in the morning. Lang had the wit not to tell the police that when a fellow called to make inquiries, pretending to be an old friend of mine. But Bryce said they were palpably shaken when he disclosed the fact."

"I don't quite see how it helped you?"

"They were in difficulty about the carving-knife. I would have had to have taken it with me. Sheila swore she packed for me and watched me dress. The last wasn't true, but they can't disprove it. No carving-knife—no murder."

"That makes things simpler for me."

"What on earth do you mean? I should have thought it made them simpler for me."

"For both of us, Derek. Harold Bryce sounds a bright young man. Do you think he would help me?"

"Of course. But why do you need help?"

"I shall be a witness at the trial—if I can't stop the trial altogether."

"There's no one to try, is there?"

"Oh yes, there is. They have arrested someone else."

"I didn't know that. It wasn't in the evening papers."

"There wasn't time for that. You can take my word that it is true, because I was present when it happened."

"Heavens, Jess, you do live! But you don't need legal advice. All you have to do is to identify the chap—if you can identify him."

"That's just what I don't want to do."

"Why ever not? Who is he, anyway?"

"The man who has been charged is Dr. Jerome Leigh."

"But he's the fellow who took Seely to hospital."

"That didn't stop him from being arrested."

"Well, but did he stab Seely?"

"I'm not going to drag you into this, Derek. You've been involved enough already. Whether Dr. Leigh stabbed Seely or not makes no difference. I want to know the best way to defend him."

Derek whistled. "So you are in love with the fellow. What is he like? Dark and handsome, I suppose?"

"He isn't dark, and I dislike the word 'handsome' as much as you do the word 'mistress'."

"But you love him! No wonder you agreed so tamely to a divorce. Really, Jess, I think you've let me down. Here have I been hankering after you for a whole year, and when I am able at last to see you, I find you have fallen in love with a murdering doctor!"

"You could have seen me any time if you hadn't been under Rupert's thumb. As for your hankering, give me someone next time who doesn't hanker, that's all!"

"Well, I've told you Sheila was just an outlet for everything I had to repress. It was because I missed you that I turned to her. That was all it was at first, I assure you. I've admitted that I've been a weak fool. But I always thought you had a stronger character than me. I did think you would have been faithful to me for one year, at least."

"That's another word I'd like to expunge from the dictionary, Derek—in that sense, at least. But I can tell you I haven't had a chance in this benighted hole of being anything else but faithful. I've been much too faithful to tell you the truth. My hankering after you didn't take the form of living with another man."

"Jess, you look almost beautiful when you're angry. I noticed directly I arrived that you look much younger than you did a year ago. I suppose that's because you're in love with this Jerome Leigh."

"Yes, I am, if you will make me say it. And I don't want to look young or beautiful. I want to make plans to get him off."

"Why did he do it?"

"I haven't said he did. The police have ferreted out some garbled story giving him a motive. Don't ask any more questions, Derek. What about Harold Bryce? I was just writing to him when you appeared."

"Harold's a marvel. If anyone can help you, he can. I'll tell you what, Jess. Come up to town with me to-morrow morning and I'll take you to see him."

"That's a good idea."

"I don't mind leaving you so much to-night if we're going to spend the day together to-morrow. I think I ought to go now; they probably shut the place up at midnight. We'll meet at the station then?"

"I'll be there at ten o'clock. Good night, Derek."

"I can't go without kissing you, Jess. We're still married. . . ."

"Poor Derek! Perhaps Sheila will help you to grow up better than I did."

"She likes me as I am," said Derek, pausing for breath between embraces.

"So do I, but I want you to be happy and you won't be till you're properly settled down with her. You must go now, Derek dear. This isn't doing either of us any good."

"I wish I could stay the night."

"You'd wish you hadn't afterwards."

Jess gently piloted a dishevelled Derek out into the hall. "Till to-morrow, then," he said regretfully, as he gave her a last kiss on the doorstep. She opened the door and pushed him over the threshold.

Three more hours wasted—no, not wasted, because Derek was always Derek—but three hours gone and nothing done about Jerome Leigh, Jess thought as she went upstairs to bed. Except the appointment with the lawyer, and it seemed that she was banking all her faith on a somewhat slight foundation. But Bryce had found ways and means to clear Derek, and there might be similar unknown factors which could be marshalled in Jerome Leigh's defence. She undressed quickly, resolved to do no more thinking until she had had expert advice to guide her. She set her alarm clock for half-past seven; on no account must she oversleep and miss the train. There were only seven hours for sleep, and she must be fresh in the morning. She was glad to find that she felt physically tired, and very soon began to feel drowsy—perhaps it was the effect of the artificial sunlight. She fell asleep and dreamed she was having a sun-bath, and took off the eye-shield to find Jerome Leigh standing over her with a knife raised to stab her in the back. You couldn't see properly with the glasses; they turned red to black and toned down all colour so that the room had looked like a photograph. She had known she ought not to have worn them in Leigh's presence; she ought not to have let him move out of her sight. And now it was too late. Unable to cry out, she waited for the blade to fall. Why couldn't she scream as Seely had screamed . . .? It was odd she had not seen Derek, but he was there, and the doctor had turned the blade towards him. Still she could not scream and the two men were swaying and struggling in front of her eyes. March was in the room now, saying quietly that he was not another patient. He carried a black scroll and began to read aloud from it, without taking any notice of the fight. He spoke to her, repeating a question—"Leigh or Derek?" There was a gallows in the room which now had no walls, and was open to a grey sky. "Leigh or Derek?" They were going to hang either . . . or . . . and they were waiting for her to speak. "Which? . . . Which?" She tried to spring at a man holding a bandage; he was going to blindfold Leigh —no—Derek, but her knees collapsed beneath her and she was falling down and down into a wet, slimy pit. . . .

The alarm clock pierced the air with its shrill summons. Jess opened her eyes in a sweat of fear, and stared around her. There was nothing to see in the half-light which filtered through the curtains but the bedroom furniture and her blue dressing-gown hanging over the foot of the bed. She would never again believe the theory that a dream lasted only a few seconds. She had lived all night in the shadow of a frightful nightmare. She went to the bathroom and turned on the taps with a sense of urgency. Everything depended now on Harold Bryce.

She paid little attention to Derek's conversation in the train. They had a first-class carriage to themselves and a rather pale sun was shining on the autumn landscape. She looked out of the window and silently rehearsed the words she must say to the lawyer. It was vital to make him grasp the whole of the crazy situation as quickly as possible so that he might set to work at once to plan her course of action. She thought of Jerome Leigh and wondered what he was thinking about in his cell. She supposed he had slept in a cell and the thought made her shiver.

"Anything wrong, Jess?" asked Derek. "Like the window closed?"

"No, I like the air. I was only thinking what to say to Harold Bryce."

"You'll have to tell him the whole truth if you want him to advise you."

"Yes, I mean to. Is he shockable?"

"Harold? Not the least. He revels in other people's disreputable secrets."

"Disreputable? That isn't the word I would have chosen. But I'm going to give him something to think about."

"I like you in that hat, Jess. It's a new one, isn't it?"

"I've had it nearly a year. I bought it in Heathmere just after I took the cottage."

"You couldn't have been very broken-hearted if you had the spirit to buy a new hat."

"I had to eat and sleep and dress, Derek, whatever the state of my heart. But I want to think for a bit. Perhaps you could read the paper."

"Perhaps I could. Oh, Jess, you make me feel so completely married to you when you talk to me like that. I suppose we couldn't——"

"No, Derek, we could not."

Jess looked out of the window again and Derek disconsolately unfolded *The Times*.

33

HAROLD BRYCE was bright-eyed and dapper and reminded Jess of a contented robin. One expected him every moment to make a quick dart with his round head and snatch up a crumb with his mouth. He sat at his desk in a sunny office and twittered a question now and again to help Jess out with her story. She told it much more smoothly than she had expected, packing all the outstanding incidents of the past ten days into the short space of half an hour.

"Is there any hope?" she asked when she had finished.

"Do smoke, Mrs. Garle," said Harold, handing her a tortoiseshell cigarette case. "Hope? Of course there is hope. I don't know yet exactly what the police case against Leigh is. They would hardly have dared to arrest him simply because Seely pinched his girl sixteen years ago, and subsequently tormented her until she was driven to suicide, particularly in view of your refusal to identify him as Seely's assailant. There must be more to it than that. I shall have to come down to Grassmere and try to find out what other evidence they have. You don't know whether Leigh has taken legal advice?"

"No, he just went off with the police without a word. He comes from the west country though; he isn't likely to know a solicitor on the spot."

"Perhaps he would let me represent him,. That would really be best, because it will give me some local standing. Business is fairly slack now. If you wait a few minutes I'll arrange things with my partner. After that, what about a spot of lunch before we entrain for Grassmere?"

"I promised to meet Derek at his club. I don't see why you shouldn't come along too."

"Derek might not approve of that. I think I'll arrange

to stay to-night at Grassmere and go home and pack a few things. How would it be if I met you at Waterloo?"

"We shan't catch anything before the three-fifteen."

"That will do. I'll meet you at the barrier."

Jess was maddened by the slowness of the train on the return journey. Now that she had secured the services of Bryce, she began to wonder what he could possibly do on Leigh's behalf. The train was lightly laden and they had not only a carriage, but the whole first-class coach to themselves.

"What will you do if Dr. Leigh refuses to let you act for him?" she asked.

"Now, don't worry, Mrs. Garle. He is bound to want legal aid in a murder charge. If he already has a lawyer, I must get in touch with him. Now, to save time, I want you to give me as many names and addresses as you can of people connected with the case. I shall have to look them all up personally."

He took out a note-book.

"There didn't seem to be anybody connected with the case except myself. Everything seems to have centred round me, and my description of Seely's assailant. That led them to Ivan Ling, and Derek, and cleared George King."

"We'll leave out Derek. But there you are, you see. I must see Ling and King—funny their names should rhyme, isn't it?"

"I hadn't thought of that. Ivan Ling is a young farmer who lives at Cairn Farm, not far from my cottage. I don't think he can tell you anything, because he was in a cowhouse at the time of the murder. George King was employed at Beech House with his wife. They are still there. I think that is all."

The train stopped at Bogmore, and one passenger entered the first-class coach and got into the empty carriage next door. Jess uttered an exclamation of astonishment.

"That was old Dr. Tom Leigh, Jerome Leigh's uncle. He didn't see me."

"Well, he's going to see you straight away. What a

piece of luck! Do you mind making yourself known to him and asking him to join us in here?"

Jess obeyed promptly and returned with the white-haired doctor in tow just as the train was moving out of the station. The old man was tall and held himself upright, but his face betrayed the anguish of mind he was suffering. When Jess had introduced Bryce, he told his story briefly. He had received a telephone message the previous evening telling him of his nephew's arrest for the murder of Ambrose Seely. He understood that Jerome wanted him to return home at once and make legal arrangements for his defence. He had accomplished the first part of his journey that night, sleeping *en route*, and found that he could complete it most rapidly by coming on across country to Bogmore. He had heard of the firm of Bryce and Drayton and thought it would be a capital plan for Harold Bryce, since he was already *au fait* with the circumstances of Seely's death, to act for his nephew.

"But I can't understand how Jerome has got into this mess," Tom Leigh said distractedly. "I knew he had some trouble about a girl when he was a medical student, but I never heard the full story, and I thought he had got over it years ago. He and Seely showed no signs of recognizing one another when I introduced them a month ago. I can't believe that Jerome would be such a rash fool—— But whatever he has done, we have got to save him—even if it takes every farthing of my savings. He would have had my money after my death, so he may as well have it now."

Bryce was leaning forward looking more like a robin than ever, his bright eyes darting from Leigh to Jess, and back to the doctor again.

"I think, sir, we shall do best if we face the fact that your nephew killed Seely—under intolerable provocation, no doubt—but that Seely died by his hand there is no doubt. Mrs. G——, I mean Miss Munro here, saw him strike the fatal blow."

The old man looked bewildered, and Jess once again recapitulated her strange adventure.

"Then Jerome is done for," the doctor muttered.

"On the contrary," Bryce said cheerfully, "Miss Munro is his one hope of salvation. She is resolved not to identify him. But she can't save him off her own bat. This is where you and I come in, sir. A guilty man can get off if the prosecution can't prove their case. Your nephew won't even be brought to trial unless a *prima facie* case is made out against him. The police must believe at this moment that they are in a position to do that. They must have some evidence that we know nothing about. I doubt if your nephew himself knows it, but if you will persuade him to see me, I can very likely get at it indirectly by questioning him. Then I shall test the value of the evidence by contacting the witnesses concerned."

"Persuade him! I'll make the young fool see you. He must put himself in your hands unreservedly. I see you have some luggage with you. You will put up at my house, won't you? I have plenty of room."

"I shall be delighted. We ought, I think, to go on in this train to Heathmere, and lose no time in seeing your nephew. The police can't refuse him legal aid—that's one thing."

"The Deputy Chief Constable is an old friend of mine. He'll give me every facility for seeing Jerome, I am certain."

Leaving the two men planning and plotting together, Jess slipped quietly on to the platform at Grassmere. She had hardly washed up her tea things when Peter appeared on the doorstep.

"Oh, Peter, I forgot I had asked you to supper, and anyhow I told you not to come before seven. It's lucky for you I'm at home; I've been up to London for the day."

"I am a little early," Peter admitted. "But I didn't know what to do to kill time. With Dr. Leigh under arrest, my part in the case seems rather to have fizzled out."

"Well, since you are here, tell me the news."

"There isn't any. I suppose there is no harm in my telling you that so far Leigh has refused to make any statement or answer any questions. I believe he is waiting for his uncle to arrive from the north of England, or somewhere."

"Have you seen him?"

"I haven't but the Chief Inspector has."

"Is that all that's happened?"

"They didn't take his pulse but I believe he is in good health. That's what you wanted to know, I take it."

"Is he fairly comfortable, Peter?"

"I haven't seen his lowly abode. I wouldn't worry, Jess. Leigh is tough enough to come to no harm in his present quarters. No doubt thinking of you is keeping him warm."

"Shut up, Peter. Or talk sense."

"I was just going to tell you there's a hell of a row on at police headquarters at Heathmere. It was rather rich, I must say. Mr. Norton and Inspector Norman had made elaborate arrangements for all Leigh's movements to be watched and when I escorted you to the surgery there wasn't a 'tec to be seen. They'd fixed for one chap to be at the garage in the road near Leigh's house, complete with motor cycle. That part of the scheme was all right. I didn't see him because I didn't look for him there. But the other should have been concealed in some bushes behind Leigh's garage, and should have hailed me when I went round to the back of the house. But at the moment the silly oaf was yards away in the outdoor lavatory. So I missed him and went haring off to the telephone."

"I don't see what you could have done if you had found him."

"I knew March was after a warrant for Leigh's arrest. If there had been two of us, we could have entered the house and detained Leigh until the others arrived. As it is, I consider I practically saved your life by my prompt action, Jess."

"Rubbish! I was not in the slightest danger. If you thought I was, why didn't you venture into the house alone?"

"I am much too wily to do a thing like that. Leigh would have laid us both out and then who would have telephoned for help? The doctor would have vamoosed while the fellow who ought to have warned his colleague in the garage was still otherwise engaged. But I didn't expect any gratitude. 'Blow, blow, thou winter wind, thou art not . . .' "

"Peter, any more of your tags and no mushroom omelette. Come out into the meadow and help me pick some mushrooms. If you will billet yourself on me, you'll have to work for your living."

Jess fetched a basket and led the way through the garden to the rich green meadow beyond, Peter following meekly in her wake.

34

"Journey's end!" said Bruce Norton to Christopher March when at length they were able to relax by the fireside on Monday evening, after their spectacular dash to Grassmere. He did not beg for his usual game of chess. "I never thought it would end this way, Chris. Poor old Tom Leigh. He will feel responsible for Jerome's crime, because Jerome met his old enemy while acting as locum for him. I wish Leigh had decided to make a statement. One would know then what chance the fellow has."

"You know, Bruce, your sympathies have veered over to the side of the criminal, which is a little discouraging for me. Leigh was very wise to keep his mouth shut. I wish he would speak; it would give me some idea how to get on with the police case."

"It seems to me you have your case already. Leigh can't possibly produce an alibi. He can't even fake an alibi now; it is too late."

"His only hope is Jessica Munro. She ought to be our star witness, but she'll be over on the other side. She will have to face a stiff cross-examination though. It depends on the relative impression she and Sibyl King make on the jury. But that is some way off yet. By the way, I was just going to tell you when John Derwent's call came through that I got Norman to take me over to see the mother of the baby Leigh visited on the night of the crime, while you were all fixing up a warrant for Leigh's arrest. That woman's evidence isn't going to help him any. She says the child was so much better that she was astonished at the doctor turning out in such a storm to see it. He had told her when he called the previous time that there was no more cause for anxiety. Moreover he was out of the house by half-past eight, and you're not going to tell me that he took twenty-five minutes to drive to the spot where he pretends he drew up on account of the storm. He was allowing a wide margin to get that gate open, and drive his car out of sight behind the trees in the field. I'll bet he was under that tree at the corner of Cairn Lane waiting to spring out on Seely by quarter to nine at latest; Miss Munro had passed on her way to the pillar-box before that. That was how he got his hair so wet that it looked black. I called at the hospital too, and ascertained that Leigh was soaked through when he took Seely in, and his hair was dripping. He wouldn't have got very wet just hopping out of his car to pick Seely up. I'm itching to know what sort of defence the fellow is going to put up."

"So am I. He's expecting that his uncle will be here by to-morrow evening and arrange for a solicitor to represent him when he appears before the magistrates on Wednesday morning."

"He will simply deny the charge and reserve his defence. That's the normal procedure when no previous statement has been made."

"Chris, I suppose you would loathe the idea of popping out to a cinema? I feel I can't sit here the whole evening worrying about poor old Tom Leigh. He was like a father to me when I broke my leg in the black-out. I couldn't concentrate on chess—even my type of concentration."

"Come on," said March cheerfully. "A change of scene will do me good too. One doesn't burst into a doctor's surgery and arrest the practitioner in the presence of a naked nymph every day of one's life."

Bruce smiled wanly as he consulted the local paper to choose a suitable film for the dark mood of the moment.

The film, however, was only a transitory diversion, and all the next day Norton was fretting and fidgeting for Tom Leigh to arrive and yet dreading the ordeal of facing him when the moment came. He cursed hell out of the young constable who had been absent from his post when Peter Cowie sought for him and even took Inspector Norman to task for not having made better arrangements for liaison between the members of the group responsible for watching Dr. Leigh and Miss Munro.

"Damn fools we should have looked if Leigh had done some mischief to Miss Munro, while our key man was in the lavatory," he grumbled.

"It was fortunate Cowie acted on his own initiative, sir," Norman admitted, trying to conceal his chagrin.

But he had said the wrong thing. "We don't want the Yard to get the impression that the local police can't do a simple job like shadowing a dangerous man without calling on them to pull our chestnuts out of the fire," Norton spluttered. "Oh, clear out, Norman; it's no use crying over spilt milk. Let me know at once if Dr. Tom Leigh turns up, or if Jerome Leigh expresses a wish to make a statement, will you?"

"Very good, sir, but I don't think Leigh will make a statement to-day. He is busy with some correspondence now."

March, with exemplary patience, bore with his friend's cantankerous mood, and went quietly about his own business, forbearing to mention the case when he and Norton were together.

The Deputy Chief Constable returned home to a late tea in the same dour frame of mind and found March waiting for him. They had scarcely begun the meal when Norton's housekeeper entered and announced Dr. Leigh and Mr. Bryce.

An embarrassing moment ensued. Oblivious of the presence of two onlookers, old Dr. Tom and Bruce Norton clasped hands and stared wordlessly into each other's eyes. March got up and strolled over to the window. Bryce hovered discreetly in the doorway.

Then Bruce broke the tension by ringing for more tea, and insisting that the doctor should have some refreshment after his long journey before calling to see his nephew. "You won't lose anything by it," he declared. "I've arranged for you to have every facility at the——" His voice trailed away and he looked unhappily at March, who said nothing. "Every facility," Norton repeated.

The doctor introduced Harold Bryce and the party split up into two groups, Leigh and Norton conversing in undertones by the window, and March being left to entertain the lawyer on the other side of the fireplace. The Chief Inspector was about to start some non-committal topic when Bryce, perking his bird-like head forward, gave him a cheeky smile.

"This is an amusing situation," he observed. "Dr. Leigh didn't tell you he has booked me to represent his nephew. We're in hostile camps. I've certainly never before sat down to afternoon tea with the official who has built up the case I propose to break down."

March smiled. "Neither have I partaken of a meal with the man charged with refuting the case I propose to prove," he retorted.

"We ought to make something of the novel situation," said Bryce. "I suppose you think you've got young Leigh on toast, eh?"

"I'd rather be in my shoes than his."

"I haven't seen my client yet, so I can talk without prejudice to him. There is such a thing as justifiable homicide, I dare say you know."

"I seem to have heard of it, but never, I think, applied in a case where a strong man stabs a small man in the back."

Bryce's bright eyes did not flinch. "Juries are not very fond of evidence which is over ten years old," he said. "They prefer something up to date."

"Yes, and you would like to know whether I've got it, wouldn't you?"

"Nothing I should like better. If you show your hand, I'll show mine."

"Thank you, no. Your hand is a yarborough."

"I have one ace, I may tell you."

"I will concede you one Queen, and no more. I don't want to see her, thank you; I have already had that honour."

"She is the Queen of Hearts," said Bryce, grinning.

"So I thought."

"And she's going to play merry hell with your case, my good sir."

"We're straying rather far away from the metaphor. You can keep your Queen of Hearts, Mr. Bryce. She can only take one trick, and it won't win the game for you."

Dr. Tom had finished his tea and was anxious to be moving. Norton insisted on getting out his car to drive him and his companion to their destination, the name of which he steadily refused to pronounce. March saw them off and, returning to the sitting-room, poured himself some more tea and lit a cigarette. His lips broke into a slow smile at the memory of his duel with Bryce. Show his hand, indeed! When he knew every card in his opponent's. There was only one of any value—Jessica Munro, who was probably even now plotting to turn one trick into the rubber.

Norman had interpreted the word "facilities" liberally and, remembering the Deputy Chief Constable's captious mood, had arranged for a small well-lit room opening out of the charge-room to be prepared for Leigh's interview with his uncle and the solicitor. Bruce approved the arrangements and went home, Dr. Tom declaring that he and Bryce were prepared for a long session and that he would prefer to telephone for a taxi when they were ready to go home.

The two visitors were shown into the room allocated to the interview, and a few minutes later Jerome Leigh was brought in by a constable, who closed the door behind him and stood on guard outside.

"Nice of you to come so quickly, Uncle Tom," said Jerome, extending his hand. His eyes looked tired but his voice was cheerful.

Tom Leigh could hardly speak for emotion as he wrung his nephew's hand. Harold Bryce had to introduce himself. Jerome gently released his hand from his uncle's grip and extended it to the lawyer. "It's good of you to come forward, Bryce. I'm afraid you'll have the hell of a job to get me out of this mess."

They all sat round a small deal table and Bryce produced his note-book.

"I'll get you out of it all right, Leigh, if I have to lie

my head off. Now, before we have a proper consultation, just tell me one or two things. I was trying to pump Chief Inspector March just now. Couldn't squeeze much out of him, but the chance was too good to go begging. I'm sure of one thing though. He's ferreted out some recent evidence to incriminate you. Any notion what it is?"

"Not an idea in the world. Do smoke your pipe, Uncle Tom, while we're talking. Afraid I haven't a cigarette to offer you."

Bryce took out his case and he and Leigh lit up, while the old doctor filled an ancient pipe.

"No, Bryce, I'm utterly stumped," Jerome repeated. "I was flabbergasted when March burst into my surgery. I thought I was as safe as the Bank of England—bar Miss Munro's evidence—and she had just sworn she wasn't going to identify me. I can't think now what put March on to me. I can only suppose sweet Jessica must have double-crossed me."

"You can put that idea out of your head right now. Jess Munro came up to London this morning to ask me to help her to save you."

"Did she, by Jove! Then I'm still stumped."

"The position is this, Leigh. The police have dug up the old story about Delia Martin. That gives you a motive."

"That was my motive, but——"

"One minute. You haven't answered any questions or made a statement to the police since they arrested you, have you?"

"I haven't uttered a damned syllable. I've bitten my lips until they're raw. I was too much taken by surprise to speak at the time, and when I'd had time to think, I saw I could only harm myself by saying anything."

"Good. And you hadn't expected them to dig out the events of fourteen years ago."

"No, I hadn't. I supposed they could do so if they suspected me. But until I heard that Miss Munro had seen me, I saw no reason why I should come under suspicion."

"Well, they've got the whole story now. We can't help that. But they positively and absolutely must have traced some more recent connection between you and Seely to be ready to show a *prima facie* case against you. You hadn't seen Seely for fourteen years when you came here?"

"Not for sixteen."

"Well, for God's sake, think then. What is it they could know? Something which happened since you came here?"

"Oh, I told March myself that Seely called me in the day before he died——"

"The devil you did! What occurred on that occasion?"

"Well, I must tell you my uncle introduced me to Seely the very evening I arrived here to take charge of the practice. We pretended not to know one another. It was arranged that I was to keep an eye on him while my uncle was away, but I hadn't the smallest intention of going within a mile of the brute. Then on the eighteenth of September—the Thursday—I got a message asking me to call that day at Beech House. My aunt took the message on the telephone and I found it on the pad when I came in. The caller didn't say who was ill, so I couldn't ignore the summons. For all I knew a servant might be seriously ill. So I took the car out and went round. Imagine my disgust to find that filthy swine Seely had sent for me to see him. He wasn't in any real need of medical attention. He thought he was going to order me to call round to see him every other day and give him some kind of injections that he had had before, so as to force me to listen to his foul gibes and gloating about my—about Delia. He murdered that girl, if the word murder has any real meaning. And he dared to mention her name to me, and to smile at me with his thin cruel lips. I don't know why I didn't take him by the throat and choke the life out of him then and there. A knife was far too clean an end for Seely."

"What did you do?"

"I frightened the little rat till his teeth chattered. I can't remember what I said. I was in a blind rage. Literally, I saw red, and could hardly find my way out to my car."

"That's the clue I'm looking for, I expect, Leigh. Did you actually threaten to kill Seely?"

"I forget, but I probably did, as I had every intention of killing him—when one's mad with temper the mouth speaks out of the fullness of the heart."

"Who was in the house besides Seely?"

"King was away. His wife let me in, but I saw myself out—or rather I groped my way out in a fog of fury."

"That must be it then. Mrs. King heard the quarrel and the threats and no doubt the police have heard her story."

"It's damned queer though, not that she should have told what she heard, but that she didn't tell it sooner. They suspected her husband at first."

"There may be some reason. I'll have to see Mrs. King of course. There isn't a doubt in my mind though. Hearing angry voices one can't wonder if she did a spot of eaves-dropping. She probably knows what you said better than you know yourself."

"I shouldn't wonder."

"Well, Leigh, now we know what we are up against. And now I know what March's Ace of Trumps is. No wonder he wouldn't show his hand. Well, we'll have to outwit him somehow. And we haven't a hope of outwitting March unless we face our position squarely before we lay our plans. The position is that twenty-four hours before you killed Seely, someone is prepared to swear in the witness box that she heard you threaten to take his life——"

"What?" said Jerome Leigh, sitting forward with a jerk that nearly upset the table. "Oh, but I didn't kill Seely, Bryce!"

35

It was Bryce's turn to overbalance himself.

"You—didn't—kill—Seely! Then what the devil is all the fuss about?"

Dr. Tom was staring incredulously at his nephew.

"Why didn't you tell us that, Jerome, directly we arrived?"

"Nobody asked me, and I didn't suppose you would conclude me guilty until I acknowledged my guilt. I was beginning to explain when Bryce interrupted me."

"But Miss Munro actually saw you stab Seely and she seems to be the best friend you have," Bryce protested. "Of course, I believed her."

"May I tell my story quietly in my own way," asked Jerome. "I don't feel quick-witted to-night, and having kept mum for twenty-four hours it's hard to collect my thoughts."

"Take your time by all means," agreed Bryce, lighting a fresh cigarette. "Your uncle looks as if he could do with a breather too."

"No, I'm anxious to hear what Jerome has to say at once. I feel bewildered by the sudden change of outlook, that is all. The relief to my feelings is indescribable."

"I'm afraid you won't feel so relieved when you have heard my story, Uncle Tom. It is true I did not kill Seely, but I might almost as well have done for all the chance I have of proving it."

"I don't understand, Jerome."

"I don't wonder. I feel sure you will believe me, but I doubt if Bryce will. I certainly wouldn't believe him if he spun a yarn like the one I'm going to spin. But here it is. I went out of Seely's house that day with black murder in my heart. I didn't care how I killed him so long as I rid the earth of his presence. But I didn't intend to sacri-

fice my own life in the process. So I made plans—not
very good plans, as it turned out, but then I was a novice
at the murder game. I saw, however, that I must kill
him on neutral ground and that I must have a natural
reason for crossing his path. The fellow presented me with
the opportunity himself. He told me he wouldn't begin
his treatment before Saturday as he would be in London
on Friday, not coming home till the last train. I ascertained
that he always walked home and on that particular night
couldn't have got a taxi if he had wanted one. Not a soul
turned up to the Friday evening surgery on account of the
rain, but I waited until after eight before manufacturing
a call which would bring me back via Pillar-box Lane.
The weather was in my favour. I reached the lane in good
time and parked my car in a field some little distance from
the corner. I got behind a tree and waited. I had with
me a dagger of my uncle's which he keeps in a glass case.
It was sharpened to a fine edge.

"I waited for about ten minutes and then Seely came.
It was so dark and wet I was only aware that the moment
had come just in time to hurl myself at him. Simultaneously
there came a terrific flash of forked lightning and a deafening roar of thunder. I grabbed Seely by the collar and I
raised the knife to strike. And then the little rat let out
the most bloodcurdling wail I ever heard. I hadn't thought
he would cry before he was struck. It shook my nerve and
made me remember that I am a doctor whose job is to
heal pain, not inflict it. Or else I felt that I couldn't soil
my hands with Seely's foul blood. I believe it was a mixture
of both motives that stayed my hand.

"The blade came down, but it didn't enter Seely's back.
He wouldn't have been alive three hours later if it had, I
know that. I diverted the blow and loosed my hold of
Seely's collar. He went down like a stone, and I went back
to the car. When I drove back to the corner, curiosity
made me pull up and look to see whether Seely had picked
himself up and gone home. He hadn't. I supposed he had
fainted from shock and terror, so I took a light and stooped
over him. I saw that someone else had completed the job

I had begun. I began to think quickly. I decided to take him to hospital and to account for my headlights having picked him up, I marked the spot where I found him as being nearer to the corner than it actually was. I helped in the effort to save his life but he died at midnight. That carving-knife wasn't as sharp as Uncle Tom's dagger, but it was sharp enough."

"But, Jerome, what do you think happened after you left him?"

"I think he had fainted dead away and never got on his feet again. That is explicable in view of the fact that he was a nervous man, not in robust health, and that he had had a nerve-racking walk in the storm, before the shock of my attack. Well, you both see now, don't you, that although I didn't kill Seely, I am still completely in Jessica Munro's power? Or don't you believe the story, Bryce?"

"Well, it takes some swallowing, Leigh, but I accept it, if only because I can't imagine you in your present state thinking up anything so ingenious."

"Thanks, that is better than rank disbelief. But Jessica Munro is convinced that I killed Seely. You see, the lightning faded out just as the blade descended and then she fainted herself. The girl is given to fainting when she becomes excited, and the episode must have seemed highly melodramatic. I didn't even trouble to explain to her yesterday what really happened. I was much more interested to know how much she intended to tell the police."

"You are perfectly safe in her hands," Bryce declared. "She will have to know the truth, of course. If we can believe it, she can. But as she didn't see the sequel, that won't help us with the police. We've got to set to work to find the chap who finished Seely off. I hope to God it wasn't Derek Garle! That *would* queer my pitch. I couldn't act for both of you."

"What is Garle's position?" asked Jerome.

"Well, he seemed in the clear when attention was focused on you. But he hasn't the ghost of an alibi. I had to pull some wires, or to get a girl friend of Derek's to pull them for me, to get him released. She only threw doubt on the possibility of his having taken a carving-knife with him on the trip. The fact that he was wandering about Grassmere that night is not disputed."

"Don't you think, Bryce," said Tom Leigh, "that you had better leave the police to find the real criminal? You may burn your fingers if you get too deeply involved in the case. Why not let me go to Bruce now and tell him my nephew's story?"

"My dear sir, he will never believe it. And you will put the police in the position of knowing what they're up against, whereas they're not sure now. It will be much wiser for your nephew to reserve his defence and spring his story on them at the trial."

"But I don't want there to be a trial. I don't even want Jerome to face a preliminary hearing if it can be avoided."

"There is my practice to be thought of," put in Jerome. "Why not let my uncle have a shot at Norton, anyway? I don't see that he can do much harm. He can take the dagger I borrowed for the murder that didn't come off. Perhaps that will do the trick."

"No, I shall go straight back to Norton's house now," the old doctor said with determination. "I'm immensely grateful to you, Bryce, for all you have done and I still wish to retain your services on my nephew's behalf. In ordinary circumstances I should give you a perfectly free hand, but it wouldn't be much use for Jerome to be acquitted of murder if he lost his practice. We must take risks which might be unjustifiable if my nephew was a coalheaver. I'll leave you here, Bryce, and ask the constable to call a taxi. The visit will seem more informal if I go alone."

"As you wish, sir," said Bryce. "It isn't the line of action I recommend, but all the same I shall await your return with interest."

"So shall I, by Jove," declared Jerome. "Good luck, Uncle Tom. Put us out of our misery as quickly as you can."

"I'll be back within an hour," the old man promised.

He was very tired when he got out of his taxi and walked

up the path to Norton's house again. He found the two men where he had left them. March was reading, and Norton writing at his desk. There was no change in the room except that the tea-things had been removed, and the light was failing though the curtains had not yet been drawn. This seemed strange to Dr. Tom; the whole world had changed for him in the space of an hour, but for others everything was the same; they went on reading and writing in the same homely surroundings. It was a pity he felt so tired just now when he had so much to say, but the hope and joy in his heart had not imparted youth to his body; he was feeling the strain of his long journey, and the successive shocks of agony and relief.

He took the chair Bruce silently offered him and answered the question in his friend's eyes.

"I had to come back, Bruce. The news is so good; I had to tell you. Jerome is innocent."

The news did not have the effect he expected, for nobody spoke. Bruce drew up a chair close to the old doctor's and his questioning eyes were still sad.

"Of course," said Tom Leigh, "it is no use my telling you that without any evidence to support the assertion. I have begun at the wrong end of the story—Jerome's story. You must forgive me, Bruce; the knowledge means everything to me and I had to blurt it out like a schoolboy. You will want all the details, of course."

He looked at his listeners for sympathy. Bruce looked at the carpet, his face twitching with embarrassment. It was March who spoke.

"We shall be glad to hear your nephew's line of defence, Dr. Leigh. It will, of course, have to be embodied in a formal statement before it will be valid as evidence, but if you think it in his interest to tell us about it informally now, please do so."

"It isn't a line of defence, Mr. March. It is a complete denial of guilt."

"Well, that is the best defence of all, isn't it?"

"Why, yes. The best defence of all. Jerome did not kill Seely; I have his own word for it. He might lie to the police, but he would not lie to me. Let me tell you his story."

Speaking haltingly and with emotion, the old man related the explanation of the events of the night of the murder which he had just heard from his nephew's lips. He plodded doggedly on to the end, fighting his growing fatigue, and controlling the break in his voice, though with ever increasing difficulty. It was clear he had no conception of how thin the story sounded, for when at last he reached the end of his recital he said simply:

"So, you see, my nephew is innocent of the crime, though he admits that he meant to kill Seely, and would have done so if his better judgment had not triumphed at the eleventh hour."

The silence lasted for a long minute while the clock on the mantelpiece ticked its message that time was passing. Dr. Tom was looking at his hearers, first confidently and then anxiously.

"You understand, don't you, Bruce? You believe that Jerome is speaking the truth?"

Bruce remained silent, the dusk masking his features, and it was March who spoke again.

"You, for your part, will understand, Dr. Leigh, that the police cannot express any opinion until they have heard the story direct from your nephew, and obtained his signed statement. I think it will be better to let that stand over until the morning. It is late to put him through a long ordeal now. You have had a long journey and you must be very tired. Will you go home and rest, and leave us to take the next step? I can assure you that that will be the best course in the long run for everybody."

"Yes, I am tired. Perhaps I had better do as you say. But what am I to tell my nephew?"

"You can tell him that I will come to see him the first thing in the morning, prepared to take a statement from him if he wishes to make one. Bryce will no doubt advise him in the matter, and can be present at the interview. Let us say half-past nine, shall we? That will allow ample time; the hearing is not until noon."

"Thank you, Mr. March. Yes, I am very tired; I will go home now. Thank you, Bruce. No, don't get up, my dear boy. I have a taxi waiting outside."

When he had seen the old man into his taxi, Bruce returned to March. "Good God, wasn't that painful?"

"I suppose you found it so, Bruce. He's a fine old chap, the doctor. He quite believes his nephew's story himself."

"Obviously, but what are we to do about it?"

"It will have to be looked into, of course. Jerome Leigh's manner when I question him may tell me something. I left him over till the morning because I want to see Jessica Munro to-night."

"I'll drive you over directly after supper. You don't believe Jerome's story, do you?"

"Not at present, of course. But I suppose there is about one chance in a thousand that it may be true. I've got to probe that thousandth chance. I mustn't refuse to believe in anything except an impossibility. Jerome Leigh's story is an improbability; it reaches the highest degree of improbability that I can conceive of. But it does just qualify for inclusion in the category of improbabilities rather than of impossibilities. Perhaps I am influenced by the fact that if the thousandth chance comes off, I shan't be forced to eat humble pie. My deductions as to Jerome Leigh's actions on the night of the crime were perfectly accurate— up to the point where he raised the knife to strike Seely."

"I'm afraid it is only a chance in a million, Chris. For Seely was stabbed with a knife, and to suppose that someone else was hanging about waiting to finish Leigh's work strains one's imagination beyond breaking-point. . . . There's the phone. Excuse me a minute—we'll have supper as soon as I've taken the call."

Bruce was back in three minutes.

"Chris, I don't know whether I'm on my head or my heels! That was Blackie, Seely's solicitor. He says that, owing to heavy pressure of work, he has only to-night completed the task of going through Seely's papers."

"Well?"

"He has found a letter to Seely which he thinks we ought

to see. He wouldn't name the writer on the telephone, but the letter threatens Seely with violence. He is bringing it round to show us at once. We can expect him in half an hour. What do you think of that?"

"I don't think I'd better say anything until I have seen the letter and know who wrote it. What about getting our meal over so that we are all set to receive Blackie when he turns up."

36

Mr. Blackie was a fat little man who seemed to enjoy living in a perpetual bustle. He hadn't time to sit down, he declared, he had a special appointment with a client in half an hour.

"But I wouldn't let this letter out of my hands," he added. "I should have found it before if I hadn't been so rushed. One of your sergeants gave me the key of Seely's desk a week ago, and I promised to hand over to the police anything I found which concerned you. Having done so I have discharged my obligations and I really must fly, or I shall be late for my appointment."

As he spoke he flew, as fast as his short legs and stout body permitted. The letter was on light blue note-paper of good quality. Bruce read it aloud to March. The address was that of a West End club.

"Dear Seely,

Your review of *The Eiderdown* passes the bounds of legitimate criticism. It is permissible to find fault, but not to distort facts. There was not a line in the play to suggest that Valmar knew of his wife's infidelity before the night of her birthday. You completely missed the point of the third act which was to reveal the consistency of Valmar's conduct with his earlier history. It would not surprise me to hear that you left the theatre before the act began.

All this would not matter if it were merely a question of your own opinion. But you abused the high standing of *Intelligentsia*. Knowing as you must that complete condemnation in this paper is enough to kill a play, you did not hesitate to deal out death with your pen.

Death to the play and to the author if he cannot earn his bread and butter. But the author does not propose to die, Seely. If he strikes it will not be with a pen.

D. G."

March held out his hand for the letter.

"Undated, and the stamp has been torn off the envelope, presumably by Seely himself," he commented. "But it was posted to the office of *Intelligentsia* and forwarded on from there to Beech House. And it must have been written soon after *The Eiderdown* was produced last winter. Written in a blind rage, too. Well, it is more than ever important for me to see Jessica Munro. But first I must ring up Derwent and make sure that adequate arrangements are still being made to have Garle shadowed."

He came back with his overcoat on. "John hasn't relaxed the watch on Garle. Garle came down here last night and spent the night at the Station Hotel at Grassmere. John rang up Cooper who had a room at the hotel and he went back to London on the same train as Garle and Jessica Munro. They went to Bryce's office, which shows that Miss Munro is still working against us. I must talk to her without letting her know that something fresh has cropped up concerning her husband. The plot thickens, doesn't it?"

"It is so thick I can't see an inch into it. I hope you can."

"I'll talk in the car. Come on."

"There are two possibilities which we must focus attention on at present to the exclusion of others," March continued as they drove out of Heathmere. "Let's assume for the sake of argument that Jerome Leigh's story is substantially true. One possibility is that Miss Munro saw Leigh appear to stab Seely and then fainted. Garle had been concealed somewhere at hand and stabbed Seely while Jess was unconscious and made off. The other is that the first attack took place before Jess arrived on the scene, that Seely had scrambled to his feet again, and that what she saw was Garle really stab Seely. The question is, did she see the knife actually driven into the body?"

"But, Chris, what she saw was by the light of that flash of forked lightning."

"I know. That is not conclusive though. Leigh may have invented the first story he told to account for the time he took to reach Cairn Corner, but he may really have been back in his car when Beech House was struck. I am only supposing his story to be substantially true—that is, as regards his own innocence."

"But he would have nothing to fear if he attacked Seely in the dark."

"I told him, Bruce, that Miss Munro had seen a man of about his height attack Seely. He must have concluded at once that it was himself she had seen. The idea of the real murderer also being a man six foot tall would hardly occur to him. The darkness was only intermittent. When one is on the verge of killing a man, one wouldn't notice an ordinary flash of lightning. Leigh therefore was convinced at once that Miss Munro had somehow managed to see him well enough to identify him if she were so minded. In some ways it fits better that Garle should be the man Jess saw. Before she had any interest in deceiving us, she was so very persistent that the assailant seemed vaguely familiar to her and that he had coal black hair."

"Oh hades!" exclaimed Bruce. "I wouldn't wonder if we woke up to find Miss Munro dreamt the entire episode. You don't want me to come into the cottage, do you? I'd much rather have a rest in the car; my head is swimming."

"Have your rest. No doubt Peter will be inside."

Peter was playing the piano and Jess was half singing and half humming an old ballad. March felt that he was not very welcome.

"Do go on singing, Miss Munro," he begged. "My business is not urgent; it can wait."

"I wasn't really singing."

"Come on, Jess," urged Peter, striking a chord invitingly. "Sing the last verse. You've got quite a nice voice if only you would breathe in the proper places."

Jess sang half-heartedly and left Peter to put away the music. "What is it, Mr. March?" she asked.

"I want you to help me clear up a point which has just cropped up, Miss Munro. You recall telling me that you saw Seely's assailant raise his weapon, and that the lightning flashed on the blade of the knife?"

"I shall never forget it."

"I thought not. Peter, give me that paper-knife. Now, Miss Munro, we are going to act a scene in dumb crambo. Peter, you are Seely and I am the assailant whom Miss Munro saw. Miss Munro, will you watch us carefully and call out at the precise moment where you believe you fainted and saw no more."

"I saw no more after the lightning died away: I reeled about a bit before I fainted. I'll stand here so that I get the distance and angle both right. Peter is too tall for Seely and you are not quite tall enough for—for the attacker."

"Crouch down, Peter. I'm afraid I can't grow, Miss Munro. I'll stand on tiptoe. Now, Peter, reproduce that blood-curdling yell of yours, and collapse when the knife strikes you."

March caught Peter by the coat collar and, holding the paper-knife in his right hand, flexed his arm and drove the blade forwards. Peter shrieked as the knife caught him fair and square under his left shoulder blade. He let his knees sag and pitched forward. March looked at Jess who had remained silent

"That was all wrong," she said, frowning. "It wasn't a bit like what I saw."

"Coach us, then," said March, "and we'll do the scene again."

"Let me think. . . . Well, first you flexed your arm and brought your hand back behind your shoulder. You should have kept your arm straight and raised it high above your head. Then you should have brought it straight down—like this. Instead of which you jabbed the knife forwards so that it struck Peter at right angles——"

"Like hell, it did," groaned Peter. "I've got a foul pain where it caught me; I wouldn't wonder if it broke the skin."

"Then you, Peter," Jess continued, "didn't shriek quickly enough. You must start to yell directly Mr. March grabs you, so that you have time to reach a crescendo before you fall."

The two men got into position again and Jess looked on critically. March brought the knife straight down and struck Peter a glancing blow. Jess's warning shout coincided with the falling of the blade, and drowned Peter's wail which had begun to die away.

"Was that better?" asked March.

"Perfect. It was just as I saw it happen."

"You didn't actually see Seely fall?"

"No, the lightning didn't last long enough."

"Are you certain we were correct in every detail?"

"Positive. It is so much easier to remember what you saw when you have two alternatives to choose from than when you try to describe your impressions *in vacuo.*"

"But your impression was that the knife had entered Seely's back and killed him?"

"Of course. His shriek sounded like a dying wail. I expected to find a dead body when I climbed out of the ditch."

"Did it occur to you?—no, it wouldn't be fair to ask you that."

"Nothing occurred to me as an alternative to my having witnessed a murder except the possibility that the whole episode was an hallucination. Next morning, when I heard Mr. Seely had been murdered, I chose between the two alternatives without much difficulty."

"Naturally. And inevitably when you tried to reconstruct the scene for me, you started from the assumption of Seely's death. Thank you, Miss Munro. I'll leave Peter to entertain you now. Don't let him keep you up too late. I understand you have been up to London to-day."

Jess had no time to reply before March was gone.

"Well, I'm damned if I know what all that was about," said Peter. "But I know I've got a jolly sore spot in my back. I think the Chief Inspector might have practised on a cushion."

"You ass, Peter. I can see what it was about, and you're supposed to be a detective."

"Supposed to be! I like that. March would never have solved this case without my help."

"The point is that he hasn't solved it. He's back again just where he started from. It will be one of those unsolved crimes that will be written about and speculated on for centuries—like the case of Sir Edmund Godfrey. Let's do something to celebrate, Peter."

"Celebrate what?"

"Oh, just that I feel happy."

"Come to the station pub and have a drink. They've got plenty of gin there; I only discovered it last night."

They walked gaily past Cairn Corner, talking and laughing.

"Home again?" asked Bruce, as March re-entered the car.

"Call at Dr. Leigh's house, will you, Bruce? I want to collect that dagger. After that, home for you, but do you mind if I take the car out by myself?"

"Going to make a night of it?"

"Possibly."

Outside the Deputy Chief Constable's house March changed into the driver's seat, and drove to the outskirts of the town, where Matthews, the surgeon who had attended Seely in hospital, lived at the top of a block of flats. Matthews was alone and expressed himself as entirely at the Chief Inspector's service.

"I don't want to prejudice your mind in any way, Matthews," said March. "But the case has taken a new turn. I want to go into the matter of the type of blow which inflicted a fatal wound on Seely and the angle at which the blade of the knife entered the body, in as much detail as possible."

"I can't help being prejudiced to a certain extent by the knowledge that you have arrested Leigh. If I had stabbed Seely, I would have made a neater job of it than the murderer did. I am certain he would not have lived to reach hospital."

"But you are a surgeon."

"So is Leigh—a physician and surgeon—but he doesn't do as many operations as I do, I admit."

"But you would have expected him to finish Seely off quickly."

"With a whacking great carving-knife such as I took out of Seely's back—definitely."

"Well, forget Leigh, will you? I want you to be completely objective and tell me how you think the blow was struck."

"I have prints of the post mortem photographs here. . . . The blow was struck with more force than judgment. A little more of the latter, and less of the former would have been called for, and it would have been a cleaner job altogether. The blade entered almost at right angles to the body."

"How would the striker have held the knife?"

"If Seely were standing up—like this."

Matthews picked up a ruler to demonstrate the point. He flexed his arm and raised his hand behind his shoulder. "The attacker's wrist would have moved forward and slightly downward—so."

"But you said nothing before about 'if Seely had been standing'."

"Neither, if I remember rightly, did you. I supposed that he was probably struck—from behind, of course—as he was walking along. The wound was quite consistent with that supposition."

"You're quite right; I didn't raise the point of Seely not being upright when he was struck. As a matter of fact, I had some reason to suppose that he was on his feet. I noticed that just now you did not raise your arm above your head at all. You flexed your arm and your hand was only just above the level of your shoulder."

"That is the only way to combine the two factors: the necessary force and the angle of the blade."

"The only way if Seely had been in the position you describe. What other position could he have been in?"

"Well, obviously his back was exposed to the blow. He might have been lying on his face. The wound was equally consistent with such a theory."

"Equally?"

"I couldn't swear in a court of law to whether Seely was upright or recumbent when he was struck. I should have to admit the possibility of either position and refuse to differentiate between them."

"Well, that is definite, anyhow. What sort of wound would you have expected to find if the striker had held the knife high above his head and brought the blade straight down?"

"If he were standing behind Seely with the knife held over his own head and brought it *straight* down, the blade would have missed Seely altogether. You don't mean that, of course. You mean that the blade came downwards and forwards, and that he steered it to the spot he wanted to hit. In that case the angle would have been quite different, of course, and the nature of the wound would also have been different. I can draw it for you roughly, if you like. . . ."

"Thank you," said March, examining the sketch the surgeon had made. "I'll keep this if I may. That is all I wanted to know."

"Well, I hope it lets Leigh out."

"We shall see."

"Is that all you're going to say?"

March smiled. "It is possible that the first blow did miss Seely altogether."

Matthews whistled, and then grinned at the Chief Inspector's refusal to commit himself further.

"I suppose it will all come out in due course?"

"I hope so, indeed."

March would say no more, and Matthews, still grinning broadly, let him out of the flat.

37

MARCH was up early the next morning. He asked Norton to postpone his interview with Jerome Leigh until ten o'clock.

"But why, Chris? You have oceans of time."

"I have other fish to fry, or rather other daggers to collect."

"What the devil are you talking about?"

"Perhaps you can help me. I want to collect eight or ten daggers as similar as possible to the one Leigh claims he meant to use to kill Seely. If he really carried that knife around with him, with intent to do murder with it, he will have studied it pretty closely. If he only cooked up that yarn at the police station yesterday, because he remembered seeing a dagger in a glass case at his uncle's house, the test may floor him."

"Ten daggers is a tall order. I've got a pair upstairs; they were given me years ago in Manchester and they're like enough to Tom Leigh's—a fraction smaller perhaps. I don't know where the dickens you'll get the rest from though. You might try Fenwick's—the antique shop in the High Street."

"I'll lay hands on half a dozen more if I have to scour the countryside. Lend me Norman and a car when I've finished with Leigh, will you? I'm taking your car now; I'll be back before you start for the office."

"I shall never get Norman back into harness again when you've gone—but all right."

"I'm going back to London this afternoon—I hope."

Fenwick supplied March with a pair of daggers on loan and told him where he could borrow a couple more. With his half-dozen, in addition to Tom Leigh's, the Chief Inspector had to be content for time was getting on. He drove Bruce to his office, arriving a few minutes before ten o'clock.

Jerome Leigh picked out his uncle's dagger without hesitation. "I carried it in its sheath, of course," he explained, eyeing March with intense curiosity.

"Yes, I purposely did not produce the sheath now. I shall have a bit of a job putting all these murderous weapons back in the right cases. Now I'm going to sheath your uncle's dagger, Leigh; I think it will be safer. I want you to show me exactly how you handled it when you aimed the blow at Seely."

Leigh raised his arm straight above his head and brought the knife down. "At the last split second, I dropped my wrist and missed Seely by a hair's breadth," he said.

"When did he start to scream out?"

"The second I grabbed his collar."

March began to put all the daggers back in their sheaths, talking to Leigh on the other side of the table as he did so. "Your uncle told us your story last night, Leigh. It didn't sound true at the time, but it is beginning to seem true now. Fortunately for you, you were not the only person with a grievance against Seely known to have been out in the storm that night. I shan't take you through your story now; I haven't the time to spare. But I warn you to be prepared to make a signed statement later on."

"Where to, sir?" asked Norman, who was waiting outside with a car.

"Cairn Cottage, for, I hope, the last time, Norman."

Jess was in the garden extracting plantains from the lawn with a kitchen knife. Mrs. Bradshaw, puffing importantly, showed March the way out through the sitting-room window. He led Jess to a tiny summer-house at the bottom of the garden. Jess wiped her hands on her overall and chose the cleanest corner she could find to sit in. Regardless of his trousers, the Chief Inspector seated himself opposite her.

"The time has come, Miss Munro," he said, "for you to tell the truth."

"The whole truth and nothing but the truth," Jess finished for him promptly. "You know, that optimistic phrase always makes me smile. You know the truth now, though not, I suspect, the whole truth. So why not let me sink back into obscurity?"

"When you have acknowledged one fact, you may do so, so far as I am concerned."

"Very well. Jerome Leigh was the man I saw spring out on Seely."

"Thank you. That is all you need say."

"It is all I mean to say."

March smiled and said good-bye. Norman had turned the car and was sitting at the wheel reading a newspaper.

"You've been quick, sir!"

"The interview was short and sweet. Drive slowly up the lane, Norman, and stop when you get to the scene of the crime."

Norman obeyed instructions without speaking. March was evidently thinking hard, and in no mood for converse.

"We'll get out here," said the Chief Inspector. He walked about for a few minutes and then returned to the car, but he did not get in. "Better lock it, Norman. I don't want my overcoat pinched. That's right, now we'll go this way, I think."

He climbed the stile into the meadow leading to Beech House and did not speak again until they were inside the drive gate. "Keep King occupied while I have a few minutes' talk with his wife, Norman."

"Right you are, sir."

Sibyl King was busy in the kitchen. March spent ten minutes with her and then went into the front room where King was Hoovering a carpet. Norman was standing by the window, talking through the noise of the vacuum cleaner. "I always think these machines leave the surface dirt untouched," he was saying as the Chief Inspector entered.

"Switch that off, King," said March. "The game is up. I'm taking you back to Heathmere with me, and there you will be arrested and charged with murdering Ambrose Seely, on the night of Friday, the nineteenth of September."

"You can't do that," King said hoarsely, after a pause

during which the purport of March's grim words slowly seeped into his brain, leaving his face as ashen grey as his hair. "You took me once and you had to let me go again."

"We shan't let you go this time. If you insist on talking here, it is my duty to tell you that anything you say will be taken down and may be used in evidence."

"I never touched Seely. I was here when the house was struck."

"I know you were, but Seely was not killed when the house was struck. He was stabbed about three or four minutes later; stabbed in the back with the carving-knife missing from this house, while he was lying on the ground in a faint. You can run all right, King. You won the two hundred and fifty yards race in the Victory sports here. You meant to do for Seely that night because of what he did to your wife two nights earlier while you were away in Leeds. You couldn't go to meet him sooner, because Hannah Green was here, but the second she was out of the house, you licked across that meadow. You had no time to lose, and if Seely hadn't fainted you would have met him nearer home. As it was——"

"Don't go over it all again," King shouted, while a frenzied look appeared in his eyes. "How could I help it if the . . . had fainted? Would you have had me rouse him before I croaked him? You should have *seen* my wife the night I got home. A knife was too clean an end for Seely."

"I know you had great provocation, King. Come quietly now. We'll see that your wife is looked after."

The little procession trailed across the meadow, March leading the way and Norman, who was almost as white as King, bringing up the rear.

"You leave me gasping, Chris," Norton complained when he was asked to procure a warrant for the arrest of George King. "What about Garle?"

"As soon as I had worked it out on paper, I saw that Garle could not have stabbed Seely after Leigh left him lying in a faint and got back to the station in time to book a ticket just before the London train came in at nine-twelve. Leigh saw nothing of him—neither did Jess Munro. He had to get to the spot where Seely was lying, stab him and make for the station. He left the station ahead of Seely. Where was he when Leigh made his attack? Where did he go when he had finished Seely off? He didn't know his way about; he had no time to look for footpaths. Garle had written a foolish letter to Seely in a fit of injured exasperation because Seely had mortally damaged the thing he had created. He said that *if* he struck, it would not be with a pen. I think he meant no more than to threaten Seely with a beating up if he was unfair to his second play. What seemed to clear King was the apparent synchronization of the murder with the flash of lightning which struck Beech House. Destroy that synchronization and you destroy King's alibi. Admit the possibility that the man Miss Munro saw was not the murderer, and King's build and colouring no longer rule him out. Realizing that, I considered again that odd carving-fork. An odd fork is more significant than an odd knife, because the safety catch on a fork often breaks, whereas a knife lasts almost indefinitely. King ought to have got rid of the fork: it was, I think, his only mistake.

"Then there was that story of Mrs. Martin's about her daughter. Seely did to Sibyl King what he did to his first wife, but he only had Sibyl in his power for one night. It is hard to blame George King and he had the decency not to want his wife to give evidence incriminating Jerome Leigh. By the way, I believe we can construe Seely's dying message now. I told you we should probably do so when we knew all the facts.

"I believe he could not answer Matthews' first question as to who attacked him. But when Matthews asked whether anyone had a grudge against him, he answered, in the light of his knowledge that he had given two men serious cause of offence: 'Leigh or King'."

"Which might sound like: 'I didn't see a thing' or like some delirious remark about 'forked lightning'."

"Exactly. Well, I must catch the first train after lunch, Bruce. I want to see the A.C. as soon as possible."

"Very well, Chris. Thank God anyhow that poor old Tom Leigh will be put out of his misery. And thank you more than I can say——"

"Don't trouble."

"I shall miss our games of chess."

Peter had gone back to London with the Chief Inspector and Jess was alone when her door-bell rang at nine o'clock that evening. She looked at herself in the mirror before she admitted Jerome Leigh.

"I thought you might come," she said.

"I'm off on Saturday. I wanted to see you first. I'm sorry your sunlight treatment was interrupted. I should advise you to let my uncle carry on with the good work. You're looking a better colour. Oh, as regards your nervous trouble, I hear your husband has been down here and I suppose you made it up with him?"

"I did not. At least we are on very good terms again, but Derek came to see me to ask for a divorce. He is going to marry an extremely nice girl; I can really give him my blessing."

"Oh, I see. Well, that puts rather a different complexion on things, doesn't it? If I am not particularly eligible, I am rather more so than I was the last time I saw you. At least I am no longer in your power."

"You couldn't be more eligible, and you will always be completely in my power," said Jess.